SUMMER
Holiday

SUMMER
Holiday

Nancy Campbell Allen

Sarah M. Eden

Annette Lyon

Mirror Press

Copyright © 2018 Mirror Press
Print edition
All rights reserved

No part of this book may be reproduced in any form whatsoever without prior written permission of the publisher, except in the case of brief passages embodied in critical reviews and articles. These novels are works of fiction. The characters, names, incidents, places, and dialog are products of the authors' imaginations and are not to be construed as real.

Interior Design by Cora Johnson
Edited by Jennie Stevens and Lisa Shepherd
Cover design by Rachael Anderson
Cover Photo Credit: Richard Jenkins Photography

Published by Mirror Press, LLC

ISBN-13: 978-1-947152-36-6

TIMELESS VICTORIAN COLLECTIONS
Summer Holiday
A Grand Tour
The Orient Express
The Queen's Ball

TIMELESS REGENCY COLLECTIONS
Autumn Masquerade
A Midwinter Ball
Spring in Hyde Park
Summer House Party
A Country Christmas
A Season in London
Falling for a Duke
A Night in Grosvenor Square
Road to Gretna Green
Wedding Wagers

TABLE OF CONTENTS

Breakfast at Sommerpool's
by Nancy Campbell Allen

However Long the Wait
by Sarah M. Eden

The Last Summer at Ivy House
by Annette Lyon

Nancy Campbell Allen

Chapter One

Tessa Baker stood in the managers' offices at Sommerpool Department and Mercantile and silently fumed. She tapped a sealed envelope against her fingertips and counted first to ten, and then fifteen. The manager, Mr. Neville Blight, watched Tessa and her fellow employee, Grover Welsey, with a gleam in his eye.

"The winner will be promoted to the position of supervisor of shopgirls in the Linens, Gloves, and Ribbons Department."

The man probably thought Tessa and Grover would brawl with each other right there in the office, and she dearly would have loved to prove him correct. Aunt Valentine's husband, Max, was a former prizefighter and had taught her to fight quite effectively. She sucked in a deep breath instead.

"Very well," Tessa said. "A contest, it is. And may the best person win."

Grover smirked. "I am certain he will."

"Remember," Mr. Blight said, "each day you will be presented with an emergency scenario, which you must solve to my satisfaction. You will also be given a scavenger hunt list, which will show your dedication and ability to focus on detail. Whichever of you brings me the entire list by closing next Friday and successfully completes each day's emergency scenario will be the victor."

"To whom shall go the spoils." Grover grinned at Mr. Blight and then turned his obsequious charm on Tessa. "Almost seems criminal, Baker, to force you to compete with me. I trust you'll recover well enough."

She narrowed her eyes and smiled. "Mmm. I shall manage."

"Good, then!" Mr. Blight clapped and briskly rubbed his hands together. "Nothing like a friendly competition to impress our mysterious new owner to no end. Whoever wins the contest will be promoted and prove himself"—he paused grandly—"or *herself* clever and equipped to handle the responsibility."

The new owner. It was all anybody in the seaside resort town of Sommerpool had talked about for weeks. A benefactor swooped in just as the store was facing financial ruin at the hands of unscrupulous bookkeepers. Sommerpool was the place to see and be seen for summer holiday, but the store had been losing money, despite its popularity. The deceptive accountants had been apprehended, but the money was gone. The store's new mystery savior rescued it and hundreds of employees' jobs.

Tessa made her way out of the business offices on the fifth floor and hurried to ring for the lift before Welsey could catch her. She gritted her teeth when she heard his voice.

"I would also run if I were you, Baker." He joined her at the lift gate, all smiles.

"I've no idea why you're so cheery, Welsey. Your win is not a foregone conclusion." She glanced at him and returned her attention to the lift, which made its way smoothly upward. "In fact, I rather think the lady doth protest too much."

He laughed. "Very glib of you. I am not surprised you must turn to humor. Keep those spirits up and all."

The lift came to a stop, and the attendant, Henry, opened the gate. Tessa looked again at Welsey, and the thought of being contained with him in that small contraption was more than she could stomach. "I'll take the stairs. Your head occupies too much space for the lift to carry us both."

His chortle rang out behind her as she spun on her heel and made her way around the corner to the stairway. She held her skirt in her hand and clomped down three flights, each step punctuating her frustration. She had worked in Linens, Gloves, and Ribbons, or the LGR Department, for four years—the last two as an assistant to the department supervisor, a position unheard of for a woman. Old Mr. Gibbons was due to retire in a matter of weeks, and he encouraged Tessa to apply for the position. She knew the department backward and forward and had earned the respect of the shopgirls who worked it. Mr. Gibbons had taken her under his wing and taught her well; he was one of few men who believed she could handle the stresses of supervising, and she didn't want to disappoint him.

Emergency tests that mirrored actual potential scenarios made sense. But a scavenger hunt? Mr. Blight might as well call it a Wild-Goose Chase. She didn't know what sort of nonsense he carried up his sleeve; summer holiday week—the biggest of the season—was knocking at the door. They would be busier than ever with people vacationing from all over England. More specifically, the city would host those vacationers who enjoyed not only Bank Holiday but also an *additional* week's holiday from work. What had once been a summer luxury for the wealthy was now available to the middle classes, and many families saved all year for their time at the seashore.

She would be needed next week and most assuredly did not have time for a scavenger hunt. She found Mr. Gibbons organizing a display of beautiful new gloves that had arrived only that morning from France.

"I am to compete with that odious toad of a man for the position," she told her superior without preamble. "Emergency scenarios and a scavenger hunt. *A scavenger hunt!*" She paced restlessly, and Mr. Gibbons continued to calmly position the gloves to their best possible visual advantage.

He glanced at her, brows drawn. "What kind of competition is that, I wonder?"

"A ridiculous one, that's what." The more she considered it, the more she fumed. "A ridiculous waste of time that in no way showcases my skills or abilities to effectively manage a team of shopgirls and oversee this department." She stopped pacing and planted herself beside Mr. Gibbons. "I am to accomplish this ridiculous feat next week, when I shall be needed desperately here."

At her pronouncement, Mr. Gibbons's eyes widened slightly. On the mild-mannered and even-tempered gentleman, it was an expression of abject horror. "What is on this list, then? How long will it take, do you suppose?"

Tessa sighed and looked at the envelope she held but hadn't opened. Briefly closing her eyes, she retrieved a letter opener from a nearby counter and slit open the missive. She unfolded it to reveal a long list in tiny print.

Her mouth dropped in dismay as she began reading. "What on *earth*?"

Mr. Gibbons left the gloves and joined her, pulling spectacles from his pocket. "Hmm," he said, squinting and reading over her shoulder. "Seems to be a wide assortment of goods along the promenade and down the pier." He took the paper from her and studied it.

"I shall never accomplish all of that"—she motioned at the paper—"in a month's time, let alone a week!"

"An extracted tooth from the dental offices, an item of jewelry from Farr's, a ticket stub from the late-night theater signed by at least three of the main cast . . ." Mr. Gibbons shook his head. "Perhaps I ought to speak to Mr. Blight."

Tessa shook her head, eyes wide. "No, you mustn't. He will believe I've asked you to do so, which will only confirm his belief that I am ill-equipped to be a supervisor." Her shoulders slumped. "Mr. Gibbons, it was a lovely thought, and I had hoped to be the store's first female department manager, but I'm beginning to believe the prospect might as well be a wish to see the far side of the moon."

Mr. Gibbons narrowed his eyes. "You're quitting then, are you? Giving up before the fight's even begun?"

"No! But you see how ridiculous this is. I cannot be running around town next week collecting extracted body parts and jewelry while this department is overrun with excited customers ready to spend their hard-earned cash." She rubbed her forehead. "We cannot spare anyone, let alone me." She flushed. "Forgive my arrogance."

His moustache twitched. "Nothing to forgive. You're quite right. However, the thought of Grover Welsey heading this department is laughable. We've no choice. I shall borrow two of the shopgirls from Dry Goods. They're overstaffed, considering the bulk of the clientele next week will be tourists and not inclined to purchase ten pounds of flour or wheat."

"But they know nothing about this department."

"They can stand behind the counter and conduct sales transactions as easily here as downstairs. Our seven regular girls can aid customers amongst the merchandise."

Tessa sighed and closed her eyes. "This is impossible—the whole idea." She lifted her hand and dropped it back to her side. "And that such a monumental opportunity should hinge on such a ridiculous test? I am bitterly disappointed."

"Understandably. But life does have its share of disappointments. You're hardly the first to face them."

"I know." She looked at the elder gentleman. "You are patient with me and supportive always. You've taught me all I know, and my gratitude is boundless." She smiled, pained. "I did so hope to make you proud."

He waved a hand and returned the ridiculous list to her. "Already done, girl. Now, silly or not, are you going to do this or allow that toad of a boy to waltz his way over to this department hoping to waltz with every girl here?"

She smiled reluctantly. "That is his design, is it not?"

"Oh, most assuredly. Sized that one up in the first five minutes, I did."

She looked down at the list and rolled her eyes. "Of course I will do it, and I will beat him, and one day I will have Mr. Blight's position."

Mr. Gibbons beamed. "That's the spirit! Now, when can you begin the"—he motioned a hand toward the list—"hunt?"

"He said we may begin immediately. Tomorrow being Sunday could pose problems with many of the items, but not all."

Mr. Gibbons smiled. "Get to it, then. I am leaving for the Riviera next month one way or the other."

"And you deserve every sunny moment." She smiled and winked. "You shall be as fashionable as the sunbathers who now view tan skin as healthy and preferable to a chalky hue."

He chuckled. "Most would call that hue *milky* rather than *chalky*."

"Mmm. I call the whole of it *poetic justice*. I was teased

more than once about spending so much time out of doors without my bonnet." Tanned skin was becoming *de rigeur*; she was a self-sufficient young woman with a good career; and, with a little luck, she might find herself as Sommerpool Department and Mercantile's first female in a management position. Throw a handsome man into the mix, and she might consider herself charmed.

 She shook her head and made her way to the LGR Department employee room to brief the shopgirls on expectations for the following week. Five hundred handsome men could come clamoring to her door, and she'd not have time for any of them. She would be spending her time scavenging.

Chapter Two

David Bellini, second son of the Italian *Conte* Bellini and now the eldest of the three eligible bachelor brothers, smiled as he gave the department store his full regard. He looked out the window of the carriage at the five-story behemoth and felt a sense of satisfaction knowing he owned it.

"You are certain you want this much responsibility? A department store so far from home?" His friend, Mr. Maxwell, whom he called Max, eyed him dubiously from the seat opposite.

David nodded and inhaled a breath of fresh sea air mingled with a myriad of scents. Paramount amongst the olfactory delights was the delectable odor of fried fish, which made his mouth water. He'd only just arrived in Sommerpool, but fish and chips were high on his priority list. "I've rented a home near yours. I plan to remain and see the store back to sound footing."

Max raised a brow. "I am glad to hear it, of course, but is this not a bit rushed?"

David smiled. "I have been looking for this for years. The

second son of an Italian count bears the title, just as the firstborn, but he finds the world expects little of him by way of productive behavior. Matteo has his role as the eldest son and heir. This is something I can do that is mine."

"You requested in your letter that Valentine and I refrain from telling anyone you are the D&M's new owner. May I ask why?"

"I wish to observe . . . unobserved for a while." David looked out the window at the people who strolled along the promenade, enjoying the view and laughing with friends. "People are honest when they do not realize their companion is their employer."

Max chuckled. "True enough. I must tell you, however, that Valentine told her niece you were arriving today, and she knows of your family. Tessa is aware you are European nobility."

David shifted his attention back to Max. "But she does not know of my identity as the store's owner?"

Max shook his head. "She is very much Valentine's relation, though—too clever by half, the both of them. I could barely keep pace with the one." His small smile suggested he did not mind the attempt. "Now I find myself overpowered and overruled before I've even recognized the threat."

David smiled. "She has lived with you how long?"

"Six months. She lived on her own at a boarding house when Val and I moved here to open the new boxing salon. Val bullied Tessa into taking a room at our house when she realized the landlord fleeced the girls so heavily that saving wages for future security was almost impossible." Max smiled again. "Tessa put steps into motion to secure smaller lodgings for herself and a handful of others at more reasonable rents, but Valentine is persuasive."

David laughed. "Valentine is charming and delightful."

"Yes, and she charmingly and delightfully convinced Tessa that she would still be, for all intents and purposes, independent and in control of her own fate. A very strong motivator for the Baker women, apparently. What did I know? I thought it was unique to Val."

"And what is not to understand?" David caught sight of Max's wife, Valentine Baker Maxwell, exiting the department store. "There is something to be said for having a purpose all one's own."

"Indeed." Max leaned over and looked out the window. "There they are. Must have taken some doing to get her disentangled from the shopgirls. Tessa is waylaid at least five times a night while attempting to clock out."

David squinted against the setting sun that glinted off the store windows. "She is popular with them?"

"She is the Linen, Gloves, and Ribbons Department supervisor's assistant." Pride was evident in Max's voice. "First woman assistant in the store's history. Her superior is set to retire and encouraged her to apply for his position. She was to have spoken with the head store manager today."

Valentine stepped onto the street and waited, glancing behind her. A figure in a white blouse and black skirt spoke with someone at the front door while two carriages passed, blocking them from sight. By the time David's view of the women was again unobstructed, they were finally approaching the carriage, arm in arm. Valentine's niece was similar in height and frame—small and slight—and she wore a small hat perched upon curls the color of dark honey.

David raised a brow. "You never mentioned beautiful."

"Didn't seem pertinent. And besides, what should I have said? 'My wife's niece is as pretty as she is'? Makes me sound a bit lecherous."

Tessa Baker tipped her head up and smirked with an eye

roll at something Valentine said. Valentine responded, and the two paused in a fit of laughter. David found himself smiling in response. "Joyous," he murmured, and Max nodded.

"Very much so. Life at our house is lively. I had only one brother, and our living conditions as children were rather gloomy. These two provide a world I never knew existed."

The women drew closer to the carriage, and David drew in his breath. Tessa Baker was lovely. She was conventionally pretty, but there was a spark behind her eyes—something in her expression that spoke of hope and optimism and genuine joy. They finally reached the door, and the driver opened it for them. Max and David each moved over on their respective benches, and Valentine entered first, sitting beside Max with a breathless laugh.

Her niece followed and paused on the steps. "Oh! I do not mean to intrude! Val, you didn't tell me you had company. I can catch—"

"Climb in, Tess." Valentine tugged on her arm. "We'll make introductions on our way to dinner."

Tessa met David's eyes with a tentative smile and climbed into the carriage, settling next to him on the seat.

"David Bellini," he said before either Maxwell could introduce him and held his hand out.

She placed her gloved fingers in his, and he kissed her knuckles. Her eyes—gold they were, with green flecks—widened in recognition. "Oh, yes! Tessa Baker." She gestured toward Valentine. "Val's niece. A pleasure to meet you, *Conte* Bellini. Your reputation precedes you."

"David, please. Here, I am David. And the pleasure is mine, Miss Baker." And it was. She was somehow more arresting up close.

"Tessa." She laughed. "Here, I am Tessa, as well. Or hoyden or wild child or brat, if the occasion warrants it."

"Psh." Valentine waved a hand and threaded her arm through her husband's. "That was years ago when you were unmanageable and in my care while your parents went on holiday."

The driver lifted the small hatch in the roof to receive instructions from Max. The carriage soon merged into the traffic flow that continued along the promenade in starts and stops.

"Now that we're away from the store, tell us!" Valentine's eyes narrowed on her niece. "What did Mr. Blight say?"

Tessa sighed. "Oh! It is insufferable. He is insufferable. I am applying for the position against Grover Welsey, and we are to"—she rummaged in her reticule—"complete a scavenger hunt for these items." She snapped the letter open with flair and thrust it at her aunt.

"A scavenger hunt?" Max voiced David's own question. "Do you mean go to various places and retrieve specific items?" He looked over Valentine's shoulder at the list. Valentine raised a brow and looked at Tessa.

Tessa nodded, her lips thinning. "We are to have each item collected and presented to Mr. Blight by closing time on Friday."

Valentine's mouth dropped, as did the list into her lap. "And here we assumed he would question you with a series of interviews or present various scenarios."

Max retrieved the paper and frowned as he read it.

"We are to be presented with emergency scenarios to solve during store hours," Tessa said. "I've no problem with that idea. But this extra hunt . . ." Tessa glanced at David. "Forgive me—nonsense with my work."

"It's just as well he be aware of the idiocy under his employ," Valentine said, and Max closed his eyes.

An awkward silence filled the carriage, and Valentine put her hand to her mouth, blushing. "Oh, David. I'm sorry—"

He lifted a hand and shook his head. "Do not concern yourself, Valentina. Truly, it is fine."

Tessa's gaze swiveled to him. He saw comprehension dawn, and she raised a brow. "You. You are the new owner."

"Yes." He couldn't read her expression. "You are disappointed?"

She shook her head. "Oh, no! Surprised, I suppose. The store has been abuzz with speculation for weeks. I assumed the new owner would be a businessman or someone . . . older."

He laughed, gratified to see a hint of a smile on her lips. "It is a new venture for me, admittedly, yes. I do have an excellent pool of resources, however, and experience investing my own money. I am bringing in a friend of mine from Oxford, Phillip Keyes, to conduct daily operations. I plan to observe for now without alerting anyone to my role and hopefully gain an accurate portrait of the store and its dynamics."

"Yes," Valentine sighed, "and I spoiled it for you within five minutes."

Tessa's lips twitched. "You were to keep it a secret from me?"

Valentine nodded and lifted a shoulder as though to say, "Surely you see the folly."

"You studied at Oxford. That explains your flawless English." Tessa smiled when he affected modesty with a hand on his heart.

"And he still retains a hint of that delightfully romantic accent." Valentine sighed dramatically and elbowed her husband, who was still absorbed in Tessa's paper. David chuckled, appreciating her attempt to tease her husband.

Max blinked and shook his head, handing the letter across the carriage to Tessa, who took it with nostrils flared. "Tess, that is ridiculous. Perhaps the new owner may have something to say about it."

"No!" Tessa shook her head, her gaze flicking from Max to David. "Please, you mustn't."

David nodded and placed his hand on hers. "I understand. You must maintain your own sense of respectability and credibility within the store."

"Yes, yes, that is it exactly. Mr. Gibbons, my supervisor, also offered to interfere, but I cannot allow it. I will do the wretched activity, and I will beat Grover Welsey soundly."

Valentine sighed. "At least allow me to help you. I can gather most of that while you're at work next week."

Tessa shook her head, and her knee began to bounce, betraying agitation or restlessness. "Blight made a point of telling us we can be in the company of others, but we must personally locate each item. He plans to employ his team of seven teenage sons to dog our heels and ensure our adherence to the rules."

David frowned. "What is his goal? There is no guarantee this other fellow will win the prize—unless there are items that are unfeasible for you to obtain?"

Tessa shook her head again, knee still bouncing slightly. "See for yourself. The only item I might struggle with is hefting the sledgehammer in an attempt to ring the bell on the strongman carnival game. But even then, all I must do is show proof of attempting it."

David looked at the list. "He does not intend for you to win."

"What makes you think so?" Tessa chewed absently on her lip.

"Has this man, to your knowledge, ever conducted an interview process like this before?"

"Not that I'm aware."

"I imagine you and the rest of the store would have been aware of such an unusual thing. Just as the entire store will likely soon be aware of this." David waved the paper. "I do not assume to know details about each managing employee, but I know enough. Mr. Blight is a veteran manager with several years' experience. None of them, in fact, have worked in their current positions for fewer than five years."

"True." Tessa nodded.

"Suddenly he faces a female applicant for the first time, and *this* is what he decides is appropriate?"

"My application for the position is highly unusual. Truthfully, I imagine at least a few of the other managers might applaud his efforts to dissuade me."

Valentine huffed. "Just half a century ago, the only sales people ever hired or interned were men. Now see the difference! I imagine the day will come when women are managers as well. Someone must be the first, and for this store, you're it, Tess."

Tessa cast a side-glance at David, her first indication of reservation in his presence. "I do not know how you feel about such an unusual venture—my application for a supervisory position, that is. You may share concerns similar to Mr. Blight's and the others."

David shook his head. "My mother is a force, a countess who funds her own archaeological digs in Egypt and travels there frequently to conduct work on it herself. She makes no apologies for it, nor should she. So you see, I am not opposed to progress, especially when one candidate is as good as another."

"Regardless of gender?" Tessa raised a brow.

"Regardless of gender, race, creed." He shrugged. "Ability is ability; knowledge is knowledge. The source is irrelevant in determining its legitimacy or effectiveness."

Tessa studied him for a long moment, and had he not spent his entire life being examined from every angle and perspective, he might have fidgeted. "You are a progressive one, *Conte* Bellini." She smiled. "I shall not tell a soul you are the store's new owner if you agree not to speak to Mr. Blight about this." She flicked a finger at the list.

He inclined his head, charmed. "You have a deal, Miss Baker. I do have one condition."

"And that would be?"

"You allow me to accompany you on your hunt. You can introduce me at the store as your cousin or a friend of the family. Mr. Blight has stipulated that working alongside someone else is acceptable, so he can have no objection when his little spying force report back to him that I am helping you to"—he glanced down at the page—"locate a spare bolt or rivet under the Ferris wheel."

A smile touched the corner of her mouth. "Surely you have more pressing issues on your time."

"Not in the least. It allows me to observe store procedure as an outsider with nobody else the wiser. I also spend time in the company of an enchanting woman. I benefit from every side."

Tessa bit the inside of her cheek and cast a look at her aunt. "Dangerous, this one."

Max rubbed his forehead. "All the Bellinis are."

David laughed, and Tessa looked at her uncle. "Mercy, how many are there?"

"Too many. The balance will again be fair for eligible bachelors everywhere when the other three are settled down."

"It's true." Valentine's smile at her husband was wry. "Cousin Eva fell for Matteo in a matter of days."

Max cast a flat look at David. "Which is why it was fortunate indeed you were under that roof less than twelve hours, my dear."

Tessa laughed out loud. "The mighty Max feeling insecure? I can hardly countenance it!"

David waved a hand and shook his head conspiratorially at Tessa. "He speaks nonsense. Your lovely aunt had eyes for only Mr. Maxwell from the first moment. A man sees these things." He looked at Max. "Well, an *Italian* man sees these things."

"We've yet to spar, isn't that so, David?" Max eyed David in clear speculation.

David smiled. "Yes, and that is by design, my friend. I have neither a death wish nor a desire to find my face rearranged. An Italian man also guards his image."

"Hmm. Should the tenure as European nobility prove a failure?" Tessa asked.

David laughed, thoroughly disarmed. She was not awed into silence because of a desire to impress him, but she was also not one of a dozen women he'd socialized with in the last decade who'd thought *he* ought to be awed by their perfection. "Miss Baker, I do believe we shall get along famously."

Chapter Three

Jessa stood at the end of Sommerpool's South Pier just before sunrise the next morning. The world was quiet that time of day, the temperature pleasant, and the water lapped gently against the pilings below. She had never been one to sleep late into the day, and becoming a shopgirl had solidified her routine. Twelve- and thirteen-hour days standing in the shops left little time for leisure.

Shopgirls' work hours overall were improving, and that was a blessing. Since becoming Mr. Gibbons's assistant, her schedule stayed consistently at nine hours per day, and she was granted a lunch break with partial pay, which was unheard of but a direct reflection of Mr. Gibbons's kind and soft heart.

Laws passed in recent years addressed working conditions that were, in the best cases, uncomfortable and, in the worst, deadly. Children under the age of eleven were no longer allowed to work in factories, and school was now mandatory for them. Conditions for women working in factories in the larger cities improved, safety measures put into place. A working mother was less likely to lose an arm in a threading machine by stumbling too close to it in exhaustion.

Tessa had known a comfortable life as a child—her father was a successful barrister, and Tessa and her five siblings had been afforded a life that her mother always said was, "Exactly enough—not too much and not too little." As Tessa came into marriageable age and it was clear there were no prospects on her immediate horizon, she'd left their small, comfortable town and moved to Sommerpool.

The breeze picked up curls that grazed her cheeks, and she leaned on the railing, closing her eyes. She loved Sommerpool—everything about it. She loved the boisterous crowds that descended each summer, loved the noisy fair and carnival rides, the spun cotton candy, ice cream treats, the Punch and Judy puppet shows, the open-air concerts and dancing, plays and musicals on South and Middle Piers. She loved the three-tiered, balconied, upscale pavilion on the North Pier that catered to those with more elite entertainment tastes. A full orchestra, a posh restaurant, and respectable comedians were to be found there.

Even in the off-season when the town wasn't bursting at the seams with visitors, the seaside resort town still found plenty to do. Aristocratic members of society who had no wish to mingle with middle-class crowds often vacationed then, taking in the healthy sea air and enjoying North Pier entertainment. Exclusive businesses offered retreats for clientele they courted and wished to impress, and always, always there were the shops. People sometimes worked throughout the year just for a day trip to enjoy shopping and entertainment. Railroad accessibility had altered life forever for the British working class.

The water swirled around the piling in circles, and Tessa

blurred her vision, staring at the fuzzy pattern of the foam. She smiled softly; for the moment, her world was at peace. She allowed her vision to come back into sharp focus and reflected on the ridiculous scavenger hunt awaiting her and the very handsome Italian count who seemed determined to help her.

David Bellini was the stuff schoolgirl dreams were made of. The only way Tessa had been able to convince herself to relax in his presence was to acknowledge that she was nowhere near the kind of woman he would find an interest in, let alone pursue. She was a shopgirl from a provincial family in a provincial English town. He was charming and funny, as she'd learned the night before at dinner on the North Pier, and she decided to enjoy his company, accept the offer of friendship he so clearly offered, and not tie her stomach into knots worrying about whether she made a suitable impression.

"My apologies for intruding on your solitude." A masculine voice with a light Italian accent sounded at her shoulder, and she turned. There he stood, as though her thoughts had conjured him, and she smiled.

"Not at all." She straightened, and he joined her at the railing, looking out over the water. "Hard to believe we're over half a mile away from shore, is it not?"

He nodded. "I remember the first time I saw this place: I was young, and we were here on holiday. There was only the North Pier; the city has grown significantly since then. I loved everything about it, and even with my advanced age, it still holds a measure of charm."

Tessa motioned back to shore. "I arrived with stars in my eyes, believing this place was immune to poverty or children living on the streets. Still not as much as London, but there's some. A Sunday School organization is raising funds to build decent orphanages, and city leadership supports the efforts, if for no other reason than it helps with tourism."

He smiled wryly. "Every city will do whatever necessary to maintain its positive image. A truth universally acknowledged."

She turned so her back was against the railing, her elbows resting on it. "An Austen reader?" She smiled. "I hadn't imagined you the type."

"My education was a broad one indeed."

He was taller than Tessa by nearly a foot, and she angled the brim of her hat to see him better. "What are your plans for Sommerpool D&M?"

"Restore it to sound financial standing, then push forward to become the best department store in all of Europe."

She laughed, but he did not. "Forgive me, but I assumed you were teasing."

"Not in the least. I intend for the store to be better than the rest in quality of goods and services, yet still affordable for the working classes who save all year to spend their money here."

"I apologize for laughing, and while I may doubt the possibility of Sommerpool outpacing Paris in department stores, I wholeheartedly support the effort."

He leaned his elbows on the railing as she had done, and the soft breeze ruffled his dark hair. Somehow he even looked wonderful all mussed, and she shook her head with a small smile.

"I amuse you?" He turned to her, and leaning on the railing as he was, he was close enough for her to appreciate the deep blue eyes that seemed to smile right along with the rest of his perfect face.

"The hearts you must have broken, *Conte* Bellini. I was thinking it's just as well mine is guarded."

"And why is that, I wonder?"

He even smelled good! She decided her paramount goal for the day would be to find a flaw. "I've no objection to the idea of romance, but my aspirations at present rather preclude it."

"Perhaps you might make room in your life for both."

She gave him a half smile. "I might if I believed it carried potential for prolonged results. As much as I live in this place where standards are sometimes . . . relaxed, I find I have little time for dalliances or trivial flings, if you will."

His eyes twinkled. "I would imagine you are propositioned at every turn."

She laughed. "Mmm. Not at every turn. Every second turn, perhaps."

His smile broadened. "And now you are being too modest."

Mercy. It was as though she were metal filings and he was a giant magnet. Tessa made a concerted effort to refrain from swaying closer to him. "Once people realize you are the store's owner and that you've been helping me with that infernal scavenger hunt, I'll be accused of all sorts of nefarious things."

"Then we shall endeavor to protect your reputation. We are, in a sense, family. My brother Matteo is married to your Aunt Valentine's cousin."

Tessa laughed. "Yes, but Eva isn't *my* relation. She's Val's maternal cousin. Val is my father's sister."

He waved his hand. "Details. We are family and as such are entitled to a familiar relationship."

"Wonderful. You've not heard of nepotism?"

He tipped his head back and laughed. "Ah, my dear, the very word originates in Italian. *Nepotisme.* Privilege granted to nephews of popes." He leaned closer and whispered conspiratorially, "Nephews who were reported to actually be illegitimate sons." He raised an eyebrow, and she couldn't help but laugh with him.

His gaze flicked to her mouth and returned to her eyes. "You were employed at the store long before I purchased it," he murmured. "As you said yourself, our connection is tenuous, at best. We are associated enough to be seen together around town, but not so much that your work will be affected by my position."

She exhaled slowly. "I do appreciate your cooperation." She attended a Tesla demonstration once, and the charged air she'd felt then mirrored the tension she felt now between her and the handsome Italian. She shifted away slightly. "I also hope that my dissatisfaction with my coworker and superior does not color your impressions unnecessarily."

"On the contrary. I shall be ever more determined to view them with objectivity and professionalism." The corner of his mouth turned up. "I am, however, not likely to form an opinion much different than yours. You've a good head of common sense upon your shoulders, and you forget, I've seen that treasure hunt list."

She studied him for a moment and finally dared give voice to the question that had nagged her since last night in the carriage. "Forgive me, but why are you doing this?"

"Helping you?"

"No, this." She waved a hand at the department store, which stood tall and easily visible along the promenade, despite being nestled some distance away between the Middle and North Piers. "You could have any sort of life. Why take on a bankrupt department store?"

He sobered, his expression as serious and contemplative as she'd seen yet. "This is the life I want. I've played enough."

"You are an original, to be sure. I don't know too many

men who would willingly pick up a bundle of problems when he had the option of a life of leisure."

He smiled tightly. "Too much leisure is not good for anyone."

"And you've grown weary of it?"

He exhaled and turned his face toward the water. "I've grown weary of who I am with too much of it, especially when those around me are engaged in purposeful activity." He smiled a bit. "Even my mother fills her time with good deeds for the archaeological community when not in Egypt."

Tessa bit her lip before daring her next comment. She really knew nothing of the man, and insulting him could be to her detriment. "But such a large business? It is Sommerpool, of course, but the D&M is still quite a large machine. Are you certain . . ."

He looked at her, maintaining the half smile. "Certain I am qualified for the task?"

She flushed. "I do not mean to insult or show disrespect—"

"Oh, no, no, no, my dear, new friend Tessa. You are not suddenly allowed to become subservient or apologetic. I forbid it."

Her lips twitched in a reluctant smile. "Very well, if you forbid it, I shall remain humbly insubordinate."

He nodded. "Good. But your question is valid, and I am aware that hundreds of people depend on the employment the store provides. I take the responsibility very seriously, despite my annoyingly carefree nature, which I'm certain the good Doctor Freud would attribute to a defense mechanism of some sort."

She laughed. "And have you met the good doctor? He traveled through London not long ago. I admit I am curious about his methods."

"I have met him—some time ago in the early days of his practice. He said something about the influence of a strong mother and may have mentioned Oedipus, but I was very young, so the memory is rather muddled."

She laughed again, charmed despite her best intentions. "I do not suppose Oedipus is the optimal model for comfortable familial relations, but given what I've heard of the contessa, you do come from good stock."

He nodded with a smile. "That I do. Incidentally," he added, "only recently Freud abandoned his *hypnosis* phraseology and instead terms his procedures *psychoanalysis*. If you mention that in elite circles, you are sure to draw admiration for being very much in the know."

"Aha! Thank you for that. I shall remember it when faced with some of my snobbier customers. I'll drop it in casual conversation and act as though I have firsthand knowledge."

"Snobby customers, hmm?"

She rolled her eyes. "Some of the worst. But most ladies I see each day are perfectly lovely."

He studied her, and she again felt the subtle pull. "You enjoy your work."

She nodded. "I do. More than the customers, though, I enjoy working with the employees. I find I quite enjoy helping them handle their issues and concerns and being someone in whom they can confide."

"You manage people well."

She considered prevaricating, knowing it was the properly feminine thing to do, and then remembered his earlier comment about speaking plainly with him. "I do. I manage the shopgirls very well. I've even extended help to other departmental managers who come to Mr. Gibbons for advice, wondering how he handles his little realm with such success. To my eternal gratitude, he points them in my direction and gives me proper credit for my accomplishments."

David smiled. "He is a good man, then."

"A very good man." Tessa felt the surprising sting of tears. "I shall miss him dreadfully. I never knew my grandfather, and he has been very much like one for me." She closed her eyes and turned her face to the breeze with a quiet sigh. "He is responsible for the fact that I can even approach Mr. Blight with any sense of confidence in my abilities. Because of his training, I am qualified." She blinked away the moisture in her eyes.

David motioned to the sky. "The wind does kick up a bit. Quite makes one's eyes tear up."

She nodded and laughed with a sniff. "What a kind friend you are." She grimaced. "Especially as my employer! It will never do to be so emotional concerning work. Mr. Blight will call me 'hysterical' and have me locked away 'for my own good.'"

David pursed his lips in a smile. "Only shopgirls are emotional? He's clearly never met an Italian man."

She laughed again and lightly tapped his arm. "A kind friend indeed—one of your many gifts, I suspect, *Conte* Bellini. You likely find friends wherever you go."

Chapter Four

Friends. David handed Tessa a cup of Italian ice from a vendor on Middle Pier later that afternoon. Matteo often teased his wife, Eva, about her declaration that they were "the best of friends" in the early days after their first meeting. Their attraction had been instant, the pull undeniable, and she had since admitted as much—usually after giving Matteo a good whack for making her blush.

And now another Englishwoman held an Italian count in her thrall and proclaimed them fast friends. He supposed it put her at ease to convince herself the tension wasn't there, that they weren't circling each other like wary opponents in a game. David was forced to admit to himself that, for the first time, he felt unsure around a woman.

He could never remember such an anomaly occurring in his life.

The difference, he realized after spending several hours with her on Sommerpool's piers and promenade, was that he cared about the outcome. He wasn't simply on a conquest. He had the distinct and uneasy feeling in the lower regions of his heart that if he made a misstep, if he somehow ruined the association with Tessa Baker, he would live to regret it.

He knew, as one who had met more people in the course of his adult life than he could number, that she was somehow different. She was a shopgirl from modest means, who possessed a granite core of confidence to rival a queen's. Every now and again, he caught glimpses of her insecurities, but she seemed to muscle them into submission with sheer will. She shook off concerns or talked through a problem to several possible solutions. Then she seemed satisfied and again at peace.

"Thank you." She smiled and accepted the ice. "You've bought me enough treats today to last a lifetime. Now, we call this Italian ice, but you shall truly be the judge."

A soft breeze had blown all day, carrying wisps of her hair tickling across her nose and eyes. Her hat was becomingly perched atop that rich honey hair, and he fought the impulse to remove the hat and shake loose the coiffure. He wanted to see the tresses dance in the wind, uninhibited by pins. Her white blouse was tucked neatly into the small waist of a light linen skirt that was well suited to the warm summer air.

He wanted desperately to kiss her.

She took a small spoonful of ice and smiled at him, one brow raised. "Well?"

He blinked. "Yes?"

"You are woolgathering! Give it a taste, and then your honest opinion, if you please."

He cleared his throat. "You're speaking of the ice."

"Yes, the ice." She frowned. "You seem flushed."

He shoved a spoonful of the ice in his mouth, where it melted rapidly on his tongue. "Mmm." He nodded, surprised. "Quite good, actually."

"Well!" She beamed. "There's a point scored for Sommerpool." She turned and studied the crowded pier, and he studied her.

Truthfully, he'd always considered Matteo a bit addlebrained to insist he'd fallen in love with a woman he'd known for so short a time. Eva was lovely, to be sure, but such haste was unlike Matteo. He realized now he owed his elder brother an apology.

"We may actually see a band performance this evening with an illumination show since the evening trains will bring in large numbers of holiday folk." She glanced at him with a smile. "Most Sundays see limited performances, but we are on the eve of holiday week. And the crowds! You've never seen the like." She paused. "Well, you do spend time in Venice, especially during Carnival, yes?"

He nodded and told himself to focus. He was getting clumsier by the minute, finding himself awed into awkward silence. She was growing more comfortable in his presence, and he was reverting to some gawky youth.

He shoved another spoonful of ice in his mouth. *Pull yourself together, man!* "Yes," he finally managed, "and the *Biennale* always draws in the masses."

"Oh, my 'cousin' met your brother at the *Biennale*, isn't that so?" Her eyes widened slightly. "Valentine told me about their adventures. I admit it sounds too fantastical to be real—rather like an adventure novel with a heavy splash of romance." She laughed. "Truth is always stranger than fiction."

He finished his ice, and she indicated she was done as well. He took her glass cup and small spoon and, with his, returned them to the vendor with a smile of thanks.

"It bears the Italian stamp of approval, then?" the man asked him with a broad grin.

"Indeed, it certainly does." David smiled at the man's delighted chortle and returned to Tessa. He withdrew the ridiculous scavenger hunt instructions from his inner coat pocket, scrambling to remember how to be a sophisticated, urbane European nobleman and grateful beyond measure to have something to turn his focus. Perhaps the idiot Mr. Blight deserved a wage increase.

"Oh!"

David looked up. "What is it?"

Her nostrils flared, and her hands found their way to her hips before she took a deep breath and relaxed her shoulders. "It is my competition, Mr. Welsey."

A man of average height wearing a smart suit and hat approached them, a wide smile on his face. "Miss Baker," he said, removing his hat with a flourished bow. "I wonder if you've also found our required list of items quite daunting? I shouldn't be surprised if you are overwhelmed. I know I am." He placed a dramatic hand on his heart, his entire form emanating clear contradiction to his words.

"Quite the contrary, Mr. Welsey," Tessa said. "I find it to be less demanding than at first glance. But then, I have an advantage, as most people I meet are inclined to be useful and pleasant when I petition for assistance. I suspect it is more of a challenge for you, what with your obsequious and yet condescending manner."

David raised a brow, impressed.

Mr. Welsey's eyes narrowed. "Did you practice that soliloquy, Miss Baker?"

"No need, Mr. Welsey. Some of us manage effective communication quite easily."

"Ha. Ha. Ha."

David chalked another point in Tessa's favor as her nemesis proved her statement beautifully.

Mr. Welsey motioned over his shoulder with his thumb, a smirk settling back into position. "You've seen our tails, no doubt?"

Tessa frowned.

"Right there." He pointed. "And there. Mr. Blight's own spy network. Give the Yard a run for their money, I daresay."

"And a pity he must employ them at all. Some of us behave with integrity."

Mr. Welsey laughed. "You would shorten or otherwise alter that list by any means necessary if you could. Those spies are in place to keep us honest."

Tessa exhaled through her nose.

"Who's the nabob?" The man jerked a thumb at David.

Tessa's eyes widened before she recovered herself. "Where are my manners?" She smiled widely. "*Conte* David Bellini, my coworker, Mr. Grover Welsey. Mr. Welsey, the count is here on holiday, visiting with my family."

To his credit, Mr. Welsey closed his mouth quickly after it dropped open. David extended his hand with a smile and narrowed eyes.

"Mr. Welsey, a pleasure." He applied more pressure to his grip than was customary, satisfied only when the other man flinched the slightest bit.

"Count, the pleasure is mine."

David finally released his hand and held up the scavenger hunt list. "How fortuitous that I came to town in time to aid Miss Baker's quest. We have been good friends for an age, and when I heard how exhaustive this list is, in addition to a very busy upcoming workweek, it was my pleasure to offer assistance. Which, I understand, is acceptable to the quest master himself."

Welsey nodded, but added, "Mr. Blight may have issue with Miss Baker's clearly unfair advantage, however."

"What do you mean, Mr. Welsey?" Tessa asked. "If anything, I am at a disadvantage because of my department's demands in the coming days. As I understand it, the Carriage Wheel and Axle Department does not see triple the customer volume as does Linens, Gloves, and Ribbons."

Spots of color appeared high on the gentleman's cheeks. "Plenty of carriages require maintenance with the increased traffic strain! I mean that, with a count at your side, you're likely to secure everything on the list without issue!"

Tessa stepped toward Mr. Welsey, and for a moment, David pitied the man. "I plan to secure everything on that infernal list without issue whether accompanied or alone, *Grover*! Furthermore, I do not see that acquiring those items would be any different for a count or a pauper. 'A stray bolt from beneath the Ferris wheel?' One needn't be nobility to find that."

Mr. Welsey also leaned forward. "I retracted the invitation to use my Christian name," he hissed. "And we shall see what Mr. Blight has to say about your help!" He cast a glare in David's direction and left, walking stiffly down the pier toward the beach.

"Retracted the invitation?" David asked, watching the man retreat.

"Ugh. Yes, after cornering me in the stairway one afternoon with propositions I soundly refused." She glared at Welsey's back.

David felt a surge of anger. He'd not crushed the man's hand nearly enough. "You do realize that as your next of kin I'm obligated to call him out."

The tension lifted, and Tessa laughed. She swayed into him, grasping his arm. "You are not my next of kin!"

He looked down at her face, which was upturned in

genuine amusement. His lips twitched. "Then Max is responsible for it."

She shook her head, her eyes still bright with laughter. "Max doesn't know, and furthermore the situation is handled. Rest assured, I can manage *that* one."

She shifted, but he grasped her hand before she could move it away from his arm. "Are there others not so easily managed?"

She sighed. "There are always . . . It is a common occurrence for a shopgirl. Men assume that because many girls are obliged to supplement their income just to survive that *all* working girls provide additional services."

He paused, searching for language that was absent several colorful words he wanted to use. "So, am I to assume that you have been *propositioned* on multiple occasions?"

"Yes. It has become a matter of course."

"But surely not at the store. Tell me that Mr. *Weasel* there is the only one."

She lifted a shoulder. "It would be a lie. And all the shopgirls—every one of them in my department and several others—have been aggressively cornered at one point or another. Some in the store, others, well, a dark corner or a lonely stretch of road."

He stared. "Sommerpool Department and Mercantile has a reputation for excellence."

She nodded.

"But . . ."

"It is not unusual, David," she said. "Regent Street, exclusive shops in London or Paris, places where only nobility can afford to spend money? You're a man of the world. Surely you're not unaware of what often occurs abovestairs in those very shops for men who are willing to pay?"

"Yes, but . . ." He paused. "Are you suggesting those women are coerced?"

"Not forced. But who do you suppose the great majority of them are? They are not girls off the street. They are shopgirls who cannot afford to both eat and pay for a roof under which to sleep." She laughed, a little sadly. "As if a woman on the street would choose prostitution for herself either. Nobody wants it, David—very few, anyway."

His chest felt tight. He'd always turned a blind eye to those in his social circle who chose to visit a woman for a few hours and then return to hearth and home or those who were single, like himself, who considered it a matter of course and a natural right. He had no sisters. His life moved in well-bred circles where such things were ignored; he'd never been truly acquainted with a young woman in Tessa's position.

"I suppose . . ." He lifted a shoulder, still clutching her hand. "I suppose I'd not paid attention closely enough." His thoughts returned to an image of Tessa, cornered and vulnerable—at her place of employment, for heaven's sake! "And where is the building security at D&M? I've seen the records; I know we employ some."

She snorted and tugged on his hand, pulling him farther along the pier. "Security guards the goods, not the girls."

"I'm going to put someone in every blasted stairway," he muttered.

"That would be lovely." She smiled at him. "What a leader you shall be!"

He shook his head and, when she moved to release his hand, tucked hers instead in the crook of his arm. "I am amazed it is a trend not already in place. How naïve I am." He chuckled hollowly. "Words I never thought to hear myself say."

She shrugged. "I was also naïve when I first arrived here.

My home village is everything one might expect of a small town where, while neighbors might squabble occasionally, they protect each other. The first time I heard someone following me home here"—she paused and swallowed hard—"I barely outran him. I made it to the boarding house with inches to spare, and, as I slammed the door behind me, I heard his laugh echo all the way down the street. From that point forward, I made arrangements for all of us to walk in pairs or threes. Many of my bunkmates were nearly as new as I was." She smiled, but her eyes were tight. "A very quick education, it is."

He released a sigh. "Indeed. I still believe I shall call out the Weasel."

"Welsey," she laughed. "And you cannot call him out."

"I own the store."

Her eyes widened, and she squeezed his arm. "No, you promised! No professional interference in your role as owner on my behalf! David, I must do this on my own."

He glanced at her, frustrated. He wouldn't truly call the man out, but he could install her in the supervisory position she applied for with the stroke of a pen. She was more than qualified. He'd known it by the time they'd finished dinner the night before. Meeting her competition just solidified it.

She halted their steps and looked at him, unblinking. "You gave me your word."

"I can fix this whole ordeal for you, make it disappear in a matter of minutes. Why are you so opposed?"

"I have something to prove, and I will not cheat the process. I will be promoted to the position by my own merits, not because I know the owner. That would be worse than losing to Grover Welsey. If you do not wish to spend your time on this ridiculous hunt, I understand, truly. Val can help me or I can do it alone—it makes no difference—but I *will* beat them at their own silly game."

He put his hand on hers and gave her a gentle squeeze. "I would not abandon this search with you for all the tea in China—much of which I own."

His comment had the desired effect; she laughed, an unreserved, unchecked expression of delight.

He smiled. "Let's see the list." He motioned for it—at some point, he'd relinquished his hold on it and couldn't remember when. The conversation had rattled him, jarred him loose from a cocoon of relatively rosy life where unfortunate things that happened to unfortunate people were a world away, and he was absolved of guilt because of his own family's charitable contributions to good causes.

"Where are we?" He perused the list relative to their position on Middle Pier. "Oh, I neglected to get a receipt for the ices. Blast."

She loosened the strings on the reticule that hung from her right wrist and pulled out a slip of paper. "Signed by the man himself."

He stared. "When did you get that?"

"Directly after you handed him the money while his assistant was dishing it into the cups."

"Very efficient." He nodded and reached into his pocket for a fountain pen his father had gifted him on his last birthday. He unscrewed the cap as she looked at the paper he held, her hand still threaded through his arm, causing an odd mixture of anticipation and contentment.

"So, we have a receipt for the ices," she said, pointing to the item on the list, "and I have the wrapper from the cotton candy. There."

He put an *X* next to the items she indicated.

She shielded her eyes and looked down the pier. "I believe

I saw a Punch and Judy earlier. The little stage is still set up so I can retrieve"—she grimaced and looked at the list—"a small clipping of Judy's hair." She sighed. "What performer is going to allow me anywhere near the puppets with a pair of scissors?"

He was impressed with her foresight. "You have a pair of scissors?"

She shook her wrist, and her reticule swayed as she continued squinting into the distance. "Embroidery scissors. Useful for all sorts of emergencies."

He lifted a brow. "What else do you have in there?"

She turned her attention back to him and smiled. "A girl must have some secrets."

Chapter Five

Tessa walked a customer to the sales counter, trying to soothe her ruffled feathers. She carried the merchandise and smiled as the woman continued to huff under her breath about untrained sales staff.

"Monique is new here, but she is learning quickly," Tessa said. "Your patience is appreciated. Not every customer is as forgiving as you are."

"Well," the woman harrumphed, "I would hope she improves speedily. To not know which ribbons are from the newest Parisian batch is simply unthinkable. She does realize, does she not, that customers can easily take their business elsewhere? Ineptitude is simply inexcusable." She sniffed. "She is a working girl, I suppose."

Tessa continued to smile, although it felt more and more like the baring of teeth. So very many retorts shot to the tip of her tongue—comments on the woman's frayed hem, shoes at least two seasons old, a hat that was of poorer quality than Monique's crocheted lace headpiece—but she couldn't undo that which she'd taken a good twenty minutes to repair.

"Mary," she said to the girl at the counter, "please take extra care of Mrs. Featherington." Tessa handed Mary the customer's solitary length of ribbon and one pair of gloves. "She has had a most trying time, and we aim to improve her feelings for our department, as she is a valued customer and we hope for her repeated patronage."

Mary's eyes widened, and she nodded at Tessa. "Of course, Miss Baker. Mrs. Featherington, I shall gladly tally your purchases and wrap them in our finest tissue paper we ordinarily reserve for purchases totaling fifty dollars or more."

Mrs. Featherington nodded stiffly at Tessa, which was the only gesture of thanks she would receive, and Tessa cast a subtle wink at Mary, who had worked as a shopgirl for several seasons and knew how to pacify unhappy customers.

She mentally reviewed the contents of her first assignment she'd received that morning from Blight. A card bearing the following had been awaiting her, fastened to her employee cabinet door handle:

An unruly child eats your entire tray of marzipan treats before the noon hour, and you are aware that several high-spending customers plan to shop in your department that afternoon. They will expect their favorite confections, but the store's café is unable to replenish the stash in time. How will you solve the problem? Bring two-dozen marzipan treats to my office by closing today.

She'd pondered the problem all morning, deciding she would first try Mr. Frederickson's bakery, which was less than half a mile from the department store. There was another bakery a few streets to the north that she didn't frequent as often but would be a decent alternative. With any luck, neither bakery had experienced a run on marzipan that morning.

Mr. Gibbons returned to the department floor from the stockroom, carrying yards of folded muslin. Tessa scooped it from his arms and walked with him to a display table near the door, where she began arranging the new additions amongst the stock already displayed.

"Well done with Mrs. Featherington," Mr. Gibbons murmured. "If the store is fortunate, she will not spread falsehoods about our service. If *we* are fortunate, she will not return."

Tessa smiled. "Miracles happen daily, do they not?"

He chuckled. "Never took you for a religious girl."

"I know my New Testament and enough of the Old to be frightened away from licentious behavior." She smiled and waved at Mrs. Featherington, who was courteously escorted toward the main second-floor area by a very patient Mary. *Speaking of biblical*, she thought and forced herself to maintain a smile until the woman was well away from the department.

She sighed and turned to Mr. Gibbons, only to catch a flash of someone familiar. She turned her attention again to see David, handsome in his tailored clothing and charming smile. Her heart sped up and her breath caught when he spotted her, his eyes slowly sweeping her from head to toe as he approached.

"Miss Baker." He removed his hat and bowed.

"*Conte* Bellini. Allow me to introduce my superior, Mr. Gibbons." She made the proper introductions, feeding Mr. Gibbons the line about old family friendships and help with scavenger hunts. She was breathless and warm as though she'd run up a flight of stairs. Mr. Gibbons accepted David's offered hand while looking at Tessa, eyebrows raised nearly to his hairline.

"We had agreed to meet for luncheon," David said, "but I see you are quite busy at the moment."

"Yes, I'm afraid—"

"We are fine," Mr. Gibbons interrupted. "The customer flow has slowed; I believe most are heading for lunch downstairs at the café or out on the piers. Go." He checked his timepiece. "And do not return for at least two hours. If memory serves, you have a mountain of minutiae to collect."

"Mr. Gibbons," Tessa began firmly. "I cannot possibly—"

"Or you're fired."

Her mouth dropped open. "What?"

"Go, no less than two hours, or you no longer have employment here."

"You are—"

"Come along, Miss Baker," David said, tugging gently on her elbow and grinning at Mr. Gibbons, who she could have sworn might have winked back at him. "Mr. Gibbons is generous, and we'll not abuse a minute of it."

She still stared at her superior.

David shook her arm. "Shall you gather your reticule and hat?"

She nodded and then narrowed her eyes at Mr. Gibbons's wide-eyed, affected innocence. She lifted a finger, prepared to argue again when David took hold of both arms from behind and steered her toward the back of the department.

"Your belongings are back here, I assume?" he said, his voice low and deliciously close to her ear.

"He is . . . He is bluffing! And I know what that means!" She tried to ignore the spiral of heat that started somewhere in her midsection and spread throughout her limbs. "David, this lunch lull will last for perhaps thirty minutes!"

"Which cabinet is yours?" he asked as he propelled her through the curtain at the corner and into the employee area.

"That one." She pointed at the far end.

He marched her to it and turned the handle. "You have the key?"

She pulled it from her pocket and handed it to him, utterly flummoxed with Mr. Gibbons and utterly, reluctantly, entranced by her dear family friend on holiday from Italy, who appeared to be fighting a smile, if not an outright guffaw.

He swiftly unlocked her door on the long wardrobe that spanned the wall and peered inside, pulling out her reticule and hat. "It is quite warm out; I'd not bother with the shawl. In fact, I rather wish I could just leave my suit coat here."

She held the hat and reticule and looked at him dumbly while he closed and locked the cabinet. She was not attracted to him. She was not. Not beyond the most surface observations that any woman with two eyes would readily acknowledge. Yes, he was handsome and funny and intelligent; he had a good heart and was readily receptive to ideas he'd not considered. He looked at her with an intense, focused regard that made her feel as though she were the only person on earth he ever cared to look at again.

But she was not attracted to him. She was *not*.

"Did Blight deliver your instructions for the day?"

She nodded.

"Do you have them in your reticule?"

She nodded again.

He finally lost whatever internal battle he was waging and laughed. "Shall I put on your hat?"

"It would look silly on you."

He took the hat from her fingers, his lips quirked in a smug smile. "Ordinarily, I'd interpret that as a witty rejoinder. Now, however, I believe you do mean it seriously."

He settled her hat carefully on her hair, adjusting it just so and tucking a curl behind her ear. She closed her eyes briefly as his finger brushed the edge of her ear and lingered. He smelled wonderful.

"There's a breeze," he murmured, and she felt him pulling the hatpin loose and carefully securing it through the hat and into her hair. "Wouldn't want to lose this. It is a quality headpiece."

"You have a good eye."

"I most certainly do."

She tilted her face up, and he trailed his fingertip along her jaw line and down the side of her neck. He whispered something in Italian—something exquisite, she was sure—and she fought to remain upright rather than falling on him.

"You should not say such things," she said, drumming up the courage to meet his deep blue eyes.

His hand paused, and then his fingers wrapped softly around the back of her neck. "You speak Italian, *cara mia*?"

She gave a half smile. "No."

"Good."

"And why is that? What did you say?"

"Nothing you're ready to hear."

She exhaled quietly, and he pulled back. He dropped his hand and extended her key, his face an expression she couldn't read.

"Now then." He cleared his throat. "First on our agenda is to visit Mr. Blight. I want to meet him."

She eyed him warily and put away her key. They made their way to the curtain—she on legs that were oddly weak—and she shook her head. "What are you going to say to him?"

"That I am your friend and am helping you meet his ridiculous demands."

"You cannot—"

He shot her a flat look. "I am teasing, of course. I do know how to behave. You give me so little credit."

"Mm-hmm." She held up a finger. "Remember what I've said."

"Yes, madam. I will not tell anyone I am wealthy as Midas, own this entire enterprise, and am quite ready to see you advanced into the position you so rightly deserve."

She clapped a hand over his mouth. "This is only a curtain!" she hissed. She twitched it aside, relieved nobody else was within earshot. She felt him smile beneath her hand, and she realized her gloves were still inside her reticule. His lips pursed slightly against her skin, and her breath came out on a shaky sigh.

She snatched her hand back as if scorched, and he winked at her. "Incorrigible! You are a gentleman!"

"Ah," he whispered and leaned in close, "but first an Italian."

She shook her head and gave him a side-glance, fighting a smile. He was close enough to kiss, and she was tempted beyond words, if only to shock *him* for once. He lingered, silently daring her with one lifted brow, and she winked at him instead.

"Come along, then. Let us pay a visit to Mr. Blight." She smiled brightly and led the way through the department and into the large area that showcased the latest fashions in women's apparel. He followed, observing activity on the floor, his eyes flicking over shopgirls and customers as if cataloguing information.

"I took the opportunity to peruse the other departments before finding you," he said as they made their way to the elevator. "Most departments seem well-run and organized. I have accountants reviewing each area's books. Phillip Keyes has managed several large Parisian boutiques. His expertise thus far has been invaluable."

She nodded. It made sense, and as she spent more time

in his company, she'd come to realize he wasn't a carefree playboy. He made decisions carefully, listened to and absorbed everything she said, down to the tiniest detail. He occasionally took a small notebook from his pocket and jotted quickly, often asking her questions about the subject at hand for clarification.

His only absentminded lapse, in fact, had been his distraction over the Italian ices and, if memory served, he'd spent much of that hour studying her, as though working something out in his mind. She felt a small sense of feminine satisfaction that she had been the reason for that distraction. Afterward, he had continually offered his arm, guided her along with a hand on her back as they weaved through crowds, and touched her hand or shoulder to draw her attention to something he observed.

They reached the lift, and Tessa rang for it. Voices from the main store areas drifted up as though from far away, and the hallway was blissfully peaceful. "I do enjoy the crowds, I truly do," she said with a sigh, "but in contrast, the quiet can be quite wonderful."

He smiled, his hands in his pockets, and leaned against the wall. "The watching of people is one of life's greatest entertainments, but I agree. Silence is sometimes bliss."

"Where will you live?" she asked suddenly. He'd mentioned awaiting a home rental near Max and Valentine's house, but that seemed temporary.

"Here." His tone was soft. "I will live here. I'll visit home often, of course, and perhaps spend extended holidays there, but this . . ." He looked around at the store and settled his gaze back on her. "This is everything I want."

She swallowed. Could he honestly be considering settling down and taking on responsibility? He'd said as much from the beginning, but she'd believed it to be a passing fancy.

Extended time spent in his company seemed to be proving her wrong.

The lift finally arrived, saving her from trying to decipher the confused mix of emotions that tumbled through her head. She was happy with her life, loved her fellow employees, sans one in particular, and looked forward to her future in the store with optimism and anticipation. She had no room for anything else.

She stepped into the lift, and David followed. "Hello, Henry," she said with a smile. "Fifth floor, please."

"Of course, Miss Baker." He smiled and closed the lift gate.

"How are your children, Henry? On the mend, I hope?"

"Right as rain, they are. The missus—tougher than nails, that one—and the little 'uns, they've her constitution and my stubbornness."

"I am so glad to hear it," Tessa said, her sentiments genuine. He was a good man who worked long hours, and his wife took in mending. Sick and dying children were more common than not, and the poor suffered more than the rest. "Please extend my best wishes to your wife, will you?"

The elevator came to a stop on the fifth floor, and Henry opened the gate. "That I will, miss. And likewise, to you and your'n."

She exited the lift, and, as she turned to see that David followed her, she felt a tug on her heart. David had handed Henry a tip—she didn't see the amount, but the other man's eyes boggled. He stammered his thanks, and David touched his fingers to his hat brim.

He joined her in the hallway, and she bit her lip, fighting a sudden flare of emotion. He gave a lift operator a healthy tip. He hadn't saved the world, for heaven's sake. And perhaps he didn't carry small currency on his person.

Well, that wasn't true, the other side of her brain argued. He'd paid with small bills the day before. He always tipped, though, and she never saw amounts but suddenly remembered multiple expressions of shock or gratitude, not unlike the one she'd just seen on Henry.

One half of her brain argued that it was easy enough to tip well when you had more money than sense. The other half argued that he had plenty of sense and that there were plenty of wealthy people who didn't bother to tip at all. She'd seen that firsthand. David was proving himself to be a good man with a generous heart, not to mention a physical appeal that was beginning to wreak havoc on her nerves.

They reached Mr. Blight's outer office where his assistant sat at a desk. He looked up and recognized her, his face settling into its customary mask of barely veiled scorn. She didn't know how he accomplished it, but it never failed. "Mr. Devon, I have urgent business with Mr. Blight that requires a few moments of his time."

"Did you schedule these few moments beforehand? I am looking at his hourly appointment list, and I do not see your name here, Miss Baker."

"You've not even looked at the list, Mr. Devon."

"I do not need to."

David tapped one finger on the corner of the desk. "I am *Conte* David Bellini. We will speak with Mr. Blight immediately. Please inform him now, or we shall simply see ourselves in."

Mr. Devon swallowed, likely caught somewhere between suitably impressed and heartily annoyed at being outmaneuvered. "Very well." He rose stiffly and entered Blight's office after a perfunctory knock.

Tessa gritted her teeth in outrage. "I have known that

man for four years—*four years*—and he still views me as a speck of dirt on his sleeve."

"Apologies for stepping in." David did indeed look apologetic, but he settled his gaze on the closed office door, his eyes narrowed.

"It is just as well," she muttered. "We'd be waiting out here all day, otherwise."

She paced the length of the outer office, amazed that there was even a slight delay in being received. Blight was one of the most obsequious people she knew; she couldn't believe he wasn't falling all over David right now.

Finally, the door cracked open, and she spun around.

"Mr. Blight will see you now." Devon looked at Tessa. "I trust you will manage proper introductions."

She used every ounce of will she possessed to refrain from either sneering at the man in an undignified manner or clawing at his eyes. "I believe I can manage it," she said when David shifted as though ready to strike. Not sparing the assistant another glance, she entered Mr. Blight's office with David.

She did indeed manage to make proper introductions, enjoying a savage sense of satisfaction at the realization that, soon, Blight would be told the storeowner's identity and realize he'd already spent time with him unguarded. Had he said anything that might cast him in an unfavorable light? Had he offended in any way? The questions would plague him, and Tessa consoled herself with it as Blight conversed with David and completely ignored her.

He finally turned his attention back to Tessa. "Did you have a purpose in introducing me to the count? Other than simply allowing me the privilege of the association?"

She held back a roll of her eyes, but only just. Her head hurt with the effort required. "You told Welsey and me last week that as we conducted the scavenger hunt, we would not be disqualified for having companionship along on the adventure. Welsey insinuated yesterday that you would find *Conte* Bellini an unsuitable companion."

Blight shook his head vigorously. "Not at all! Not at all objectionable. I had no idea you possessed such illustrious connections, Miss Baker."

"I did not see the relevance. My associates away from the store have no bearing on my work here."

"Well, perhaps you do not appreciate the import of such alliances, but men of business certainly do."

She looked pointedly at David. Surely he'd seen enough.

"Well, then." David smiled at Blight. "Miss Baker wanted to be certain you have no objections to my help."

"None at all! Please come by again. Or perhaps one day soon you'll allow me to buy you a drink. Sommerpool pubs and taverns are among the best, you know."

David smiled. "This city offers the best of many things indeed."

Chapter Six

David held open the bakery door for Tessa and followed her inside. She was irritated with Blight's casual dismissal of her, and he couldn't find fault in that. She was justified in her frustration with the man, who clearly did not expect her to succeed with her week's tasks.

Tessa tapped her foot on the shop floor as several people were in the queue already. Finally, it was their turn. "Mr. Frederickson, how are you today?" She smiled at the man behind the glass display cabinet.

The man's weathered face broke into a smile. "Miss Baker's come to the bakery!"

She laughed. "That one never does get old. But today I have an unusual request. I am urgently searching for two-dozen marzipan favors. Do you happen to have any on hand? I didn't see any in the other two display cases."

"Ah, missy, I am sorry to tell ya, but another bloke was in here an hour ago, bought up every last marzipan confection I have."

Tessa's mouth dropped open, and she hastily closed it.

"Must be marzipan is in high demand today. Can I offer ya something else?"

Tessa took a deep breath, and David wondered how on earth he could help her find two dozen of anything that specific with half of Britain enjoying Sommerpool's seaside delights. The display cabinets in the store were fairly sparse, and a harried employee in a stained apron bustled from the back room with a tray of sweet rolls.

"Thank you anyway, Mr. Frederickson. Oh!" She opened her reticule. "When I realized I would be stopping by today, I cut a sample of our newest pink ribbon for your wife." She handed him the length of lacy pink material over the cabinet. "And will you tell her that we'll happily honor the same discount for the first thirty days again?"

"Ah, missy. She'll be delighted to hear it." He pocketed the ribbon and beamed at Tessa, who smiled in return. "I'll have marzipan aplenty tomorrow morning, if ye're still needin' it."

"Thank you ever so much. I shall be in again if I do." Tessa maintained a pleasant expression until they left the store, then she spun on David, face flushed. "Can you believe it? I can! Welsey bought up every last smidgen of the stuff so I couldn't get any!"

David looked back into the bakery. "If I offer to buy all his remaining stock, plus tomorrow's, will he close his doors and make nothing but marzipan between now and closing?"

Her shoulders slumped. "No, it would take more time, and besides, I cannot have you rushing to my rescue." She glanced at him, her brows knit. "Especially since people will know soon enough about your relationship to the store."

David knew she was right, but still, it rankled. "The weasel is certainly not opposed to playing a dirty game. I see no reason for you to avoid responding in kind."

"I want to do this the right way. And Blight is correct—suppose that scenario actually played out and Mr. Frederickson did not have what I need? I would try the next baker, a few streets that way."

David whistled and motioned for a hansom. A driver pulled alongside, slowing the horse with a low whistle. "There's nothing in Blight's rule book that dictates you must walk all over town to solve the problem. Would you travel by carriage if this situation were real?"

"Yes." She took his hand and allowed him to help her into the small cab. She gave him the name of the shop, which he relayed to the driver, who nodded and clicked to the horse.

David settled down beside her, grateful for the limited space the narrow carriage provided. Their shoulders overlapped, and hers nestled just behind his as though it had always been there. She was pressed against him from shoulder to knee, and he glanced at her, unable to suppress a grin.

"We shall travel thusly, always."

She laughed and tapped his arm, a blush staining her cheeks. Her smile lingered, and he reached for her hand, which he then threaded under his arm. He winked at her. "We'll find your marzipan."

She nodded, her lips tightening. "How in blazes did he get away from the store so early?" She shook her head. "It's as I told him: his department is substantially less crowded than mine. I knew when I began that I would not only have to be proficient, I'd have to be better than proficient."

The carriage rattled along in fits and starts, dodging rather handily around congestion. The driver turned north onto a less crowded avenue and, in a matter of minutes, pulled to a stop. Tessa checked a pocket watch she had pinned to her waist. "I shall hurry."

She jumped down from the carriage with impressive speed before either he or the driver could offer assistance. "I'll wait here," he called after her as the shop door closed. He smiled, knowing in that moment that he was done for. She'd stolen his heart, and he quite wanted her to keep it.

"I will pay you two days' wages if you will remain at our disposal for the next two hours," he said to the driver as he climbed down and approached the bakery, which was one of several small shops along the street.

"I accept!" the driver called. "I'll wait here!"

He might not have bothered getting down from the cab. Tessa opened the bakery door and headed back toward him, her face drawn. "He did the same thing here."

David's brows climbed. "He bought all their marzipan?"

"Yes!" She stood on the small walkway, nostrils flared, hands on her hips. "Think, Tessa. Who might have a stash of marzipan continually at the ready?"

David scratched his neck, entirely at sea. He could pay someone good money to make the stuff, but he had no idea where it came from.

Her eyes lit up. "Mrs. Dyer!"

"And who is Mrs. Dyer?"

"She creates wedding cakes on special order from her home, located about a mile inland from South Pier."

"Excellent." He grasped her arm and propelled her back to the carriage. "Do you have an address?"

She puffed air into her cheeks, thinking. "Just south of the corner of Verbena and Rosewood."

The driver nodded when David looked up at him. They settled into the carriage, which immediately pulled into traffic. She bounced her knee restlessly, agitating the entire carriage, and he finally clamped his hand down on her leg. She gave him a flushed side-glance and a rueful smile. "I knew it would be a lengthy day; I may have had twice my usual amount of morning coffee."

He laughed, and when he left his hand on her knee, she tilted her head toward his shoulder.

Well, an interesting development indeed. He smiled, and it remained in place all the way to the corner of Verbena and Rosewood.

She grinned at him when they came to a stop and hopped down again on her own. Deciding he didn't want to miss one moment of her negotiating skills, he followed her and entered a well-tended town house that smelled deliciously of sugary delights. The housekeeper had already stepped away to fetch her mistress, and before he could say two words to Tessa, a woman appeared, middle-aged, pleasant features, and thin as a rail.

"Must not eat her own creations," he murmured.

"Nary a bite. She has a sugar illness—something with her blood. Makes her sick and she faints."

"Tessa Baker!" The woman enveloped Tessa in a quick embrace, her own demeanor as animated as Tessa's. David supposed she'd also had a double round of coffee. "And how is your darling aunt?"

"Splendid, thank you for asking." Tessa smiled and made quick introductions, and he soon learned that Mrs. Pamela Dyer made the world's most beautiful wedding treats.

Tessa hurriedly explained her dilemma, and Mrs. Dyer snapped her fingers with a triumphant nod. "I have seven dozen in cold storage. You need two?"

"Yes, but only if it doesn't inconvenience you. I'll pay you extra, of course."

"Nonsense." She eyed David with a quick glance. "You follow me. You can carry them to the carriage."

Tessa looked at him and raised a shoulder apologetically.

"Lead the way, Mrs. Dyer," he said, and they followed her down the hall to a large kitchen.

Mrs. Dyer pulled a large tray from an icebox and made quick work of arranging the treats on a platter, which she then covered with paper. She handed it to him with an aside for Tessa. "These are fairly small. They will thaw in an hour or two. The almond in the middle may remain colder than the rest for a time."

Tessa grabbed the woman and squeezed. "You are wonderful. Here." She released Mrs. Dyer and pulled several coins from her reticule.

"No, you batty girl!" Mrs. Dyer tried to return two coins, but Tessa darted around the woman and David, who obediently held the platter.

"I shall visit soon!" she called from the foyer.

David smiled at the woman and dug into his pocket. He clinked another three coins into her hand and said, "Madam, you have truly saved the day."

He left her gaping in the kitchen and followed Tessa, who had already climbed into the carriage.

Chapter Seven

Jessa's second cup of morning coffee had worn off by midafternoon, and she was in danger of falling asleep on her feet. The trauma of locating two-dozen marzipan treats had changed to euphoria upon success, but now had her feeling drained. The crowd of customers in her department had thinned, and Mr. Gibbons was in his small office, taking a much-needed break.

A runner from the fifth floor appeared in the second floor main area, and she knew instinctively the message he carried was for her. She sighed, and when Mary pointed the boy in her direction, she held out her hand. He gave her a sealed envelope that matched the one she'd received that morning, except there was a lump inside.

She opened it, and an inexpensive, plain cameo slid into her palm. Along with the cameo was a clasp. The note inside read:

The provost's wife has a pressing engagement in a matter of hours, and she neglected to plan for alterations to her family heirloom. The last time she wore the brooch, the pin stuck her dreadfully. She has come to the department store, as the jewelers have closed their doors early for the day, and desperately seeks assistance. She must have the pin removed and the clasp attached, and it must be secure because there's certain to be dancing and revelry.

You have one hour.

Tessa stared ahead at nothing, her eyelids at half-mast. Blight had said nothing about an additional task in the same day. She exhaled and took a quick look around the department.

"Mary," she said, locating the shopgirl who was restocking blue kidskin gloves. "I must conduct a pressing errand for Mr. Blight. There is relative calm at the moment. Do you suppose you can manage until Mr. Gibbons finishes his rest? Shouldn't be more than another twenty minutes."

"Of course, Miss Baker."

Tessa dashed to her cabinet in the back and retrieved her belongings. "Jewelers are closed for the day in the scenario," she murmured aloud as she made her way down the two flights of stairs to the main level. "Am I to presume that I am forbidden to use a jeweler?"

She stood near the main doors and, on a whim, spun and hurried to the department store's small jewelry department. She explained her dilemma to the shopgirl behind the counter, who shook her head in sympathy. "I am sorry, but I am the only one present for the remainder of the afternoon, and I haven't the skills. You're the second person with a similar problem today. I had to send him away also."

Tessa stilled and cast a quick glance in each direction. "Was the other person a gentleman who works in Carriages?"

The girl's brows lifted. "Why, yes! And his brooch was nearly identical to yours."

"How long ago was he here?"

"Two hours, roughly."

Tessa gaped. "Two . . . two hours?" She'd only now received her instructions from Mr. Blight, and she'd returned from her mad marzipan dash ninety minutes earlier. "He's giving that toad a head start."

"I'm sorry?"

"Nothing. Thank you for your time, Miss . . ."

"Cloverton."

"Miss Cloverton." Tessa quickly left the jewelry department, making her way outside. There was a jeweler adjacent to the department store, an old establishment that had been in business over a century. The proprietor was the original owner's grandson, who also looked to be over a century.

She entered the shop, and a bell overhead alerted Mr. Farr to her presence. She smiled, steeling herself. The few encounters she'd had with him had been unpleasant. He detested the department store—shopgirls especially.

A few other customers moved quietly around the shop, which seemed to demand an air of reverence, and she approached cautiously. Perhaps she ought to have brought along one of the nearly thawed marzipan treats. "I wonder if you might help me, Mr. Farr."

She repeated the same tale she'd just spun for Miss Cloverton, and his expression never altered a mite. When she finally finished speaking, he looked at her for a long moment. She raised her brows and leaned forward slightly.

"Miss, I was told you would come storming in here with a tale similar to the gentleman I aided not two hours ago. He also informed me of your nefarious intentions to pass off that piece of paste nonsense as a genuine article."

Tessa gasped. "I am planning no such thing! I simply seek—"

"I know what you seek, and you will not find it here," he interrupted, and several curious gazes swiveled their way. "Forewarned is certainly forearmed. I owe the gentleman a debt of gratitude."

"Why, that little—" She cut herself off and clutched her reticule until her knuckles were white. She took in a deep breath and nodded stiffly. "I'll not disturb you further."

"I should think not."

Using every ounce of strength, she closed the door gently behind her rather than slamming it. She put a hand to her forehead, exasperated. How was she to compete when the competition's designer showed clear preference for the other side? She suddenly wished for David's solid presence beside her and scowled when she realized the direction her thoughts had wandered. She didn't need anyone. She could do this on her own.

She walked away from the store and headed south on the promenade. She paused at Middle Pier, tapping her fingertip against her lip. She scanned the buildings, and her spirits lifted. "The clockmaker!"

She dashed down the pier, calling apologies to people she bumped along the way. Mr. Timely's clock shop was a magical little world unto itself; she felt quite like a fanciful creature, a fairy, when in it. They had laughed together upon meeting that his name quite fit his profession. He admitted people remarked on it constantly, and she promised to not make a habit of it.

The gentle ticktock slowed her racing thoughts, and she smiled at the white-haired gentleman seated at a table, looking through a magnifying glass attached to his spectacles. He looked up at her, and she bit her cheek; his one eye was enormous through the glass.

"Well, then!" Mr. Timely rotated the magnifier up and

away from his face. "Trouble with the timepiece again? Beautiful old boy, that one."

She took a breath and approached him, waving him back to his seat when he moved to stand. "No, no," she said, tapping the watch pinned to her waist. "Runs like a charm. I wrote to my mother, and she was amazed you'd fixed it. She figured after all those years it was well and truly done for."

"Nothing is well and truly done for. What can I help you with today?"

Tessa sighed. "I'm not certain you can." She explained the problem, feeling like a magpie that continually repeated itself.

He rolled his eyes and held out his hand, motioning with his fingers. "And here I was hoping for a challenge."

She handed it to him, feeling a sense of hope that had dwindled alarmingly since her conversation with Miss Cloverton at the department store jewelry. She watched in amazement as he made quick work of removing the pin from the back of the brooch and fired up a tiny soldering iron to attach the clasp.

In a matter of minutes, he had completely switched out the findings and waved the piece, blowing gently to cool and solidify the metal. "And there we have it." He smiled at her and handed her the brooch.

She nearly cried. She bit her lip and cleared her throat. "I cannot thank you enough." She fumbled with her reticule strings, and he interrupted her.

"Nonsense. You've sent more business my way during the off-season that, for the first time in ages, the store isn't at the mercy of holiday week. Now, be off with you. You were in a mighty hurry when you blasted through that door."

She shook his hand, clasping it gently in both of hers. "Bless you. A million times, bless you."

He shooed her away, but she paused at the door. "Oh! Would you please tell your granddaughter that I saw the loveliest pair of pale blue gloves today? She would adore them. Send her in and have her ask for me."

Mr. Timely chuckled. "She will be thrilled. Do not be surprised to find her waiting for the doors to open tomorrow."

Tessa checked the clocks hanging on the wall and, with a quick goodbye, rushed back down the pier, nearly running. She was winded and knew she'd likely fall over before reaching the fifth floor by stair, so she waited what seemed an interminably long time for Henry and the lift.

She checked her timepiece again as she exited the lift and dashed down the hallway to Mr. Blight's office. She had ten minutes to spare. Mr. Devon guarded his post, lip curling as she approached, and she heard masculine laughter from within the inner sanctum. Snatches of conversation escaped: "And an extracted tooth! Plenty to keep her so busy she'll not possibly be able to complete the list . . ."

She gritted her teeth, prepared for battle. Mr. Devon opened his mouth, and she held up a hand, catching her breath. "If you tell me I'm not allowed in because my name is absent from the schedule, I will overturn this desk."

He narrowed his eyes but stood and knocked on Blight's door. The laughing quieted, and Tessa moved to stand beside the assistant. Mr. Blight saw her and raised a brow. Devon moved as though to block her entrance, but Blight shook his head. "Let her in."

She entered and noted the presence of two additional men—Mr. Litton from the Housewares Department and Grover Welsey. They remained seated, although Mr. Litton gifted her with a nod of acknowledgment. She managed a tight smile for each of them, clenching her hold on a temper that was charging to escape.

"Miss Baker, what brings you here?" Blight asked, leaning against his desk.

"This." She marched forward and thrust the brooch out to him. "You sent me a note fifty minutes ago with instructions to return the cameo fixed within the hour. I trust it meets with your approval, as I wore it while dancing my way to your office. Quite solid, it is."

Devon's voice sounded from the outer office, but she ignored it. She held Blight's gaze and took immense satisfaction at his shock.

She raised a brow at him. "Closing time is soon upon us, and I trust there will be no further emergencies today?"

Welsey rose quickly from his seat and stormed to Blight's side. "Let me see that!"

She held up her hand and faced him squarely, blocking his approach. "You are privy to *nothing* I do as a result of this test. You are neither my superior nor my friend, and I shall tell everyone within shouting distance of your treachery and deceit. You have blocked me repeatedly today, and yet I have still managed to complete my assigned tasks. My marzipan is downstairs as we speak, and I shall bring it up directly."

Welsey's eyes narrowed. "You do not have the marzipan."

"Because you visited all the bakeries in town and bought every last piece? How many baking establishments saw your patronage today, I wonder? Three? Four? How much marzipan candy do you have—enough to host a party?"

He closed his mouth.

"You labored under the assumption that a bakery was the only available option." She turned her attention back to Blight. "It may interest you to know that this colleague and fellow applicant received his instructions for the jewelry task two hours before I received mine. As I am certain *you* would not have given him an unfair advantage, because that would not showcase his true skills, you may consider questioning him." Welsey emitted a sound of protest, and she snapped her attention to him. "Tell me I am wrong. I have witnesses."

Blight slid a finger between his collar and neck, glancing nervously at the door. He stood straight, and in her periphery, she saw Mr. Litton stand as well. She turned around then and saw David in the entrance, leaning one shoulder against the doorjamb with his hands in his pockets. The fiery blue eyes belied his relaxed stance and his pleasant expression.

"*Conte* Bellini," she said, her heart thumping in pleasure. "I did not expect to see you until dinnertime with the family."

"One of your shopgirls said you'd been called away on an emergency, so I thought to ask Mr. Blight if he knew what that might entail."

Blight cleared his throat. "You and Mr. Welsey both performed admirably today, Miss Baker, and a busy day it has been. I will suspend the emergency scenarios tomorrow, and we'll resume again on Wednesday."

"Very wise managerial decision," David murmured. "Doesn't make much sense to exhaust key members of your staff during holiday week."

"Quite right." Blight nodded and smiled, but it slipped as his glance darted to Tessa. "Perhaps we might eliminate a handful of the items on the scavenger list. You may both dispense with five tasks of your choice."

Mr. Litton lit a cheroot. "Might I have an introduction, then?"

David straightened, his expression hard. "Another time, perhaps, when I do not enter a room where a gentleman remains seated while a lady stands."

Delicious! Tessa hurried from the room to keep her smile hidden. She would have dearly loved to command that sort of respect, but all things considered, she'd stood firm and spoken her mind. Blight hadn't fired her on the spot—probably because her accusations had hit their mark—so she would enjoy at least one more day of gainful employment.

She stopped at the lift, but David took her arm and propelled her to the stairway. They walked around the corner, hidden from view, and the door closed behind them.

"I am not going to assault you," he said.

She laughed softly, feeling some of the tension of the last hour drain away. "I never assumed that was your intent." Nor would it have been an assault. She was honest enough with herself to admit it. She sobered. "How much did you hear?"

"Enough. I've a mind to stop all this. Clean house, I believe, is the correct terminology."

She knew a moment's relief, which in turn saddened her. She shook her head. "You must do what you feel best for the store, of course, but if you think to end the contest here for my sake, please do not. Something amazing happened to me just now. I did something *amazing*."

He closed his eyes briefly. "Everything you *are* is amazing," he whispered and placed his hand alongside her cheek.

She leaned into it, weary from the surge of emotions she'd experienced over the course of a few hours.

"I'll leave things be, for now; however, I am sending for my business manager, Phillip, immediately. I'll reveal my identity next week."

She frowned. "But you wanted to observe for at least two."

"I've seen enough." His fingers slipped to her neck, and he cradled her head in both hands. "I am going to kiss you now," he murmured.

"I am going to allow it," she said with a smile, her heart pounding so loudly she was certain he must hear it.

He traced her eyebrow with this thumb. "I would hate for you to feel trapped in here."

"This is one time I do not mind," she whispered.

He lowered his head and touched his lips to hers, soft, tentative at first. He captured her sigh and deepened the kiss, moving his hands to her back and pulling her close. She put her arms around his neck and reveled in each sensation—the feel of his lips tasting hers, the smooth texture of his hair beneath her fingertips, the very smell of him.

It was the most exquisite invasion of sense and thought she'd experienced. He traced her jaw line with his lips, nipped lightly at her neck, and she shivered, amazed at the sensation such a small thing evoked. She cradled her hand against his head, which he slowly lifted to once again capture her lips in a sensual caress.

He finally pulled away and met her eyes. He drew an unsteady breath, and she felt a thrill at it—that he was as affected as she. "I must indeed install security guards in here."

She smiled, suddenly feeling shy, which was not a familiar emotion. He was a man of the world, though, and she was an untutored shopgirl. She'd never been kissed so thoroughly or well, and her own inexperience left her feeling vulnerable.

"I do not . . . That is, I do not know how . . ." She frowned, unable to find the words.

He laughed, his expression pained. "Oh yes, *cara mia*, you most certainly do know how." He pulled her close again and kissed her, slowly and thoroughly, finally pulling back with a regretful sigh. "But we must go before we are discovered and your credibility here is in tatters."

"You truly heard my diatribe, then?"

"*Mia bella*, it was the most arousing set-down I have ever witnessed. If I hadn't been so angry on your behalf, I would have applauded. And then kissed you soundly right there in that office."

She laughed and reluctantly stepped out of his arms. She straightened her blouse and felt her hair, repositioning a few pins. Her legs felt wobbly, but she didn't want to return to the lift for fear of encountering one of the other men. That would tarnish a beautiful moment she wanted to hold in her heart forever. David Bellini had a mouth made for scandal, and she'd been a happy recipient. As much as she relished his hand on her shoulder as they walked down the stairs, she was mortally afraid for the state of her heart. She was falling rapidly down a hole she'd desperately wanted to avoid.

Chapter Eight

David reclined in a chaise lounge on the balcony adjoining his guest suite at the Maxwell home. The stars were out in full force, and he closed his eyes, enjoying the cool evening air. He held an after-dinner drink that he sipped slowly and eventually set on the small round table at his elbow.

He'd arrived at several decisions that would have surprised him a week before. He would bring in his friend, Phillip Keyes, as soon as possible, as well as the paperwork and records he'd had delivered to his friend in London months ago. He would stay out of Phillip's way and allow him the freedom to do what he did best: operate a successful and profitable retail establishment. But David was no longer content in his role as a silent partner. He wanted to be more involved, to be apprised of not only the bigger picture but some of the smaller ones as well. Over the course of a couple days, he had met people—real people, both in the store and on the crowded piers—whose lives were affected by decisions other men made.

Tessa had been glorious in her cold fury earlier in Blight's office. She had been calm and professional, but justifiably angry. She had demanded integrity from men who ought to be displaying it as a matter of course. She had made them aware she was not ignorant of their tactics, that she knew full well what they were about and that it was wrong.

By the time they had delivered the blasted marzipan to Blight's office—which was notably empty but for the man himself—and then closed out the day with Mr. Gibbons, Tessa had drooped with fatigue and, at Valentine's insistence, retired early. David had chatted for some time with Max and Valentine in the library, discussing Max's business dealings and details he hadn't known to ask before now.

Valentine had excused herself earlier than the gentlemen, saying she felt under the weather. Max mentioned that she seemed to have contracted some sort of illness—she had been oddly nauseous for several weeks. David hadn't voiced his opinion about that, but smiled.

He now breathed deeply of the clean air and exhaled. While Tessa had been sent off on a mission apparently designed to fail, he had wandered the store, taking in details and observing employees. He'd learned much in a few days from his association with Tessa and now noticed things he'd have missed. He was also trying to give her some time to actually do her job—he knew she would be distracted if he hovered, so he'd left her in peace. Only he'd then found she hadn't been in peace at all.

He'd found her upstairs, upbraiding a trio of men he would label 'men' only in the loosest of terms. Upset for her sake and aroused beyond bearing, he'd taken her into the stairwell, of all places, and kissed her.

He felt a surge of heat at the memory of her hands in his hair, her contented and yet urgent sigh against his lips. Every new little piece of her he learned or explored deepened his rapidly growing affection, and he knew he would either convince her to marry him or die trying.

A firework lit the sky, and he heard a distant pop, signaling continued revelry on the beaches and piers. He fully intended to experience it all with Tessa, but perhaps it would have to wait until after frenetic holiday week had passed. There was still the matter of the extra items on the scavenger hunt list, though, and the deadline was Friday. Perhaps they would tackle that tomorrow night when she was rested.

He wished he knew the true nature of Blight's goal. Did he hope to force Tessa into such impossible situations that she would voluntarily withdraw? Would he fairly judge the two candidates for the position? David snorted and rubbed his eyes. That much was clearly impossible—if Blight were an impartial judge, he'd have already offered the position to Tessa. She worked in the department in question, knew it inside and out, and had established relationships with the staff, not only in her own department, but elsewhere. She seemed to know people on every floor. She was even friends with Henry, the lift operator.

She was eminently more qualified than the weasel. He supposed the trick would be to ensure she received the position she deserved—even if Blight sabotaged her efforts—without lending credence to any suspicion that she had been given the promotion because of her friendship with him.

Friendship.

He smiled. He would write soon to Matteo and admit he finally understood. A deep and abiding connection with another soul could indeed form quickly and without warning. David had always appreciated beautiful women, but all others paled in comparison to Tessa. He dozed on the balcony, a small smile on his face as he envisioned hers.

The following day was an uneventful yet busy one for

Tessa, as much as David could ascertain. He stopped in at lunchtime to find the department swamped with people. This time, she didn't let Mr. Gibbons bully her into taking more than a fifteen-minute lunch, standing in the employee rest area next to her cabinet. He couldn't even entice her to the store's café on the main level.

David spent the afternoon telegraphing his associates and going about the business of advancing his timeline. There were details yet to confirm, and his rental home was nearly ready, but he put everything away at the end of the business day to meet Tessa in the department store lobby.

He spied her exiting the stairway, where she was waylaid by no fewer than three shopgirls who apparently had questions for her. She paused, smiled, offered information, and then finally reached him by the doors. A becoming flush tinged her cheeks. They'd not had occasion to talk alone for more than a few snippets of conversation since the day before. Did she regret the kiss? Did she resent him? Did she hope to repeat it?

He took her hand and kissed her fingers, and she swayed closer, which he interpreted as a very good sign. "I told Max and Valentine I would treat you to dinner this evening on North Pier, if you've no objections. Afterward, we could gather some more of those ridiculous bits of miscellany for Blight."

She wrinkled her nose. "I will enjoy dinner. I may even enjoy gathering the stray items, but thinking of that man is still causing my blood to boil." She tucked her hand in his arm, and they left the building. "This week will be over before I know it, and I will either have proven myself or find myself working for Grover Welsey."

He stilled on the sidewalk. "You will work for him?"

She nodded. "That seems to be the natural course. If he

is advanced to Mr. Gibbons's position, I will work under him and assuredly be demoted from my responsibilities as the assistant."

He exhaled and, when she tugged on his arm, began moving again. "You cannot work with that man."

"I could request a transfer to a different department, but I enjoy being with the girls in LGR." She sighed. "I will ponder that over the weekend, if necessary."

He was quiet as they strolled down the street to a relatively empty spot where he could hail a cab. He would die a thousand deaths before allowing the weasel a position anywhere near Tessa, let alone in a supervisory capacity. The smarmy man lacked integrity, that was abundantly clear; David hoped it would be a short matter of time before he could fire him altogether.

David instructed the hansom driver to North Pier, and he settled in beside Tessa. He laced his fingers with hers and settled their joined hands on his leg. After a moment, he realized he was bouncing his knee restlessly as she frequently did.

"I shall work it through," Tessa told him quietly. "I can manage him. It would be a disappointment, but I would devise a plan for myself."

"That should not be an issue to solve." He glanced at her, knowing she would balk at his interference. "I will take care of it."

"No, you will not."

"He abuses women in stairways."

"Nobody will believe it."

He looked at her flatly. "Everybody will believe it. Anybody who has spent even a moment in his company will believe it."

"We are putting the cart before the horse. Perhaps it will not be an issue."

He pursed his lips, stewing.

"Why are you helping me?" she asked, and the question caught him off-guard.

"Because I l—like you. I enjoy your company. I respect you, and you make me laugh." He looked at her, trying to gauge her mood, the direction of her thoughts. His heart beat a little harder. What was she attempting to *not* say? "Are we not friends?"

She wiggled her fingers still wrapped in his. "Are you very familiar with all your friends? I know, I know." She waved her free hand. "You are Italian. But still I wonder."

What response would least likely send her fleeing? She was accomplished and determined to further her prospects as a woman of independent means. The thought of scaring her away was not one he relished.

He finally posed the question itself. "Which answer will make you the most comfortable?"

Her mouth lifted just a bit. "I would hear the truth, above all else. I suppose I am wondering how much of my . . . emotion I should invest. Such casual familiarity is not customary for me."

"You believe I view you casually?"

She shrugged. "I do not know what to believe."

"What do you want to believe?" He felt as though he walked on slippery banana peels.

She exhaled in frustration. "The truth! I would know the truth, and yet I suppose I am an inexperienced, naïve schoolgirl for even having the awkwardness to ask."

He looked at her carefully and realized her eyes held an element of something he'd not seen in her: fear. "Tessa Baker, you are the only woman I have ever met who has caused me to consider my future—my true, permanent future. You do not know me well. You have preconceived notions of my past, some of which may be justified. You also have goals for your life, and you will probably accomplish more than you can even imagine now. I would not expect you to allow anything to interfere with that; perhaps at some future date, however, you may find a way to blend other elements into that life, as well."

She bit her lip. "So much is happening right now, I hardly know what to think."

"Perhaps you needn't think quite so much. Take one step at a time."

"But I do not like not knowing what to expect."

He smiled. "Suppose you simply leave your heart open to possibilities?"

"I do not want it to get broken." She looked away when she whispered it.

He lifted their joined hands to his lips and kissed hers. "I would be the last man on earth to do it."

Chapter Nine

Jessa eyed the strongman contraption dubiously. The hammer alone probably weighed more than she did, and the scavenger hunt stipulated she must wield it on her own.

"It is quite heavy," David said, having rung the bell three times already. "I suppose that might seem daunting."

She glared at him and grabbed the handle. He smirked at her, not bothering to hide it, and she realized she'd been had. She thrust his coat at him—she'd held it while he exhibited his admittedly impressive prowess—and narrowed her eyes.

The crowd around them cheered, and she lifted the large hammer. She maneuvered herself into place and swung the thing experimentally, knowing full well she would never be able to arc it up and over in a large sweep.

She moved closer to the mechanism she was supposed to hit and dropped the hammer down onto it, still maintaining a grip on the handle. She was met with a chorus of good-natured laughs and boos, and she glanced at the onlookers with a smile.

She sighed and looked back at David. "I cannot bring myself to admit defeat, but I'll never manage proper form."

He stepped onto the platform and took the hammer, his hand brushing against hers. "You require a bit of extra help, that's all." He grinned at her, and her heart thudded against her ribs. Since his veiled declaration of affection earlier in the carriage, she'd thought of little else.

"Now, then." He nudged her back into place, encircled her arms with his, and set her hands close together on the mallet.

The crowd cheered and whistled, and she felt herself blushing furiously. He placed his hands on the handle, one above, one below hers and lifted, swinging the heavy mallet slightly, like a pendulum.

She looked over her shoulder, and he lowered his mouth to her ear. "Would you prefer to try it alone again?"

His breath was warm against her skin, and she shivered, shaking her head. "You are scandalous and an incorrigible flirt."

Her lips twitched as he raised his brows, all innocence. "Having never engaged in such activity, I cannot imagine what you mean."

She snorted a laugh, and he winked at her.

"Now, relax your arms. Let me guide you. We shall swing back in a wide arc and come around on top of it."

She nodded.

"By 'relax your arms,' I mean to say, do not do anything at all other than keep your hands on the mallet, or we shall both require shoulder splints."

She laughed again, as did several people standing next to the game.

"We will swing twice, like so," he said, demonstrating. "And then on the third, we ring the bell."

She tipped her head to the side, eyes wide. "This suddenly seems very foolhardy."

"Nonsense. One. Two. And three!"

She kept her arms as limp as possible and allowed him to do the work. He shortened the arc considerably to adjust for her height and reach, and she wanted to slow the moment. The length of him pressed against her back from head to toe, his arms completely enveloping her, his quick inhale as he hefted the weight for both of them. He was warm and solid and so very much alive.

The mallet head came down on the contraption, and the large rubber pellet shot upward. It didn't reach the bell, but it was certainly a better result than she'd achieved on her own. She laughed, the crowd cheered, and she noticed every touch, every sensation associated with him. He handed the mallet back to the game master but left his other hand on her hip.

She drew in a shaky breath. He was turning her insides to mush.

"Yes, please initial the back of this ticket." David laughed as the game operator shook his head. "We need verification that she did indeed swing the mallet." David turned his attention back to her and smiled, still lingering close, touching her in a deliciously familiar way—as though they were together, as though she belonged to him and he to her. She wanted it to be true so badly it felt like an ache.

He tilted his head. "Are you well?" He took the ticket from the bemused operator, nodded his thanks, and accepted his jacket from an onlooker who had held it for him. He drew her away from the crowd and looked at her closely. "Did I hurt your arm?"

"No, no." She shook her head and drew in a deep breath. "I feel as though the sand is shifting beneath my feet."

He studied her in silence.

"I am . . . completely lost. At sea."

He lifted the corner of his mouth in a gentle smile. "Do you swim?"

"Some. Not well."

"I have a very strong stroke. All you need to do is stay on the surface and work with me. Not so much unlike that, yes?" He motioned with his chin to the strongman game.

She felt her eyes burn and looked away from him, embarrassed. She exhaled through pursed lips and chewed on the inside of her cheek. "I am so overwhelmed."

She saw him shrug into his coat from the corner of her eye and looked at him as he held her hand and led her away from the carnival and onto the promenade. It was late, and she would be tired come morning, but she didn't want to go home, didn't want to go to sleep. Even confused, she didn't want to be anywhere but with him.

"Walk with me onto the pier; it's quieter there." He nodded toward South Pier.

She nodded, and he laced their fingers together. Late-night revelers thronged the promenade, and she breathed a small sigh of relief when they reached the pier. Activity still flourished farther down as a small band played for an open-air dance, but midway along the wide wooden bridge, there were spots absent people and glaring light and noise.

He released her hand and leaned forward on the wooden railing. She breathed deeply and sighed, standing close to him, wanting to be near and not knowing how to articulate it.

He looked to the side at her, his blue eyes serious. "I will wait for you. I am not searching for a bride. I did not come here looking to start a family, but I did come here hoping to move to a different place in life." The light Italian accent—she would never tire of hearing it.

He examined his forefinger, picking at a splinter. "I

suppose what I am saying, Tessa, is that I do not just want a wife. I want you. I am not looking for the sake of looking. If you were to refuse to see me again after this moment and leave me here, I would not refocus my efforts on finding someone new."

She studied him—his handsome profile, thick hair, solemn expression.

He cleared his throat. "I am not asking for anything from you, other than to know that I am building my life here, I am not going anywhere, and I very much would like you to consider getting to know me better. I do not expect you to leave your work. I do not expect you to rearrange anything in your life, except perhaps to allow me to plead my case."

She laughed, a quiet exhalation. She leaned on the railing next to him and turned her face into the ocean breeze. "I want a family of my own. I want a home and a husband and children. I also want to continue to work at the store, and I do not know how to reconcile the two."

"Must one negate the other?"

"David, I do not know a man on earth who would countenance a wife working anywhere other than at home. I want to work at least a few hours during the week." She lifted her shoulders. "Unless I am single or widowed, it is not done."

"Do you know another thing that was simply 'not done'? Women working as shopgirls. It was unheard of half a century ago. And something 'not done' now? Women working in supervisory positions in retail, in business, anywhere. And yet?"

She turned toward him fully, one arm on the rail, the other hand on her hip. "Do you honestly mean to tell me that you would have no objections to having a wife who worked outside the home?"

He smiled. "You've not met my mother." He paused.

"Anyone I marry will presumably spend her time sponsoring charity events and attending social gatherings. This is time spent away from home. Why should it matter to me if that time is spent in a department store?"

She snorted. "Because you're a *count*, for one thing!"

He rolled his eyes. "*Cara mia*, I could not care less." His eyes roamed over her face, settled on her lips, and then her eyes. "I am not in a rush; I certainly do not mean to cause you a moment's distress. It is only that . . ." For the first time, he seemed vulnerable. "I did not expect you," he admitted quietly. "I find myself rather at sea too. You are not the only one with a heart at risk of breaking."

"Mercy," she murmured, and her eyes stung. She leaned into him on impulse and touched her lips softly to his. He returned the gentle kiss but remained still, following her lead. She pulled back and touched her forehead to his. "And I would be the last woman on earth to do it."

Chapter Ten

Jessa passed the next three days on a cloud. Even Grover Welsey couldn't dampen her mood, although she noticed that Wednesday's emergency assignments from Mr. Blight were ridiculously easy in comparison to the fiasco Welsey had created for her on Monday.

Wednesday's tasks included securing extra lengths of certain fabrics that were housed in storage containers at the shipping docks and handling an imaginary squabble between two shopgirls in the children's department that began in the employee room and moved into the store proper. She admitted feeling a slight advantage with that scenario. She knew both shopgirls, had helped them a few months back with housing issues, and her solutions were guided by the fact that she could work with what she knew of their personalities. She crossed five items off the scavenger list, beginning with the extracted tooth.

Thursday afforded them another break from emergency scenarios, but she used the evening hours with David, Max, and Valentine for locating the last of the trivial items on the list. She indeed found a bolt beneath the Ferris wheel, and the operator, who was with her during the search, was comfortable signing a paper to that effect. She added both paper and bolt to her growing collection of oddities that ranged from candy wrappers to puppet hair.

They watched a water polo match and obtained signatures from each member of the winning team. David covered her eyes when the men emerged from the water in dripping wet bathing suits. She couldn't deny the thrill she felt that he of all people would be jealous of her attention to other men.

They attended an informal production on Middle Pier, after which she jotted a summary of the plot onto the back of the printed program. She obtained signatures from each cast member, and "for luck," the leading lady kissed the paper with her bright, red-rouged lips.

It was Friday now, early afternoon, and she had yet to receive instructions from the fifth floor. Mr. Gibbons checked personally to be certain she'd not been missed—either accidentally or intentionally—but all had been quiet on that front. The department itself, however, was a madhouse, and she'd not taken a proper lunch.

She was helping a group of young girls decide which ribbons complemented their new glove choices when she heard the loud yip of a puppy and a crying baby. Two runners, both looking frantic, found her and handed her the familiar envelope, the puppy, and the baby.

Her mouth dropped open. "What? What is this?"

The boys backed away. "Beggin' yer pardon, miss. Read the message." She blinked, and they were gone.

The customers around her erupted into a flurry of delighted squeals and horrified shock. One of the girls she'd been helping took the puppy from her hand, but not before it leaked urine onto Tessa's white shirt. With one hand free, she held the baby on her hip and tore open the envelope.

Mrs. Grimbsy-Jones has suffered a stroke on your department floor. Her son was charged with keeping the puppy outside while she shopped with the baby, but when the medics carried his mother out, he lost track of the puppy, which followed its mistress's scent to your area.

She was holding the baby when she fell, and the crying child has no milk, crackers, or diapers. You receive word that Mr. Grimbsy-Jones will arrive as soon as possible, but is at home in London and will have to take the next train, which will not arrive in Sommerpool until tonight at 9:00 p.m.

Your customers are disgusted by both dog and baby.

She stared at the letter open-mouthed, stunned, before turning to Mr. Gibbons and Mary. "This has literally never happened here! He is certifiably insane!"

The puppy squirmed and barked, and the high pitch echoed off the ceiling in a piercing aural assault. "For the love!" She took a deep breath and closed her eyes briefly as the puppy again lost its bladder, this time on one of the girls, who screamed and dropped the animal on the floor.

Tessa dashed forward, calling to Mary, "Grab the dog!" It slipped through Tessa's fingers, but thankfully Mary caught it in her skirt and scooped it into her arms.

"Monique, please cut a length of the grosgrain ribbon"—Tessa motioned the girl closer—"from the puce-colored spool we cannot seem to give away." The girl nodded, wide-eyed, and dashed over to the ribbons. "Long enough to use as a leash," she called to Monique.

The baby began to wail, and Tessa bounced instinctively, suddenly remembering how it had been each time her mother had had another child. She'd never minded, truthfully, but the incessant crying used to give her headaches. She now realized adulthood had not made her immune to that.

"Ssshhh," she murmured as customers around them continued to gawk and comment on the chaos. She patted the child—a girl?—gently on the back and murmured in her ear. Her best guess put the baby at four, perhaps five months old. She hugged her close. She had no idea whom the child belonged to and wasn't about to hand her off to a stranger.

Monique appeared with the length of ribbon nobody wanted to purchase, and Tessa took it with a nod of thanks. "Mrs. Pendleton is over at the linen table, Monique. Will you see to it she receives help? Her hands are arthritic, and she doesn't manage it well but always wants to examine each length."

Mr. Gibbons worked at soothing the angry teen and her equally angry mother, offering to replace the soiled skirt. Tessa motioned to Mary and the puppy and handed the girl the ribbon. "Tie it securely—and I do mean securely—on the collar." She glanced up to take in a rough customer count presently in the store. "Listen carefully. I want you to find a young boy named Charlie Grant. He runs errands for Mr. Frederickson, the baker, and I've seen him several times walking tourists' dogs while they use the bathing machines. Offer him twice his usual fee to care for this puppy until closing time. Tell him to bring the dog here at the end of the day, and I will pay him and take the puppy."

"Yes, Miss Baker." Mary glanced over her shoulder. "You may have noticed Mrs. Featherington. She entered a moment ago, and I thought perhaps to assign her a different shopgirl than Monique."

"Excellent idea." Tessa nodded her approval and managed a smile for the girl, who beamed at the validation.

Tessa lightly bounced the baby and rubbed circles on her

back. The child must have been exhausted. She eventually relaxed her tense, little body and leaned her head against Tessa's neck. She viewed the relative calm that settled again over the store as customers returned to their shopping and Mr. Gibbons mollified the angry mother and daughter duo with a pair of gloves, the entire spool of puce ribbon, and half a yard of their most expensive silk.

She took a deep breath, realizing she'd crushed the letter and envelope in the hand that cradled the baby. She looked at her tightened fist and shook her head at Blight. His audacity had reached new heights. Whose baby had he recruited for this?

Two gentlemen stood in the main ladies' wear area, mouths slack. David's eyes met hers, his brows high. She shrugged.

He tapped his companion, another handsome fellow Oxford student presumably, and her suspicions proved correct when the pair reached her and David hastily introduced him as Phillip Keyes, his business manager.

"A pleasure," the man said, looking as baffled as she felt.

"Likewise," she nodded with a smile.

"You handled that admirably, I must say," he told her and looked around the room at happy customers and no barking puppies. "This is a test?" He looked at David.

David shook his head. "I'll explain everything later. Tessa, is there something you'd like to tell me?" He looked pointedly at the baby.

She laughed, wincing and rubbing the little back again when the infant jerked at the sudden noise. "I have no idea whose baby this is. None. I plan to give him a piece of my mind because this is beyond the pale. Did you see the puppy?"

He nodded. "Where did you send the shopgirl?"

She explained about the baker's young helper who

walked dogs for supplemental income. "I'll keep this one with me, however. I do not trust a soul."

"Will you chat with me a moment somewhere quiet?"

She nodded. "What is it?"

"I'll explain." She led him to the employee area. She walked to the back of the room so they wouldn't be overheard.

"Something happened?" She looked at him and Phillip, who didn't seem overly grave, so she tried to refrain from panic.

"Nothing catastrophic. One of my accountants must leave town this evening for a family emergency, so I am forced to meet with the business staff now."

She nodded.

"Meaning I will use the offices on the other end of the fifth floor. Word will spread quickly."

"Ah." She paused as the implication set in. "So Blight and Welsey will know of your role in the store within the hour."

He nodded and winced. "I am sorry, Tessa. I had planned to wait until next week. I would hold the meeting elsewhere, but the files are all here, and . . ."

"You do not owe me the slightest explanation. Truly, David, you've helped me more than I could ever have expected or hoped. You must run your business now."

He sighed, shoving his hands in his pockets. "Do you have your collection of assorted items?"

She nodded. "In a satchel." She motioned toward her cabinet.

"If I am still in meetings—" He broke off and rubbed the back of his head. "I wanted to be there when you turned this mess in to Blight."

"David, I shall be fine."

"I know. I had hoped to—"

Phillip had glanced at his timepiece and now cleared his

throat. "Apologies, Bellini, but the accountant and solicitors are most likely already upstairs."

David muttered something in Italian that Tessa could only assume was a curse.

"Go." She shoved his arm.

The curtain was flung suddenly aside, and Blight stormed in, followed closely by Welsey and Mr. Litton, who looked at David with disdain.

"*You* own the store?" Blight growled at David. "You stood in my office and withheld that information?"

David straightened to his full height, and Tessa watched as before her eyes, the man she loved put on his mantle of aristocracy, laced with a healthy dose of intimidation that felt somehow palpable. "I was not aware I owed you an explanation, Mr. Blight."

Blight opened his mouth and closed it again. His eyes fixed on Tessa, who still held the baby he'd abducted from some poor mother. "And you!" He stabbed a finger in the air at her. "You pretended such superiority and dared to call me to task over a lack of integrity when you were nothing but the new owner's light skirt! Did you believe that favoring him would somehow force my hand to promote you over Welsey?"

She gaped, outraged, and the baby fussed. Before she could string together two coherent words, however, David moved forward in a flash and smashed his fist into Blight's jaw. The man hit the ground and was still. David stood over him, breathing heavily.

Litton looked at David with a smirk. "You going to hit all of us, then, *Conte*?"

David squinted at him. "You do realize I am going to fire you."

Welsey shoved into the fray, eyes bulging. "I do not care what you do to me, but *she* is finished!" He glared at Tessa. "I am going upstairs to meet with your business associates, Mr. Bellini. When I tell them that you helped Miss Baker procure the items required for the emergency scenarios and that she spends inordinate amounts of time in your company—you, her employer—they will insist she be cast out on her ear. And if they do not act, I shall inform the *Daily Herald*!"

He ran from the room. Litton eyed her insolently, rolled his eyes at David, and followed Welsey.

Tessa sat back against a table, her legs suddenly weak. Everything she'd been working for was about to be upended by a horrible man she despised. What was worse, she knew he would be believed. The room upstairs was filled with men, and her reputation would be destroyed.

David looked at Phillip. "I'm going to kill them."

Phillip shook his head. "You are not going to kill them. Let's go up there and control the flow of idiocy."

"It won't matter," Tessa said hollowly. Her eyes were dry; she couldn't even summon any grief. "He will tell the newspaper. He will spew far and wide that I'm nothing but my employer's mistress."

David shook his head. "Tessa—"

"It will not matter one whit that it isn't true, David. You don't understand. The world does not favor women. Welsey has won."

He approached her swiftly, telling Phillip to await him upstairs. Phillip looked at Tessa with sympathy and left the room, dragging the unconscious Blight out of the employee area. She heard the low rumble of his voice as he instructed Mr. Gibbons to see to him.

David cradled her head and turned her face to his. "This is not over. It has not even begun. And I will bury that little man." He was fierce—the count had returned—and his fingers tightened in her hair. "You do not quit, Tessa Baker. That is not what you do. Will you trust me? Will you let me fix this, just for once?"

Her eyes finally filled with tears. "I know you want to," she whispered, "but I'm afraid there are some people even David Bellini cannot charm."

He smiled darkly. "I've said nothing of charm." He kissed her, hard and quick. "I love you. And I will fix this."

Chapter Eleven

David stood in his large fifth-floor office and looked out over the promenade and beyond that, South Pier and the ocean. An even larger conference room adjoined his office, and a cast of thousands gathered behind the door. He'd spent the last hour sending messages via courier and telegraph, gathering forces and resources.

Tessa's face haunted him. She'd not crumbled or screamed or yelled. Those beautiful green eyes had filled with tears that silently overflowed.

A brisk knock sounded at the door, and Phillip stuck his head in. "It's time."

"Everybody is here?"

"Everybody and then some."

David entered the boardroom. The large table had been removed, and he'd had the room filled with chairs. He turned to his business team, the city provost, and the *Herald*'s managing editor. "Thank you all for being here on such short notice. I would not have requested it were it not urgent." He extended his welcome to several other familiar faces, who watched with interest. Max stood at the back of the room and nodded his support.

He explained to his gathered guests his new role in the company, the reason for his visit, his purpose behind observing before anyone knew who he truly was. He explained the department changes, Mr. Gibbons's pending retirement—Mr. Gibbons nodded gravely—and the ensuing application process for his replacement.

He told them about the stipulations, the emergency scenarios, the scavenger hunt. He detailed his observations of Miss Baker, his role as a family friend, her desire to succeed by her own merits, and then told them exactly how she'd done it.

The room was silent as he spoke, his listeners focused. He then told them of the events of the day and how they had come to be gathered in that room. He included details—all except for the desperate kiss he'd given Tessa—and his own participation in the mayhem by rendering Blight unconscious. He received several nods of satisfaction with that detail.

"Miss Baker is under the impression that there will be those who doubt her, especially if Mr. Welsey spreads false tales not only about Miss Baker's handling of the application activities, but also the slanderous lie that her relationship with me is inappropriate or scandalous. The woman is above reproach; she has more integrity than a good majority of the men I've met who manage this company.

"To allay not only her fears but to nip any potential gossip, I've called several character witnesses to Miss Baker's defense and ask that they now explain to you their involvement with her in the last week."

He stood back and handed the floor first to Mr. Frederickson, who explained that Tessa's competition had purchased his entire stock, then Mrs. Dyer, who had sold Tessa the marzipan treats. They heard from Mr. Farr, who grudgingly admitted Tessa's competition had told him lies about her and his subsequent refusal to help, and Mr. Timely, the clockmaker. Next was the storage-unit manager at the docks, who explained Tessa's arrangements to have the missing material packaged, tracked, and delivered to the store in under an hour. Lastly, Mr. Gibbons, Mary, and Monique recounted the events of the day, including the puppy and the baby. Young Charles, the dog walker, was even on hand to tell about his adventures with the dog and Tessa's monetary reward, which was indeed twice his usual fee.

David thanked the gathered character witnesses and excused them, but before they left, Mr. Timely asked for the floor.

"Ya should all know that Miss Baker is one of the kindest, smartest women I have known in my life, and the amount of business she continually sends my way has increased my profits by nearly forty percent."

Mr. Frederickson nodded. "She sends folk to the bakery, and she remembers my wife's favorite ribbons."

Mrs. Dyer added her two cents at the door before exiting. "That girl came to my rescue once during a wedding where all of my sheet cakes and favors had been destroyed by my sister's hellion ten-year-old. Miss Baker spent her entire Saturday with me when she heard—helped me finish and deliver every last item on time." She shook her head. "That some buffoon thinks to besmirch her name and malign her character is criminal."

The room was quiet after Tessa's supporters had left. The newspaper editor raised his hand. "Where are Mr. Blight and Mr. Welsey now?"

"Mr. Blight is nursing an aching jaw and looking for a new job. Mr. Welsey has been arrested on assault charges and slander. Fifteen of the store's shopgirls are rendering depositions to the Yard as we speak. He is a predator who waits in secret to attack unsuspecting, vulnerable women."

The editor's pencil scratched in his notebook. "And the slander charges?"

"Filed by the company on behalf of Miss Baker for spreading potentially harmful vitriol and maligning her character and reputation."

The city provost nodded. "Seems the store has needed a good scrubbing. The city is grateful for your influence. I hope to see you or a representative at our commerce meetings."

David nodded, thanked the remaining guests, and excused them. When he was left with Phillip, two accountants, and a solicitor, he sank into a chair next to them.

Phillip clapped him on the shoulder. "Nicely done. And while we're here, I have a matter to put to the lot of you, and it concerns Miss Baker's future with the store. I do not believe she is meant for the department supervisory position she seeks."

Chapter Twelve

The hour was late, the store was closed, and Tessa climbed the final stairs to the fifth floor. The store was enormous and eerie in the dark. Security guards walked patrol, but David was correct—they needed more. Several gentlemen passed her in the hallway outside the large conference room doors, introduced themselves, tipped their hats, and filed out. She stared after them, deciding David must have put the fear of God into every male employee the store had.

She entered the conference room to see Phillip Keyes, who stood and beckoned to her. "Miss Baker, thank you for returning to the store. I hope you'd not gone all the way home?"

She shook her head. "I was on South Pier with my aunt and uncle." She was tired, weary, and she hadn't spoken to or seen David since his hasty departure earlier, after a desperate kiss and a promise.

"Please have a seat. I won't keep you long, but wanted to discuss something for your consideration over the weekend. I believe your talents on one department alone are wasted, to be frank. What I witnessed today was unlike anything I've seen. After asking around each department, I realized that you know at least a handful of shopgirls in every department and have favorable relationships with the majority of department managers."

She nodded, unsure of his intentions.

"I have seen a trend in other large companies. There is benefit to having a central employee who sees to the concerns and potential issues of the employee network as a whole. In short, I would like to offer you, with the business team's approval, a position as general manager over all the shopgirls. Your duties would include building relationships, training, aiding with paperwork, checking references, those sorts of things."

Her head spun.

"We are prepared to offer a respectable salary increase, of course. I'll not ask for your answer tonight, but be aware that if you decide against it, your original application for shopgirl manager of the Linens, Gloves, and Ribbons Department has been approved. You may accept that position instead."

Tessa inhaled and straightened in her seat. "I am incredibly honored and will have a decision for you Monday morning."

He smiled. "Excellent. And now, I am off to enjoy a rousing variety and musical show on Middle Pier. I hear this town's entertainments rival all others."

"I've found that to be true." They stood, and he shook her hand.

"Until Monday, then."

He left, and she stared at the door he closed quietly behind him. She put a hand to her forehead, wondering if she'd been knocked in the head. Movement caught her eye, and she saw David leaning against the doorjamb between his office and the conference room.

He watched her quietly, a smile lifting on one side.

The answer to her next question would fill her with emotion, whether joy or sadness she didn't know. "Did you suggest that to him? Was it your idea?"

He shook his head. "On the life of my family and all I hold dear, it was Phillip's suggestion after watching you today. He'd intended the position to be implemented regardless, and he witnessed a master ringleader at work."

She put her hand to her midsection and exhaled. A laugh bubbled up and escaped, and she doubled over. David was at her side in a flash.

"You realize, of course, that Blight helped me after all?"

His brow wrinkled.

"Had he not thrown the puppy and baby at me today, I'd not have had a circus to perform in."

"Did you ever locate the mother?"

She nodded. "A flower girl."

He shook his head and managed a grim smile. "I hate him." He took both of her hands. "You were never able to turn in your scavenger hunt items, though, and I'm disappointed about that, so I am going to present them to you instead. I convinced Mr. Gibbons to open your cabinet and give me the satchel. Come."

He pulled her into his office and patted his desktop. While she sat, he closed the drapes over the large windows that overlooked the promenade. "All that work to preserve your reputation, and here we sit behind glass for all to see."

She laughed, and he plunked the satchel next to her on the desk.

"Here is what I find meaningful in these objects. This one." He pulled out a small piece of paper. "This is a receipt for the Italian ice we were eating when I realized I was falling in love with you."

She bit her lip, and he turned her hand palm up and placed the paper in it.

"This envelope contains the hair from a Judy puppet. It is significant because it represents your resourcefulness in carrying scissors at the ready and your amazing ability to charm anyone, anywhere." He added the small envelope to her hand.

"This is marzipan candy I bought earlier from Mr. Frederickson. I was angry that, after all our running around, we weren't able to enjoy even one piece of it. You were resourceful and clever, even when your opponent cheated." The treat joined the pile in her hand.

"This cameo is quite the most hideous thing I've ever seen, but it is perhaps one of your most amazing accomplishments. You were clever to think of Mr. Timely, but not only that, you had built a relationship with him beforehand that helped facilitate this small, ugly miracle."

She laughed, feeling misty-eyed again, and he clipped the brooch to her blouse.

"This bolt from beneath the Ferris wheel reinforced your clear ability to follow through. Max and I both offered to get a bolt for you, but you insisted on following the rules of that ridiculous search and did it the right way.

"This is the ribbon you used today to make a leash for that ridiculous dog, who has no known owner, I understand."

She nodded and sniffed. "Val has it."

"I was never prouder of someone in my life than watching you today." He tied the ribbon around her wrist in a big bow. "These bite marks in the ribbon show where the puppy rebelled."

She laughed.

"This is the paper signed by the water polo team, all of whom ogled you like lechers."

She scoffed.

"True, it's true. But you let me cover your eyes in good fun, and you laughed. And it made me realize, as if I needed the reminder, that I was fortunate indeed to be the man by your side."

She shook her head, tears building in earnest.

"And my favorite piece of the lot." He pulled out the strongman receipt. He grinned and stepped between her knees. "Must I truly explain why?"

She laughed, and the tears spilled over. He took the items piled in her hand and set them aside. Without bothering with any further sentiments or pretty words, he slid his arms around her and lowered his lips to hers. He waged a gentle assault against her senses, and a slow burn began in her midsection, spreading until she thought she'd go up in flames.

She clutched his lapels, knowing that even if he kissed her forever, it wouldn't be long enough. She sighed, exhausted and euphoric. And every painful, emotional moment had been worth the reward. She would accept the first position Phillip had offered, and she would set a trend for other shopgirls to follow. She'd reconciled herself to the fact that David had helped her—half the town had helped her—and despite not doing it all on her own, she was better for it.

Perhaps the most amazing thing of all was that she'd fallen in love with a man she'd known for a week. She knew it in her heart, deep down where she kept the hopes and dreams she thought she'd outgrown. He pulled her closer, and she sighed as he trailed his lips along her neck.

"I adore you, Tessa Baker."

She smiled and closed her eyes. "And I you, *Conte Bellini*."

One Year Later

Valentine fluffed Tessa's long wedding train and smiled encouragingly at her. "You're stunning," she murmured, "and your groom is absolutely besotted."

They stood just outside the enormous chapel doors in the largest church Tessa had ever seen. A month spent in Italy with David and his family still hadn't prepared her for the butterflies that now plagued her insides. His parents were kind and welcoming, his mother especially hilarious. His brothers were charming; Valentine's cousin Eva had become a friend and confidante; and Tessa loved David so much it was like a lovely ache.

She was deliriously happy and wondered if she should pinch herself. Valentine had given birth four months earlier to a baby boy Tessa adored. Her work was challenging yet rewarding, and David had been patient enough to postpone the wedding until Tessa was well and truly settled into her new job. His patience was especially impressive, given the fact that he'd asked her to marry him one short month after that fateful, crazy day filled with urinating puppies, a crying mystery baby, and more mayhem than the store had ever seen. For eleven months now, she'd been busy but anxious to know she and David were well and truly bound.

Her father cracked the door open from inside the chapel and smiled. "Are we ready, then?"

"More than ready."

"That is good because I believe the groom will faint if you don't show your face—and soon."

Tessa glanced back at Valentine, who held the train with

teary eyes and blew her a kiss. Her father helped her place her veil, and she threaded her arm through his. He nodded to the page boys, the doors swung open, and the aisle stretched interminably. At the end, however, stood David, too handsome for words, watching her approach slowly.

She was impatient suddenly and wanted to run the length of the aisle, throw her arms around him, and kiss him soundly in front of the whole world. She smiled, and when her father relinquished her hand to David's, she breathed a sigh of relief. He was her home, her heart, her other half. He caught her gaze through the filmy veil and winked. He linked their fingers together, despite the fact that such was not a part of their scripted ceremony, and her lips twitched in a smile as she held her bouquet with one hand.

The words of the ceremony washed over her in Latin, Italian, English—she didn't even know—but finally they spoke their vows, placed their rings, and he lifted the veil away. He placed his hands on either side of her face and kissed her, maintaining the contact long enough that his brothers chortled. A cheer echoed to the ceiling, and she laughed.

He smiled, his eyes suspiciously bright. "*Cara mia*," David murmured in her ear. "*Ti amo.*"

"*Ti amo*, my handsome *conte. Ti amo moltissimo.*"

The End

About Nancy Campbell Allen

Nancy Campbell Allen (N.C. Allen) is the author of 11 published novels, which encompass a variety of genres from contemporary romantic suspense to historical fiction. Her Civil War series, Faith of our Fathers, won the Utah Best of State award in 2005 and all three of her historicals featuring Isabelle Webb, Pinkerton spy, have been nominated for the Whitney Award. Her formal schooling includes a B.S. in Elementary Education from Weber State University and she has worked as a freelance editor, contributing to the recent release, *We Knew Howard Hughes,* by Jim Whetton.

Nancy served as the Teen Writers Conference chair in 2011 and 2012, and has presented at numerous conferences and events since her initial publication in 1999 with Covenant Communications. Her agent is Pam Victorio of D4EO Literary, and she is currently writing a series of Gothic

Steampunk novels and other short novellas. Nancy loves to read, write, travel and research, and enjoys spending time laughing with family and friends. She and her husband have three children, and she lives in Ogden, Utah with her family and one very large Siberian Husky named Thor.

Visit Nancy's blog: http://NCAllen.blogspot.com
Twitter: @necallen

OTHER WORKS BY NANCY CAMPBELL ALLEN

My Fair Gentleman
Beauty and the Clockwork Beast
Kiss of the Spindle
The Secret of the India Orchard
Autumn Masquerade
The Orient Express
From Cairo, With Love
European Collection

ISABELLE WEBB SERIES
The Pharaoh's Daughter
Legend of the Jewel
The Grecian Princess

FAITH OF OUR FATHERS SERIES
A House Divided
To Make Men Free
Through the Perilous Fight
One Nation Under God

Sarah M. Eden

Chapter One

Rafton, Staffordshire, 1870

There were few sights Carina Herrick found more inspiring than the billow of steam rising from a distant train. The back meadow of her family estate afforded a view of the tracks crossing the plain below. She never tired of watching it and wondering who sat inside, where they were going, if they would return. A train held hundreds of stories, each unique, each important in its own way.

Did the passengers ever glance up this hill and wonder who she was, where she dreamed of going, how she imagined her life playing out? Hers was not an exciting tale with a mysterious ending, but she thought it lovely just the same. Indeed, her reason for standing at the far end of the meadow was a fine one, a glorious one. This was where she came each day to talk with Grant Ambrose, the gentleman she meant to one day marry.

She had known him a couple of years, though their connection had only grown romantic over the past few months. He was good and kind. He treated her with tenderness and real regard. She was happier in his company than in anyone else's.

Her days were spent counting down the hours until she could meet him in their designated place. Here, amongst the trees and flowers, the vista of fields and rolling valleys, and the puff of passing trains, she'd fallen endlessly in love with him.

He'd told her not a fortnight earlier of his dream to one day oversee a portfolio of investments, to have his hand in new and exciting business ventures. Her family was what society called "old money." While she did not doubt her father invested in various undertakings, such things were not discussed or mentioned. To be directly involved in business of any kind was considered beneath their dignity. For Grant to share that dream with her showed enormous trust, something that touched her more than he likely knew. He wanted her to be a part of his hopes and his ambitions. He'd asked after hers as well.

When she'd told him of her time spent watching the train and imagining far-off places and adventures, he hadn't laughed, neither had he insisted she be sensible, as her mother had on the one occasion Carina had been foolish enough to divulge her wonderings. Grant had urged her to speak more of it, to imagine more specifically, to share with him the places she longed to see and visit, not merely those she imagined others traveling to.

With him, she felt alive and valued, as if all things were possible. With him, she felt loved.

He turned the corner of the shrubbery lined path he always took from his family home to this particular spot. A warm blanket of peace and contentment settled over her as she watched him approach.

Someday, I will have his companionship in more than mere snippets. Someday, his home and mine will be the same.

Grant moved at a faster clip than usual, his movements filled with purpose and an unmistakable eagerness. Did he have news? His uncle, a vastly successful man of business, was visiting from Lancashire, and Grant had hoped to find some favor in the man's eyes. He wished to learn all he could about the path he meant to pursue.

His eyes met hers, and Grant began to run. He reached her side in no time at all and, unlike their usual staid greetings, he wrapped his arms about her and lifted her from the ground, spinning her in a gleeful circle. The colorful trees all around them blurred into a rainbow of autumn hues.

A giggle escaped her lips, which did not happen often. She laughed out the syllable of his name. He was a happy person, but this degree of joy was unprecedented.

He set her on her feet but did not release his hold on her. "I spoke with my uncle."

He could not seem to hold entirely still, as if the words he held back danced inside him. His eyes shone with excitement. He made no effort to conceal his smile.

"Tell me all before you burst." Her own enthusiasm grew with every heartbeat. She did not know precisely what he meant to say, but his eagerness was contagious.

Grant took her hands in his, his eyes sparkling. "I told him all I am learning and studying. I also told him of my interest in business pursuits. He was impressed, Carina. He said as much himself."

"How could he not be?" Her words bounced about with the excitement building inside her.

He grinned. "You may think highly of me, but that is not a universal opinion."

"Nonsense."

How she loved the sound of his quiet, gentle laugh. It suited him perfectly. "Never let it be said that you are not a fierce defender of those you care for."

"As are you," she reminded him. "I will never forget you coming to my rescue when Mr. Baskon was being so terrible." Mr. Baskon, a widower nearly three times her age, had been unrelenting in his unwanted attention to her at a local assembly a few weeks earlier. Grant had neatly removed him from the room and, though she did not know what transpired between the two men, Mr. Baskon had not returned. Somehow, Grant had managed it without drawing undue attention.

"He has not continued to bother you, has he?" True concern touched his words.

"He has not," she assured him. "I am grateful for that."

"As am I." He pulled her arm through his and walked with her along the edge of the meadow.

"What transpired in your discussion with your uncle?" she pressed.

"He was impressed with the knowledge I have already acquired and says I have a good head on my shoulders." He beamed with pride. Carina felt certain her own pride shone on her face as well. "He wishes to take me under his wing, to personally oversee my continued education in business matters and pursuits. I am to be a junior partner."

"Oh, Grant." This was all they could possibly have hoped for.

"He has no sons of his own, and neither of his daughters married men who are interested in joining their father-in-law's business."

"He has no heir?"

Grant made a gesture somewhere between a shrug and a shake of his head. "It is not quite the same as inherited estates.

He will leave a great deal of money to his daughters, but the interests of the company, the future running of it, is independent of that."

Her family, he knew well, belonged to the world of entailments and the need for heirs to protect future generations. His family, though of good standing and firmly entrenched in the gentry, were not as tied to those things. Their status had grown in only two generations from the bottom rung, with little beyond a bit of land here and there to sustain them, to a family of significant and increasing wealth accumulated through shrewd investments and the active pursuit of industry.

She did not entirely understand the world in which his past and present existed, but neither did he entirely understand hers. It was the future that most concerned them, not the past. And for many weeks they had spoken of that future in terms of togetherness.

"Your uncle, then, wishes you to take over the running of the businesses when he is no longer able or no longer wishes to do so?"

He nodded. "Those businesses are very successful, and he will teach me to keep them that way. The path before me has always seemed uncertain, but I need no longer worry on that score."

He would have an income and stability. They might at last move from vague ideas of their future together to actually planning and building it. She could not hold back her joy. His smile spoke of the same feelings.

"I will have to work swiftly tonight to have everything in readiness," he said as they continued walking, a light breeze rustling the stiff leaves around them, sending a few fluttering to the ground. "My uncle is generous, but he is also very strict.

I fear if I delay him at all in the morning, I will simply be left behind."

As if nature herself were as stunned as Carina, the wind grew still.

"In the morning?" The question emerged quieter than she'd intended.

"He does not wish to be away from his office for long. The train for Preston leaves shortly after breakfast, and he intends to be on it. If I am to accept his offer, I need to be as well."

She had not thought about the possibility that his ambitions would take him away from Rafton. She ought to have. Rafton was agricultural—vast expanses of fields, grand estates, farmland. There was nothing here for a man of business. Still, her heart had been ill prepared for the blow he had just dealt.

Her feet continued to move her forward, though she hardly noted the world around her. "You will be so far away."

For the first time, he seemed to sense her unease. He stopped walking and faced her. "We will be apart for a time," he acknowledged. "That cannot be helped. My uncle will give me a room in his house, but I will not have a home of my own for some time. I will work hard and learn all I can, earning my way until I am independent enough to build a life for myself."

"Our life?" she pressed.

He took her face gently in his hands. "Our life," he repeated. "I love you, my dear."

"What will I do without you here?" She posed the question more to herself than to him, yet he was the one who answered.

"You will fill your days as you always have. When I return on visits to my family, we will see each other again, in this spot." He dropped his hands to hers and held them reassuringly. "You will continue to watch the train and imagine far-off places. And I will work as hard as I know how so we need not be apart long. And I will yearn for you and miss you and dream of the day we will be together again."

She took a fortifying breath, squared her shoulders, and looked up once more into his beloved face. "I wish it were permissible for a gentleman and lady to write to one another. I should dearly like to know how you are and have that connection to you."

Were there an understanding between them, an engagement, they would be permitted that luxury.

"Allow me to raise my position in the world so your parents will accept a situation in which we would be permitted letters." Such sincerity shone in his eyes. "As it stands now, they would reject my request."

That was likely true, though she wanted to believe that his uncle's offer of junior partnership and his expectations of a fine and stable income, coupled with his family's place amongst the gentry, would be enough for her parents to grant a furtherance of their relationship. Still, she understood they were tiptoeing those bounds as it was, meeting each day and sharing such personal confidences. It likely was not wise to press harder.

"I can be patient," she vowed. "A person can endure a great many things for true love."

"How fortunate I am to have the love of so dear and wonderful a lady." He kissed her fingers, as he so often did. "I will not keep you waiting long."

He pulled her into his embrace and held her as the wind danced around them. She committed to memory the feel of his coat, of his arms wrapped about her, the warmth of him, the scent of his soap. She could, indeed, be patient, for this was a man worth waiting for, however long the wait might prove to be.

Chapter Two

Five years later

"I understand you've refused Mr. Baskon," Mother said without looking up from her needlepoint. "Again."

"I do not love him, Mother." Carina did not even like him.

The objection only increased the frustration on her mother's face. She lowered her sewing to her lap. "You are twenty-three years old, Carina. There are other things to consider."

Carina maintained the air of calm serenity she had perfected over the last five years. "I have also taken into consideration the fact that his late wife's misery was obvious and well-known to all in the neighborhood. I should not like to live the life she did."

Mother's expression hardened. "You would do well not to cast aspersions on the character of a gentleman of his importance."

"He is not important to me." She would stand firm on this matter.

Mother sighed, her shoulders drooping. "I thought you had put this foolishness behind you. Five years is time enough—"

"I long ago abandoned my hopes for Mr. Ambrose," she insisted. "I have no expectations in that quarter, neither am I nursing a broken heart. I was wounded at the time, but I am no longer pained."

That was not entirely true. Grant Ambrose had fractured her heart, and the fissures remained. Those deep scars were not, however, the reason for her rejection of Mr. Baskon. Though Mother objected to gossip, all of Rafton considered the most recent Mrs. Baskon, to whom Mr. Baskon had been married only a year upon her death, to have been a tragic figure. He was a hard and unfeeling man who had made her life a misery. Everyone knew it, whether or not they spoke of it openly. Carina would not resign herself to that fate.

"Perhaps your father can talk sense into you." Mother turned in her chair and faced Father, who sat not far distant in his own high-backed chair on the opposite side of the sitting room fireplace, watching, listening.

"I doubt you will receive offers from any other gentlemen." Father spoke by way of warning but without the warmth or concern a daughter might hope for. Carina had long since grown accustomed to that. Her parents' disappointment in her had become palpable over the years.

"I know, Father."

His gaze narrowed. "And the prospect of spinsterhood does not concern you?"

"Not as much as the current alternative."

His mouth pursed, pulling his narrow mustache down sharply. He and Mother exchanged sharp, knowing looks.

Mother nodded. So did he. Then Father turned his gaze on Carina once more. The hardness she saw in his eyes sent a shiver down her arms. While he had never truly been cruel, he could be unrelenting when he was determined to get his way.

"Your Great-Aunt Chadwick suffered a fall a few days ago."

Carina did not know why he'd undertaken such a drastic change of topic, but she was decidedly wary. She knew little of her great-aunt beyond what her father had told her over the years. She was cantankerous, difficult, and generally unpersonable. The only thing she'd done that any of the family remotely approved of was never visiting them.

"She is in need of someone to look after her and see to her needs while she recovers," Father said. "You will be traveling to Wilkington on the train tomorrow."

"Wilkington?"

"Where she lives," Father clarified. "If you are so enamored of spinsterhood, you will be excited at this opportunity to observe it firsthand."

"I did not say I was enamored—"

"Any no-longer-*young* lady who would turn down repeated offers of marriage must be eager for it," Mother insisted. "Now you can, for the length of the summer, go live the life you are seeking."

"That is not—"

"The train leaves in the morning." Father raised his paper, ending their conversation.

Carina turned to her mother but could see in an instant there would be no help from that quarter. Her exile had, it seemed, been planned before this moment. Her parents intended to change her mind and punish her in the undertaking.

Very well. She had learned these past five years to look out for herself, to be her own advocate. It was a lesson she had learned in painful ways, but one for which she was grateful. She might not have emerged whole of heart, but she was stronger.

"If acting as the poor relation and lady's companion to my great-aunt is the price I must pay to avoid marriage to an unkind man, then that is a forfeiture I will willingly make." Carina stood, not allowing hurt or uncertainty to show in her expression or posture. "You, my own parents, may not value me enough to want what is best for me, but I do."

A look of shock bordering on horror immediately crossed Mother's face. "That is not at all—"

"I shall begin packing so that I will be ready to flee to my safe haven as early tomorrow as possible."

She left with all the dignity she could summon. Father's voice echoed from the room before she'd gone far enough to avoid overhearing it.

"The life Aunt Chadwick lives will cure Carina of this stubbornness," he said. "She will see the wisdom in seizing what opportunities she has."

"Mr. Baskon?" Mother at least sounded a little hesitant.

"Whatever opportunities she has."

Carina stood on the train platform the next morning with an unshakable sense of dread. She had not allowed herself to dream of far-off places and adventurous train rides in nearly three years. She had clung to those childish dreams for a long while, but eventually life had required her to mature, to set aside fantasies for rational expectations.

"You will watch the trains and dream of adventures,"

Grant had said on the day he'd left her behind. She had actually believed that for a time.

But he hadn't come back. He'd sent a few notes and messages by way of his sister, but those had quickly become fewer and further between. Within six months, those notes had stopped altogether.

After another six months, she'd ceased imagining herself boarding a train in this very station, bound for Preston. She'd eventually stopped imagining anything.

Dreams die, she'd discovered. And the dreamers move on.

The train had arrived some minutes ago, and her trunk had already been brought on board. Yet there she stood, paralyzed. She had never before been on a train. And, though she hated to admit as much, she was afraid.

She feared neither the journey nor the massive machine that would carry her to her destination. She feared what awaited her at the end of the tracks. She had only ever heard her great-aunt described as a terror. Perhaps Mr. Baskon would not have been a worse alternative.

But memories of the late Mrs. Baskon—the third to bear that name—haunted her. She had been nearly Carina's age, sweet-natured and friendly. The poor lady had grown more withdrawn, isolated, and miserable. Carina did not remember the first two Mrs. Baskons, they having passed on many years earlier. Had they been equally unhappy?

No. Mr. Baskon was not the better choice, no matter how difficult or troubling her great-aunt was. She might not be bubbling over with happiness in Wilkington, but she could not imagine the temporary situation awaiting her there would be as awful as the permanent misery of a life with Mr. Baskon.

"The train is boarding, miss," a porter announced, waving her forward.

One foot in front of the other. Had she been making this journey five years ago, no matter the destination, she would have been overjoyed, brimming with excitement. All she felt in this moment was tired.

The din of voices inside struck her like hail in a winter storm. It was not the soft rustle she'd always imagined. The long, narrow passage was dim and uninviting. She peeked inside compartment after compartment, hoping to find one empty where she might be alone with her thoughts.

At last she came upon one. She stepped inside and set her small carpetbag on the sparsely padded seat before placing herself beside it. She took a breath, then another.

A cloud of white and gray rushed past the window. She knew it on the instant, having watched trains pull away from the platform and charge down the tracks. The engine had released its first puff of steam. She could not help thinking back on her eighteen-year-old self and how majestic she'd always found that sight.

The train lurched forward, pulling itself as if fighting a backward push. One jolt at a time, it picked up speed. The station slid from view, then the stand of trees just beyond it. Soon, the fields were visible from the windows of her compartment. The scenery moved faster and faster until the train settled into a rhythm.

Imagine far-off places. She could hear Grant Ambrose's voice so clearly in her mind, could feel his warm embrace. Heaven help her, thinking back on those magical times still set her heart aflutter.

Mr. Baskon was not an option she would consider, but neither would she wallow away her life daydreaming of past hopes and expectations. This time with her great-aunt was meant to serve as a cautionary experience, showing her that a husband, any husband, was better than spinsterhood. She meant to make it a learning endeavor of a different kind.

Great-Aunt Chadwick was an unhappy woman, made miserable by her circumstances. Carina would watch, see what caused her suffering and unhappiness, and simply resolve to approach her own life of solitude in precisely the opposite way. She would be happy. One way or another, she would be.

Chapter Three

Wilkington, Lancashire

Grant inspected the last crates of cotton. The quality was acceptable, but they had not received the full shipment. He eyed his shipping foreman.

"We're short, Cobb."

Cobb gave a quick nod. "I've noted it. Are we to accept the shipment and reduce our payment or leave it in hold until the rest arrives?"

Leaving it in hold would send a stronger message to the supplier, as they'd have to wait for payment, but the factory needed cotton. Without the shipment, production would stall. Curse the suppliers, they knew as much.

"Tally what we did receive," Grant said. "We'll not pay for anything that didn't arrive."

Cobb's attention turned fully to the crates once more. He could be relied upon; Grant didn't employ anyone who couldn't be.

Grant stepped away from the shipment and paced down

the station platform. A passenger train had arrived on the opposite track. Wilkington was a busy enough stop that people would soon be swarming about. He chose a bench against the wall of the ticket office. He'd wait until the platform was calm again before making his way back to his offices. He needed a moment to think through the situation.

Their supplier had been unreliable of late. The agreed-upon amounts were not consistently delivered and didn't always arrive on time. The prices Grant was paying were lower than any he'd found elsewhere, but it might be time to consider paying more for cotton he could depend on. His final product required raw material.

He rubbed his forehead and took a few deep breaths. His mill was profitable. Their fabric was good quality and sought after. Yet it was a struggle. Nothing had run as smoothly as his uncle had expected it to. If this factory, a smaller one than the others Uncle owned, proved too much for him to manage, he could not hope to be entrusted with anything grander or more significant. All his hopes of taking over the entirety of the family business would be dashed.

It had seemed quite simple five years earlier. He'd been rather naive, truth be told. He would simply step into this new life with no difficulties or delays. His situation would be stable and enviable. He'd soon enough have a wife, a family, a home of his own.

Five years later, he was still living in rooms above his office at the mill, still trying to prove himself to his uncle.

"Mr. Ambrose, what a pleasure to see you."

He knew well that voice and hearing it eased some of his doubts. Miss Beaumont was the only daughter of a successful merchant in Wilkington. The Beaumonts had taken a liking to him early on, treating him as the success he hoped to be. Their confidence had more than once bolstered his own.

He rose and offered Miss Beaumont a bow of acknowledgment, then offered another to Mrs. Beaumont, who stood beside her. "What brings you to the station today?"

"We have only just journeyed back from Birmingham," Mrs. Beaumont said.

"Where your parents live," he remembered.

Mrs. Beaumont's pleasure at his recollection of their previous conversations blossomed on her face. "I believe your parents live in Rafton."

"They do."

"We passed by there on our way home—a very small station."

"It is a very small town." The same aching fondness that always gripped him at the thought of Rafton seized him once more. "But a very dear one."

Miss Beaumont set her hand lightly on his arm. "If only you had come with us, we might have disembarked and spent a little time there. You could have seen your home again."

His immediate response was to agree that such a thing would have been ideal, but then, as always happened, his mind and heart retreated from the idea. He could not go back home, not truly. It would not be the same place it once was. Too much had changed.

"Was yours an uneventful journey?" he asked the Beaumont ladies.

Mrs. Beaumont listed the discomforts she'd endured, while her daughter countered those light complaints with a list of pleasurable experiences. They were enjoyable companions, both for one another and for those fortunate enough to make their acquaintance. Grant had valued their company from the time Mr. Beaumont first undertook the introductions. Wilkington had been a far less lonely place from that moment on.

The platform buzzed with activity, travelers boarding the train, those newly arrived searching out their parties or winding their way toward the street beyond. Grant hadn't always found the commotion of the station uncomfortable, but that feeling had grown more pronounced over the years. Neither did he care for the sound of the train whistle, no matter how distant. It echoed inside him, hollowing him out and rendering him as empty as a bone-dry well.

But trains were necessary, especially to one whose livelihood depended on the goods they delivered. He could endure it.

Again, he felt the delicate weight of Miss Beaumont's hand on his. "You do not care for the train station. I have noticed that before."

He pulled himself together enough to acknowledge her observation with a brief nod.

"Why is that?" she asked. "It cannot be the crowd, as you walk about your factory and the busy streets of Wilkington without difficulty."

"It is not the crowd."

"The train, then?" Mrs. Beaumont guessed. "Some people find them disconcerting."

He could actually smile at that. "I am not frightened of trains." He glanced over at Cobb, standing beside the shipping crates, waiting. "When the platform is crowded, I am unable to see to business matters as efficiently as I would prefer."

"Ah." Miss Beaumont dipped her head in understanding. "You are a busy man. We know that all too well. And, knowing that, we will not keep you from it."

"I did not mean to imply—" His words stopped.

A face appeared in the crowd. Briefly. The mere length of a heartbeat. His mind had played this particularly cruel trick on him before, filling in gaps with the grief he tried so hard to forget.

Carina. She was always there, lingering in the background, entering his thoughts when he least expected. How, after the passage of so many years and the pain of feeling them drift apart, did she still have a claim on his affections? Clinging to what was not meant to be was neither wise nor logical.

He forced the imagined sight of her from his thoughts and attempted to recall what he had been saying to his companions. His distraction must have been short-lived, as neither of the Beaumonts appeared to notice.

"Will you join us for dinner this evening?" Mrs. Beaumont asked. This was a familiar invitation, one he had accepted many times before.

"I would be honored." In the instant before asking what time he ought to arrive at their home, he saw once more his earlier illusion, Carina's face in the crowd.

The all-too-familiar aberration did not quickly disappear, as it usually did, but turned and walked in the direction of the road. He could see nothing but the back of the phantom's dark bonnet. Wisps of hair in Carina's same shade of deep brown hung free and visible. This was a far more complete mirage than those he'd experienced before.

Could it be truly her? No. Surely not. She had no reason to be in Wilkington. He watched a moment longer. The lady who had, at least upon first glance, borne that once-beloved countenance did not walk with the same bounce in her step and eagerness in her posture that his Carina had. There was a heaviness, a forced purposefulness that did not fit the lady he'd known.

His mind, as it was too often wont to do when fatigued and overburdened, had conjured up the impossible.

"We will take our evening meal at seven o'clock," Mrs.

Beaumont said. "Send word if you are unable to join us. Otherwise, we will happily see you then."

He dipped his head in apology. "My thoughts are wandering just now, but I commit myself to better manners and offering my undivided attention tonight—at seven o'clock."

Mrs. Beaumont's expression turned utterly maternal, her daughter's concerned. He attempted to appear reassuring, but he doubted his success. Years had passed since the last time he'd struggled so much to put Carina Herrick from his thoughts. Failing to do so inevitably led to heartache, an emotional indulgence he could ill afford.

"Until tonight," he said.

They smiled at his poorly executed acceptance and made their way from the station with all the grace he had come to expect from them.

Though Grant returned to his work and his duties, focusing on both for the remainder of the day, the furthest reaches of his mind spun and churned like a waterwheel. Why had his one-time sweetheart invaded his consciousness now, after all this time? He was, at long last, building a life for himself. If he allowed those regrets, those losses a place in his world again, it would all fall apart.

Chapter Four

Carina expected Wilkington to be a small town not unlike Rafton. She had filled her thoughts with fields and farms, stone cottages and grand estates. She had not been at all prepared for the bustling industrial center she found instead.

The station was filled with a crush of humanity. She feared she would never manage the short distance between the tracks and the road beyond. Movement was slow, painstakingly so, but she at last freed herself from the press of people. She inquired at three different carriages before finding the one her great-aunt had sent to fetch her.

The coachman whistled as he held the door for her, as he closed it, and as he climbed onto his perch at the front of the conveyance. He likely continued his whistling as he drove, but the cacophony of sounds and voices drowned out any noise he might have made.

She hoped for a quiet drive to her home for the summer, but fate was not ever that kind. The din seeping in through the rattling windows of the carriage kept her on edge, uncertain, and overwhelmed.

I am meant to be miserable here, but I will not give in to it. She could not. The moment she accepted that spinsterhood was a repugnant path in life, one to be avoided at all costs, her determination might falter. She could not allow that.

On and on the coach drove, bumping and jerking over uneven cobblestone, winding around ever-narrowing lanes, before it began to climb an unpaved road, one without buildings on either side. Open country lay in both directions, though it did not extend far. She could see the city encroaching on its edges, staking ever more territory.

Great-Aunt Chadwick did not live in the heart of the city, it seemed. That was a most welcome realization. The estate would be far quieter, far more peaceful, even if the woman herself was not. If Carina were truly fortunate, her presence would not be regularly needed and she could escape to the fields and trees, explore nature, perhaps even find an isolated spot she could make her own.

The carriage slowed, curving around a short drive. Carina leaned toward the window. Her bonnet brim pressed against the glass. The home was not grand, only slightly larger than the vicarage in Rafton. It had a stone edifice with two rows of windows and a pitched roof. Two identical potted shrubs trimmed into an upward swirling pattern adorned either side of the door. A rainbow of flowers filled the low garden boxes beneath the front windows.

The house might not have been a grand one, but it was clearly meticulously cared for. A woman with salt-and-pepper hair tucked neatly into a crisp white cap stepped outside and waited on the front step. She straightened her spotless apron and smoothed her puffed sleeves. Carina knew a housekeeper when she saw one.

The coachman opened the carriage door and handed her down. Carina held herself with dignity, knowing that these first interactions would set the tone for the remainder of her time in this household. She walked at an appropriately sedate pace directly to where the servants—the housekeeper had been joined by the butler, a footman, and two maids—waited for her.

Carina dipped her head in acknowledgment. The staff bowed and curtsied as appropriate. Then the housekeeper... hugged her.

So tremendous was Carina's shock that, for the length of several heartbeats, she did not move or breathe. Never in all her life had a member of another household's staff embraced her. She remembered the nursemaid who had looked after her when she was a young child doing so, as well as her governess. While her lady's maid had never been quite so intimate, they had shared a few confidences over the years and were known to laugh together. This degree of friendliness, however, was utterly foreign.

"We are so pleased you've come," the housekeeper said, still holding Carina close. "Miss Chadwick's so lonely for company."

Carina was set back once more. The staff all smiled broadly at her, eagerness in every face. Was she expected to say something? Her family didn't often make visits, but when they did, their arrivals were far swifter and quieter, consisting of little more than being ushered inside and shown to their assigned bedchambers to recover from their journey.

"I am grateful I can offer her a bit of company." The statement held a note of uncertainty that could not be helped. She was not on familiar ground.

"Come in. Come in." The housekeeper waved her inside, a grin permanently affixed to her face. "Johnny'll see to it your trunk and bag are taken upstairs. Miss Chadwick'll want to see you straight off."

"I am not to go to my room first?" Carina had been hoping for even a moment of quiet before beginning this new and dreaded chapter in her life.

It was not to be.

The housekeeper moved quickly, pausing now and then to allow Carina to catch up. After the third pause, the housekeeper remained with her, slowing her own steps.

"I am Mrs. Jones, housekeeper here at Chadwick House." Her enthusiasm had not abated in the least. How isolated a life did Great-Aunt Chadwick live that Carina's arrival should inspire such excitement? "Miss Chadwick has not stopped speaking of your arrival. The entire staff is abuzz with it. Abuzz. All seven of us."

Seven? This was, indeed, a small estate. That, though, would be nice for a change. Her family home sat somewhere in the middle of that spectrum: small enough to not be truly overwhelming, but too large to be deemed comforting or inviting. Perhaps that was the reason Great-Aunt Chadwick's staff had been so friendly and welcoming, because a smaller home allowed it.

That explanation might have easily settled on her as the appropriate one if not for what she knew of the mistress of Chadwick House. Her great-aunt was too much a miser, an unhappy and bitter old woman for her influence to have created a place of warmth and hospitality. Though Carina's memory of her great-aunt's one and only visit to Rafton had been rendered vague by the passage of so many years and the undependable nature of the memories of childhood, her mind's eye clearly recalled a woman who had frightened her. Everything she had heard of her great-aunt in the years since only confirmed that impression.

"The mistress is just out here." The housekeeper

motioned to an open French door that led onto a terrace. "She'll be so pleased you've arrived."

That did not seem at all probable. Still, there was no avoiding this moment. She had come to look after her aunt, to witness the apparent torment that awaited her in her own spinsterhood. Putting off the inevitable would accomplish little.

Carina stepped through the open door. Though she intended to seek out her great-aunt first, her attention was captured by the view, and all other thoughts fled her mind. From the front, the house gave every indication of being small and quaint—nothing that would impress anyone of discernment. The garden that stretched out before her, however, stole her breath away.

Rows of hedges circling out from a star-shaped fountain sat in the center of the lawn before her. A brick wall, trellised with vines, marked the edges of the inner garden. Elaborate iron gates granted access to more gardens beyond, each with its own unique character. This expanse could be explored for weeks without ever growing tiresome.

"Beautiful," she whispered.

"I designed it myself," a voice said. "I'm rather proud of it, in fact."

Carina turned quickly toward the source of the declaration. Though she did not vividly remember her great-aunt's face from that long-ago visit, there was enough of a resemblance to her father for the speaker's identity to be easily discernible.

Carina offered a quick curtsy. "Great-Aunt Chadwick. I am pleased to see you again."

"No, you're not." Was that a laugh behind the words? "That father of yours no doubt told you how terrible these next months will be and that you ought to spend your train ride here weeping for your fate."

Those had not been his exact words, but they adequately communicated the sentiment.

"Never you fear," Great-Aunt Chadwick said. "If you find Chadwick House is not so miserable a place after all, I'll not tell him. I will even send letters delineating how badly treated you are. That ought to earn you a little peace from that quarter."

For the second time in a matter of minutes, Carina was rendered silent by shock. Nothing was playing out as she had expected.

Great-Aunt Chadwick patted the wicker chair nearest hers. "Sit by me, child. I'll not bite."

Carina took the seat she was offered, eying her hostess with uncertainty.

"You don't believe I'm harmless, do you?" Great-Aunt Chadwick's dark eyes narrowed on her. She certainly didn't look harmless. "You've been told, by your father no doubt, that I am a miserable old woman who is absolutely torturous to spend time with."

Carina didn't nod. She suspected she didn't have to.

"I will let you in on a secret." Great-Aunt Chadwick leaned closer. "He is correct."

Why, then, did she sound as though she was barely holding back a laugh?

"However," her great-aunt continued, "I would be willing to be a little less bitter and miserable if you would prefer. I am terribly accommodating, you see."

"I believe I am beginning to."

A look of pure mischief spread over her great-aunt's heavily lined face. "Then you, fortunately, did not inherit your father's level of intelligence. That is a good thing."

Though it was likely disloyal to feel so much amusement at her father's expense, Carina could not hold back her growing smile.

"You were, however, blessed with your grandmother's beauty. She was the gorgeous sister, you realize." Great-Aunt Chadwick straightened her spine dramatically. "I was the clever one."

"I believe you."

Great-Aunt Chadwick folded her wrinkled hands on her lap. Hers was an intelligent and sharp eye, unwavering in its attention, which, at the moment, was focused on Carina. "Tell me a little of yourself. What are your interests?"

It was a question she had not been asked in years.

"That you have to give it such thought is not a reassurance, Carina," Great-Aunt Chadwick said. "There must be something that brings you joy."

"Of course there is," she answered. "I simply don't get asked about my interests often—ever, truth be told."

"Because your father is a miserable old man who is absolutely torturous to spend time with?"

Carina slowly released a tense breath. "He was not always that way, only once I—" She pressed her lips closed before the words could slip out.

Great-Aunt Chadwick nodded, knowing, likely from experience, the feelings fathers too often had for daughters who did not marry as or when expected. There was no unhappiness in the expression, no pity or disapproval, simply understanding. The rarity of the experience provided Carina with a much needed bit of confidence in her new situation.

"I do have interests and joys, though some might consider them frivolous."

"I appreciate a bit of frivolity." Great-Aunt Chadwick motioned to her own pale green dress. "You will notice I am quite the fashion plate, though most ladies of my generation, those who are not yet dead, see little point in updating their wardrobe from what they wore decades earlier. I am even wearing a bustle, which is possibly the most frivolous thing in the world."

Carina had spent the day anticipating misery, yet she felt more lighthearted after only a few minutes of her great-aunt's company than she had in years. "Do you consider corsets frivolous as well?"

Her aunt shook her head. "Not at my age, dear. Without tight lacing and the heroic efforts of whalebone, nothing about a seventy-year-old figure stays where it's meant to stay."

Wouldn't Father be shocked to know their first conversation centered around ladies' unmentionables?

"What are these interests of yours?" Great-Aunt Chadwick asked. "Certainly not undergarments."

"I enjoy nature." She felt, for the first time in five years, safe to express these personal parts of herself. Somehow, this lady she was told to fear had already set her mind at ease. "Meadows and stands of trees and meandering streams. I also like gardens with pebbled paths. I enjoy reading about faraway places and the people who live there and about the history of my tiny corner of the world."

"I see nothing wrong with any of those interests," her hostess said. "How do you feel about fashion and elegance and gatherings of important people?" The tone was teasing.

Carina found she could match it. "Those are my most favorite things. Fashion above the rest. If I cannot have the appropriate bustle, I simply refuse to get out of bed."

"As do I. We are expected tonight for dinner with a local family of some standing, so I do hope your bustle befits expectations." Though Great-Aunt Chadwick still spoke with amusement, Carina felt certain the invitation was a real one.

"This is an industrial town, mind you. The influential people tend to be the merchants and the mill owners."

"Is this family we are to dine with part of that section of society?"

Great-Aunt Chadwick nodded. "They are, indeed, and fine people, if a bit pretentious."

"Do you wish to dine with them?" Carina asked. "I would willingly serve as a convenient excuse if you'd like a reason to reject the offer."

Great-Aunt Chadwick laughed, the sound deep and ringing. "I am going to like having you here, Carina Herrick."

"Does that mean dinner at home?"

"Not tonight. I do like our host and hostess, though only in short spurts. Besides, I do not intend to keep you locked up here all summer. You need to meet people if you are to be at all social these next weeks. This will be a fine way to begin."

"I am to enjoy myself?" Carina gave her a theatrically suspicious look. "That is not what my father told me."

"It can be our secret." Great-Aunt Chadwick leaned back in her chair. "Now, go rest. Sleep a little if you are able. Prepare yourself for a busy summer. I may be old, but I am not a do-nothing."

"I look forward to it, Great-Aunt Chadwick."

"None of this great-aunt nonsense. You may call me Aunt Chadwick."

Father had sent Carina to Wilkington with the sole purpose of plunging her into the depths of despair. As she walked away from the terrace, however, her heart was soaring.

Chapter Five

Grant had once been quite adept at navigating social gatherings. His family home had often hosted dinners and soirees, even the occasional ball. Though his parents could only claim a place at the fringes of old and respected families, the extended family's growing wealth and influence improved their standing significantly. Their invitations were eagerly accepted, and Grant enjoyed the events.

He didn't anymore, and he wasn't sure why.

Perhaps he was too busy, his mind too full of the concerns of his mill and other business interests. Perhaps he simply didn't have the heart for it any longer. Social gatherings hadn't done him much good in the past.

"Imogene tells me you appeared displeased at the station this afternoon," Mr. Beaumont said, interrupting Grant's moment of reflection. "Did you have trouble with the shipment of cotton?"

Grant nodded slowly and with emphasis. "I've nearly reached my limit with this supplier. Shipments are forever arriving short or behind their time. His rates might be better than others, but that price comes far too dear."

"Indeed." Mr. Beaumont's knowledge of business was second only to Grant's uncle's. If he was in agreement with Grant's analysis, that was a strong vote in favor of seeking a new supplier. "The money and time you lose tracking down your missing merchandise may be better spent on a new, more trustworthy distributor. Those increased rates will pay for themselves over time with your increased productivity and reliability."

"That is my evaluation as well." Finding a new supplier and forging a relationship took time, however. Productivity would be down while that was all arranged, unless Grant could time it such that there was no gap in deliveries. That was easier said than done.

"Let me send a wire to a few men I know in the City," Mr. Beaumont said. "They may have a few recommended suppliers for you—more reliable options."

"I would be deeply grateful."

Miss Beaumont arrived on the scene in that moment, eying them both with a playful look of scolding. "Are the two of you discussing business matters again? What will it take to convince you to set that aside long enough to enjoy a dinner?"

"My apologies, Imogene." Mr. Beaumont even bowed, though his mustache danced with mirth. "We are quite the worst of guests."

"You, Father, are not a guest," she said. "You are the host. It is for you to set a good example." She turned to Grant. "You must think us the veriest heathens."

She made comments of that nature now and then, alluding to his more exalted origins. Wouldn't she be shocked to discover that the rung he occupied on the social ladder of

Rafton and the surrounding area had been a relatively low one?

"On the contrary," he told her. "I am always pleased to be in your company."

She blushed, and he realized his mistake. She spoke of her family's impression on him, and he intended his reply to reference her family. It clearly had not been received that way. Still, correcting the misunderstanding would only embarrass her.

"If you and Father are willing to set aside your talk of cotton and investments and shipping schedules, we do have two other guests who are expected this evening," Miss Beaumont said. "One of whom is old Miss Chadwick."

Grant had interacted with Miss Chadwick on a few occasions, though nothing of a significant nature had passed between them. She was a lady of advancing years with a sizable income, known to invest in any number of ventures. Thus far, she showed only a passing interest in any of his.

"Miss Chadwick?" That was unexpected. Grant looked to Mr. Beaumont, who nodded subtly.

Miss Beaumont was smiling when he looked at her once more. "I thought that might seize your attention."

"Who is the other guest? The Queen herself?"

She shook her head. "Miss Chadwick's niece, who is only lately arrived in Wilkington. A poor relation, I believe, who has been thrust upon her aunt for the foreseeable future."

That was an unenviable position for anyone. The niece of a lady who was old enough for her age to be described as "significantly advancing" must be rather old herself. Grant remembered well the dinners with his own grandmother. They had been short affairs, owing to her low energy, and conversation had been difficult, owing to her nearly nonexistent hearing.

Perhaps the dinner would be ended quickly. That certainly met with his approval. A great deal of business awaited his attention.

"I look forward to making their acquaintance," he said.

"Look forward no more," Miss Beaumont said. "I believe I hear them in the corridor."

The Beaumonts moved closer to the door, ready to greet their guests. Grant stayed back a few paces. He had already given the impression of stronger feelings than he felt for Miss Beaumont. Inserting himself into the family's welcome would only confirm what he'd never meant to imply.

Mrs. Beaumont's voice broke the silence first. "Miss Chadwick, what a pleasure."

"Isn't it, though?" came the reply, spoken firmly despite the telltale shake of age.

Miss Chadwick was not the docile, soft-spoken octogenarian most would expect. Grant had realized that during their very first interaction. He knew not what to expect of her niece. Poor relations were often mistreated and trampled on, rendering them far more timid than they might have been otherwise.

He stepped closer to the window, granting the new arrivals space and time in which to greet their hosts. Their voices were swirling about, mixing too much for any one word to be truly discernible. The group moved in one mass farther inside the drawing room. Grant kept to his side of it. Introductions would be undertaken once doing so was convenient; he would not press for speed when it was not necessary.

His difficult mood was beginning to ebb. The past years had taught him the trick of forcing unpleasantness from his mind and summoning lighter thoughts and brighter moods to take its place.

The Beaumonts always served a fine meal, and their

conversation was without fault. Though they did not keep exclusively to the topic of business, when they did discuss such matters, Mrs. and Miss Beaumont proved themselves nearly as knowledgeable as Mr. Beaumont. On other matters, their opinions and thoughts were pleasant and interesting. No doubt Miss Chadwick and her niece would prove equally enjoyable dinner companions.

Miss Beaumont separated herself from the small group and moved toward him. "You have not suddenly become bashful, have you?"

He'd never been truly bashful, but he did prefer quiet and solitude to gatherings of people, unless those people were particularly well-known to him. Still, he knew how to be polite. "I only wished to allow your family time and space to greet your neighbors."

"You are our neighbor as well." She had perfected her tone of playful scolding. He had heard it often enough to know that for a fact. "Come greet the arrivals."

He stepped closer. The crowd parted enough for an older lady dressed in the finest fashion, leaning on a cane and moving at a slow clip, but with eyes keen and sharp, to move to the front of the group.

"Miss Chadwick." Grant offered a bow.

She answered with a dip of her head. "Mr. Ambrose. I'd like to introduce you to my great-niece, Miss Herrick."

His heart stopped at the sound of that name. The entire world, that very moment, slowed to a painful crawl as his eyes tracked in the direction of the second, yet-unseen guest. He told himself again and again in that elongated instant that the surname was a mere coincidence, that he would feel an utter fool when he saw the truth of it before him. But his heart knew. Heavens, it knew.

There she stood. Carina. No trick of the eyes, no cruel jest of the brain. Carina. In the same town as he was. The same house. The same room. Carina.

He knew he was meant to do something. Bow or dip his head or say something. His mind, however, emptied of everything except his all-encompassing shock.

She did not seem similarly bewildered. Her expression remained as serene as could be. She dipped a perfect curtsy. By sheer habit, he managed the required bow of acknowledgement.

"Miss Herrick." He hoped his voice emerged as steady as it sounded to his ears.

Carina answered with a fleeting smile, one that spoke of obligation more than any real pleasure. She lowered her eyes, her posture stiff and unyielding. That was to be the nature of their interaction? After all these years, after the loneliness and disappointment, they were to go on as if they'd never known each other, as if there was nothing between them beyond the vague interest one might feel when meeting a stranger?

He had sunk to the depths of agony as her letters had grown shorter, filled with fewer personal sentiments. He sensed no enthusiasm for the parts of his life about which he wrote. They exchanged fewer notes, fewer expressions of hope for their future or tender regard. In time, they simply drifted apart, the short distance between them proving too great a barrier. And now, here she was, entirely disinterested.

Grant steeled himself. He accepted long ago that her affections had cooled. He would not be felled now by the evidence of it.

Mrs. Beaumont announced that dinner was ready, and they proceeded to the dining room. Grant offered his arm to Miss Beaumont, as had become customary during his increasingly frequent evenings amongst the family. This time, however, the ritual was more than the result of habit; he needed a reason to look away from the unexpected materialization of half a decade of disappointed hopes.

He moved mindlessly to the dining room and sat in the chair he always occupied. If he did not allow any conscious thought, he was far less likely to dwell on the situation. Then he looked up and saw Carina directly across the table from him.

A growl of frustration nearly escaped before he muscled it back. He had not been at all prepared for this. How could he have been? He hadn't the first idea how he would manage an entire evening spent in her company without either storming out in frustration or disrupting the Beaumonts' evening by demanding to know why she'd pushed him away all those years ago and why, by the stars, she had come here to torture him further.

"Mr. Ambrose, you have been in Wilkington nearly a year now," Miss Chadwick said. "Why is it we seldom see you?"

He set his attention firmly on her and not upon her niece seated beside her. "I cannot say, other than the possibility that the demands of my business have prevented my participation in most of the social gatherings in Wilkington. The Beaumonts have been good enough to include me, but I daresay most of the other local hostesses have given up all hope of me."

He glanced at Carina out of the corner of his eye. She showed not the slightest interest in his conversation or presence, though he felt certain she was listening.

"Have they?" Something far more pointed than casual conversation lay beneath the older lady's words. Indeed, when he looked more fully at her, he could see that he was being evaluated. Perhaps, as the Beaumonts had hinted, she was considering investing in his mill. "Where did you live before coming to our fine city?"

"In Preston." It was the truth, though not all of it. If Carina did not mean to reveal their connection, he certainly wasn't going to volunteer it.

"Ah." Miss Chadwick's gaze narrowed on him. "You've family there?"

"Yes. My uncle. I am a business partner of his, currently assigned to oversee Ambrose Mill here in Wilkington."

"And are you turning a profit?" Her questions were direct, which did not surprise him in the least. His few interactions with her before now had revealed that bit of her character.

"I am turning a profit, yes." He matched her matter-of-fact tone. "I expect it to grow each year, in fact."

"Mr. Ambrose has an excellent head for business," Miss Beaumont said. "My father has declared him the *second* best business man in all of Wilkington—second to himself, of course."

That earned the expected amusement from all at the table, except Carina. Her expression did not change in the least. Indeed, her gaze did not rise above her plate.

Mr. Beaumont launched into a discussion of margins and risk assessment, joined by his wife and daughter, as well as Miss Chadwick. For his part, Grant could only half listen. Carina continually pulled his notice. She had never been one for endless prattle, but this silence was unnatural.

Was she overset at being in his company again?

Had the years since they'd last seen each other rendered a fundamental change in her?

Was she being mistreated by her aunt?

He reminded himself more than once that they were no longer sweethearts, that she had made plain her waning connection to him. His head had, logically and correctly, closed that chapter in his life with a firm and resounding snap. He simply could not allow his heart to open it once more.

Carina returned to her bedchamber at Chadwick House that night and wept.

Chapter Six

Breakfast was a quiet affair the next day. Mrs. Jones informed Carina that Aunt Chadwick did not generally rise before midmorning. So Carina indulged in a quiet walk through one of the gardens, during which she practiced putting Grant Ambrose out of her thoughts once more. His behavior toward her the night before baffled her. He had not admitted to being from Rafton. Nothing in his interaction with her even hinted at a previous acquaintance. Her heart ached recalling the coldness of his glances.

Had he not hurt her enough five years earlier? Was doing so again truly necessary?

Too many uncertainties flowed through her mind for any degree of peace or contentment despite the beauty of her surroundings. She would try not to think on him, but trying and doing were different things.

She returned to the house no less burdened than when she'd left. Her aunt had arisen and taken a seat in the sitting room. Carina joined her there, determined to pass her day with more pleasant pursuits than torturing herself with thoughts of Grant Ambrose.

"Good morning," she greeted as she sat near her aunt.

"How long have you and Mr. Ambrose known each other?" Aunt Chadwick asked without preamble. "And do not think to brush me aside with protestations: the tension between the two of you last evening could have securely suspended a bridge."

Was it so obvious? Her heart sank, weighed down by humiliation. Had everyone at the dinner noticed?

"The Ambrose family moved to Rafton seven years ago," Carina said, resigning herself to the retelling.

Aunt Chadwick's sharp gaze grew more pointed. "He, then, is not from Preston as he said."

"He moved to Preston five years ago to be a partner in his uncle's business ventures. So he was being honest, if not detailed."

Aunt Chadwick shook her head, apparently dissatisfied with that. "He went to great pains not to reveal any connection between the two of you. There must be a reason."

Carina had been trying very hard not to ponder that reason. If he had merely grown indifferent toward her over the years, as she had told herself he had, then he would have acknowledged their acquaintance and perhaps shrugged it off. To make no mention of it at all spoke of something else entirely.

"Were you sweethearts?" Aunt Chadwick asked.

With a small sigh, Carina nodded. "When he left for Preston, it was with the understanding that he would visit regularly and write to me—his sister allowed our notes to each other to be included in her correspondence with him—and that once he was established as a partner and had secured his own lodgings, he would—" She could not force the remainder of the sentence to form.

Her aunt seemed to understand what was left unspoken. "Did he write to you?"

"He wrote for a time. His earliest letters were long and detailed, delineating all he was learning and doing, the people he was meeting. He told me he missed me and longed for my company. I wrote back, sharing my thoughts and feelings, asking questions about matters of business I did not fully understand but wished to. At first, his responses were eager, allowing me to be part of all aspects of his life. They changed, though. They grew shorter, less personal. He seldom spoke of loneliness as he once had or of wishing I were with him. In time, his letters stopped entirely."

She did not dare look at her aunt. She'd spent far enough time seeing pity in the eyes of those who knew of her dashed hopes and aching heart. Last evening's painful encounter had left her even more vulnerable to it.

"Did he ever visit you?" Aunt Chadwick asked.

Carina swallowed down a lump forming in her throat. "Not even once. It seems he grew indifferent very quickly."

Aunt Chadwick snorted—actually snorted. "What I saw on young Mr. Ambrose's face last night was anything but indifference."

She had to admit that was true. "There was too much coldness for true apathy."

"And too much coldness for true coldness." Aunt Chadwick leaned back in her chair, her wrinkled face pulled in thought. "I found myself wondering again and again last night and this morning just what he *is* feeling."

"I am not certain I wish to know," Carina admitted quietly. "I have long since come to terms with his disinterest. I do not know that I could abide anything else."

"Then let us not dwell on him." Aunt Chadwick's hand swished the air. "We will spend this summer, instead, discovering who you are and what it is you want."

"My father sent me here for precisely that same reason."

Aunt Chadwick laughed softly. "Heavens, child. I know perfectly well his motivation. Do you think you are the only one of my nieces to be sent here as a warning against the perils of spinsterhood?" Again, she laughed, not bitterly or humorlessly. She seemed to truly find it amusing. "You are the fourth resigned to this fate. Two have gone on to marry wonderful gentlemen and build beautiful lives. The third did not choose to marry, but has built a beautiful life as well—one filled with work that brings her satisfaction and many, many people who consider her as close as family, whose lives she has touched. My relatives send their daughters here on the assumption that they will be miserable. I receive them on the assumption that, here, they will finally learn to be joyous."

Oh, how Carina liked the sound of that. She had not felt truly joyous in far too long.

"I have often felt these last five years as though joy hovered just out of my reach," Carina said. "I haven't any idea how to grasp it."

Aunt Chadwick nodded firmly. "Then that is our goal for this summer. We will go out amongst society, attend meetings for charitable societies, explore various pastimes. We will find what brings you happiness, and you will embrace it—all of it."

"And what of Mr. Ambrose?" She worried his presence in Wilkington would be a source of tremendous misery for her.

"We will sort him out in the midst of it. Never you fear. We will sort him out."

By the end of her first week in Wilkington, Carina was exhausted. How her aunt maintained such a whirl of activity, she did not know. They had called upon any number of local ladies, taken tea at a small tea shop in company of a Mrs. Garold, with whom Aunt Chadwick appeared to have a friendly rivalry, and spent three of the seven nights at various events around town: soirees, musicales, and the like.

Carina could hardly keep pace with her hostess.

"Where are we bound this morning?" she asked as the carriage rolled down the cobbled streets toward the far end of the city.

"A meeting of the Ladies' Aid Society, of which I am an original member."

This, then, was not a social appointment. "What does your society do?"

"We advocate for the less fortunate here in Wilkington, be they orphans or widows or poverty-stricken workers."

"And this is the kind of work your niece took up after leaving here?"

Aunt Chadwick nodded. "She saw that women can do a great deal of good in this world."

"What of your other nieces, those who married? Are they doing good in the world as well?"

"Of course they are," Aunt Chadwick said. "Their influence is felt in different ways, but it is real just the same."

"You are not nearly as grumpy as my father led me to believe," Carina said with a smile.

Aunt Chadwick's eyes twinkled. "Wouldn't he be disappointed to hear that."

"He likely would have simply locked me in my room until I agreed to marry Mr. Baskon rather than send me here."

The admission brought a return of Aunt Chadwick's

searching expression. "This is a complication I wasn't aware of. Who is Mr. Baskon, and what is your objection to him?"

"He lives in Rafton on an admittedly grand estate. He is of an age with my father, recently buried his third wife, and wishes for me to be the fourth. My objection—"

"What you just told me is objection enough," Aunt Chadwick said.

"There is more," Carina told her. "He is cruel and cold and unkind. His most recent wife was an acquaintance of mine. I watched her wither in absolute misery after their marriage. It was more than a loss of happiness in her expression. She became increasingly hermitic and quiet. She physically changed as well, dwindling to little more than a shell of a person. The fact that no one in town was surprised told me his earlier wives endured similar agony in their life with him. I choose not to tread that particular path."

"I should think not." Aunt Chadwick appeared appropriately horrified—something Carina's own parents had never managed.

"Perhaps at the end of the summer, you could explain that to my father, as I do not think he will have changed his mind."

Aunt Chadwick leaned closer. "It is your mind and not his that matters, my dear. Until you fully embrace that, you will not know how strong you truly are."

Carina had never thought of herself in those terms. Ladies did not have a great deal of say in their own lives, after all. She had steadfastly refused Mr. Baskon's advances and her parents' seeming acceptance of them. Such, though, was an act of desperation more than true strength.

"Ah, here we are." Aunt Chadwick motioned to the carriage window, outside of which rose a tall stone wall cast in shadow.

Carina had been too distracted to note where precisely they were. She still did not know. The local workhouse, perhaps. A dock building. The poor and destitute were to be found everywhere.

The coachman, whistling as always, handed them out. A great deal of noise emanated from within the walls of the yet-unidentified building. People moved about in the distance, crossing a shadowed courtyard from one building to another.

Carina followed her aunt through a narrow door and down a pokey corridor. They passed several small offices in which people were bent over desks, making notes in large bound books. This appeared to be a place of business.

They were ushered into an office. Mrs. Garold sat inside, along with two ladies Carina did not know. Aunt Chadwick took the nearest seat, then launched into an animated discussion with the other ladies on a topic that, by the sound of it, involved a previous undertaking of the Ladies' Aid Society.

Carina moved to take the only vacant seat other than the one behind the large desk. She stopped, however, at the sound of heavy footfalls directly behind her. Spinning around, she came face-to-face with the last person she expected to see.

"Mr. Ambrose," she whispered.

His brow pulled low. Apparently, he'd not anticipated her presence either. His eyes darted to Aunt Chadwick, and a look of wearied understanding filled his features. "Please be seated," he said as he walked past her to his desk.

She lowered herself into the armless chair. In the next instant, he sat as well.

"What can I do for you, ladies?" he asked, eying everyone except Carina.

"It has come to our understanding that a few families working here in your mill have fallen upon difficult times,"

Mrs. Garold said. She, like Aunt Chadwick, preferred to get straight to the point.

Carina had never known women quite like them before. Hers was a more quiet nature, though she found their directness inspiring. Perhaps more backbone would do her some good.

"We've come to ask your help in assisting them," Aunt Chadwick said. "We realize there's not much financial benefit to you, and your mill would likely be more profitable if you simply cut loose workers who—"

Grant raised his hand and stopped her. "Not all men of business are ogres. Tell me what it is you know, and we can begin discussing what is to be done."

"As easy as that?" Mrs. Garold clearly hadn't expected such easy capitulation.

His answering smile transported Carina to their meeting place all those years ago, when he would tell her something that amused him and his lips would turn up in just that way. She dropped her gaze, unprepared to face those memories.

"If I am in a position to be of help, to ease suffering," he said, "you will not have to *convince* me to do so."

"Well, this is an unfamiliar situation," Aunt Chadwick muttered.

"We'd best move forward before the gentleman comes to his senses," Mrs. Garold said.

"Do you often have difficulty securing aid in these matters?" Grant asked.

"In our experience," Aunt Chadwick said, "men of business are more motivated by profit than compassion."

"That is more often true than it should be," Grant said. "Tell me about these families who are struggling."

The ladies gave a detailed account of illnesses and loss, need and near desperation. Carina's gaze rose to Grant as the discussion continued. He took copious notes, asking questions, and listening to the ladies' suggestions while making a few of his own.

He had obviously forgotten her, which was something of a relief. She was not enduring his looks of displeasure or dismissal, but watched him unnoticed. Here, again, was his kind and tender nature, his compassion. He smiled as he once had. He clearly cared about the people he oversaw. This was how she'd imagined him in the role of businessman, the role in which she had pictured herself assisting him.

This was the Grant Ambrose she had once loved.

And he abandoned me. Do not forget that, Carina, or you will simply be hurt again.

The meeting came to a close, several approaches having been decided upon. They all rose. Grant thanked the ladies for coming, offering friendly bows and smiles. Then he turned to Carina. His expression emptied. His bow was quickly executed without meeting her eye.

"Miss Herrick. A good day to you," he said, his tone flat and insincere.

She simply watched him, not returning the pleasantry. Aunt Chadwick was right; this was not indifference. He actively disliked her.

He had hurt her almost beyond bearing five years earlier. Why must he continue to do so?

"Miss Herrick?" Her silence, apparently, confused him enough to bring his eyes to hers at last.

She hadn't the energy to argue, nor could she explain all that was weighing on her. In the end, she released her pent-up breath and whispered, "You never used to be hurtful."

She turned and followed her aunt out of the office, promising herself that, for the remainder of her time in Wilkington, she would do her utmost not to cross paths with him again. She simply couldn't bear it.

Chapter Seven

You never used to be hurtful. Hurtful. Carina's words echoed in Grant's mind for hours on end.

He hadn't been hurtful. He'd been civil and polite. He'd not embarrassed her or himself. He'd kept their interaction as serene as possible despite the many questions swirling in his mind. What more could she expect of him?

The question weighed heavily on his mind as he stepped into the Beaumonts' house that night for a society gathering. He had actually been looking forward to it. His enthusiasm, however, had waned after what transpired that morning.

She would be there. He knew she would. And those words— *You never used to be hurtful*—would follow him all evening long. There were a lot of things he never used to be, things *she* never used to be. Strangers, for one. Alone, for another. They used to have each other. Nothing had been the same since that changed.

Miss Beaumont met him not three steps inside the music room, her open, friendly manner weaving its usual spell. He felt content in her company, something he appreciated even more than usual just then.

"We have secured an unparalleled performer for this evening," she said, slipping her arm through his. "She is in demand on the opera stages in London, as well as Milan. Quite a coup for Mother."

Carina would be pleased. She had once attended a musical evening and heard an operatic soprano. She'd spoken of the experience on more than one occasion, waxing poetic about her enjoyment of the performance.

How had she entered his thoughts again?

"You seem distracted this evening," Miss Beaumont said. "Did you have difficulties at the mill?"

He smiled apologetically. "No, my thoughts are simply wandering. I believe a musical evening is precisely what I need to calm this overworked mind of mine."

"Then I am even more pleased you are here." She led him toward the rows of chairs set in place in anticipation of the evening's entertainment.

A few of the guests were seated already, but most were moving about, mingling. As his luck of late would have it, Miss Beaumont led the two of them directly to Miss Chadwick and Carina, who stood a few paces from a small gathering of attendees.

"Miss Chadwick, Miss Herrick," she greeted. "How pleased we are to see you here this evening."

Miss Chadwick's gaze darted from Grant to Miss Beaumont and back again, pausing only long enough to eye their interlinked arms. "How very gracious of you both to greet the guests so personally."

Something in that observation felt like a challenge to Grant. If Carina noticed anything odd, she did not allow it to show. Her focus remained to the side, not acknowledging the conversation going on directly before her.

Miss Beaumont noticed. "Is something amiss, Miss Herrick? You appear displeased with your company."

"Not at all." Her denial was spoken softly, not unlike the denunciation she'd offered him earlier. "I have simply had a taxing day."

"You and Mr. Ambrose both," Miss Beaumont said.

The comment brought Carina's eyes to him at last. What he saw in their brown depths pulled him back five years to the day he'd told her he was leaving Rafton: worry, uncertainty, even fear. But, on that long-ago day, those emotions had been directed at fate and the vagaries of the future. In this moment, he knew without question that what he saw in her eyes was directed entirely at him.

You never used to be hurtful.

"I have managed to pull Mr. Ambrose from his doldrums," Miss Beaumont said. "We simply must find someone to ease Miss Herrick from hers. I know any number of young gentlemen in attendance tonight who, I am certain, would be quite pleased to spend the evening at your side."

Before Carina could say a word, her aunt spoke. "You should know that Miss Herrick's parents have bestowed their blessing on a suitor who lives near their family home. I do not imagine her spending an evening on the arm of another gentleman would meet with his approval."

A suitor? Was she engaged? Promised? Her expression gave away nothing, though she blushed a little.

"These tired bones of mine need resting," Miss Chadwick said. "Let us find a place to sit, Carina."

They stepped away and moved toward a back row of chairs. Grant could not be satisfied with so uninformative an answer.

"Pardon me." He slipped his arm free of Miss Beaumont's and followed in Carina's wake, weaving around guests obstructing his path.

He reached the ladies before they sat.

Carina saw him first but didn't speak. Her attention was immediately focused on her aunt.

Miss Chadwick's brows turned up in surprise. "Did you think us incapable of finding seats on our own?"

He shook his head. "I only—" How did he explain this? He didn't know if Carina had told her elderly relative about their history. Yet he had to know. His mind would never be at ease otherwise.

"Who is he?" he asked Carina.

"Who is whom?" She wore her dignity like a shield.

"This suitor in Rafton. Robert Caraway?" He had spoken more than once of an interest in her years earlier. "George Wilson?" He was the right age, though not at all suited to her clever and quick intellect.

"You, sir, have no right to ask me such personal questions. You forfeited that privilege five years ago."

He lowered his voice, not wishing to air this grievance at full volume. "You knew perfectly well why I had to go to Preston. You agreed to it. You supported the decision."

"And you didn't come back," she added firmly. "Your life proceeded without me. You cannot object to hearing that mine has as well."

Didn't come back? He hadn't been able to in those early months; there'd been no time. By the time he was able, there'd been no reason. Their letters had long since grown impersonal and infrequent.

"Miss Beaumont appears to be wishing for your company," Carina said. "It would not do to disappoint her."

Miss Chadwick went so far as to wave Miss Beaumont

over. She sent Grant a look of challenge as she lowered herself onto her chosen chair. Carina sat beside her, once again refusing to look at him.

Miss Beaumont arrived and immediately slipped her arm through his. "Mr. Whiting wishes to speak with you. I suspect he may be interested in discussing your mill."

Normally, that bit of information would grab his entire attention, but he hesitated. Who was Carina's intended? How long had her heart been engaged elsewhere?

"Your thoughts really are wandering today." Miss Beaumont laughed as she urged him away.

One step, and Miss Chadwick spoke. She uttered only two words, but they stopped his heart. "Mr. Baskon."

Grant was afforded no opportunity to obtain an explanation—one he desperately hoped would ease his horror. Miss Beaumont kept to his side throughout the remainder of the evening, she and her parents pulling him into one conversation after another. By the time he slipped free, long after the operatic performance had ended, Carina and her aunt were already gone.

He hardly slept that night, his concern for Carina growing by the moment. He remembered Baskon all too well. There were no polite words strong enough to describe the type of man he was. Grant, being male, had been privy to even more details of Baskon's despicable nature than Carina likely was. Surely she knew enough to give the horrid man a wide berth. Surely.

If, however, she did not, she had to be warned. She had to know the life she would be choosing—one in which misery would be unavoidable and the life drained from her.

By the next morning, Grant had formulated a course of action. He sent word to the mill manager not to expect him and, instead, hied himself to the far edge of town and directly to the door of Chadwick House.

He was ushered to a small, private breakfast room where Miss Chadwick sat enjoying her morning meal, despite the morning being half over. Carina was nowhere to be seen.

"I wondered when we might be seeing you," Miss Chadwick said.

"I was expected?" Odd, considering he had decided upon this call only that morning.

"One does not live as many decades as I without learning a great deal about people." She motioned him to an empty chair at the small table.

He sat. "Is Car—Miss Herrick about?"

Miss Chadwick smiled knowingly. "She has gone for her morning walk, which gives me ample time to see to the matter of *your* version of all this."

He eyed her more closely. "Of all *what*, precisely?"

"Come now." She set herself to the task of buttering a scone. "I may be an old lady, but my wits have not gone begging."

"She told you?"

Miss Chadwick pointed at him with her butter knife. "Told me what?"

They were talking in circles now. "That we were sweethearts."

She laughed lightly. "I sorted that out on my own. I'm hoping to hear from you what ended that connection."

"What did she say ended it?"

Miss Chadwick tsked. "That would be cheating, Mr. Ambrose."

She was a formidable verbal sparring partner, that was for certain. Grant had no desire to cross swords over this; he had come on weightier matters. A quick explanation seemed best.

"We drifted apart."

Miss Chadwick appeared unimpressed—extremely so. "Is that not how she described it?"

She arched a silver brow. "That is not how she described it *to you* last evening."

Grant hadn't truly pondered much of last evening beyond the revelation that Mr. Baskon had been chosen for Carina.

"She said I left," he remembered.

"And?"

"And—And I didn't come back."

"Your explanation is that you drifted apart," Miss Chadwick said. "Her experience was that you stopped caring."

Stopped caring? How could she possibly believe that? Even after years of silence, of enduring the heartache of losing her, he still cared. She, however, had grown more distant, a shift he'd felt long before the Beaumonts' dinner party.

"Her letters were not the kind one would write to a sweetheart," Grant said. "She spoke of no tender feelings. They were nothing but questions, none of which were the least bit personal."

"Questions about your business concerns?" She seemed to already know the answer.

"Yes."

"Matters about which you had written to her but with which she had no experience and, thus, no real understanding? Things that were part of your life, your future, your concerns, all of which she felt connected to and, thus, would wish to better understand?"

Doubt began to bubble.

"She asked you questions that showed a deep interest in

all you were doing. And for that, you concluded she was . . . disinterested?" She ended on a withering tone, one that communicated her feelings on the matter quite clearly.

"But there was a change," Grant insisted. "Her earliest letters spoke of longing and tenderness."

"She told me yours did as well, but that they quickly became nothing beyond terse answers to her questions and little else."

He leaned back in his chair, mind swirling. Her letters had changed. Hers. Not his. How was her explanation to Miss Chadwick the absolute opposite of that?

"Did you write her with any questions of your own?" Miss Chadwick asked. "Did you inquire after her life and concerns? Did you ask what weighed on her heart and mind? Or did you decide her devotion was waning simply because her letters did not flatter you with a sufficient number of tender sentiments and promises of unending loyalty?"

Grant didn't know how to answer. He thought her feelings had cooled in his absence because her tone had indicated as much. What else was he to have thought?

"When you began to suspect a distance growing between you, what did you do? Did you return to Rafton? Did you rush back to see and hear for yourself the state of things?"

"I could not," he said. "My time was not my own. I was given no leeway for journeys, even short ones." It had been a hectic and exhausting time. He'd struggled to do all that was expected of him. He'd slept little and eaten poorly, not for want of a comfortable bed and ample food, but for want of time. He could not have returned. It was not possible.

"Surely you wrote to her of your concerns," Miss Chadwick said. "Surely you told her how much you loved her and that you feared those sentiments were not easily expressed through letters."

He had not. To do so when her heart had ventured elsewhere seemed a foolish endeavor. But what if . . . What if . . . "She still loved me," Grant whispered.

"She did."

He looked at Miss Chadwick once more, an ache growing inside. "Did?"

"I have no authoritative answer to the question I suspect you are asking," she said. "But I will tell you this: when she looks at you, what I see most clearly is not affection and tenderness, but pain and apprehension."

He had seen that in her eyes as well.

"You told me yesterday morning at your mill that you are not an ogre," Miss Chadwick said. "Is that true in matters of the heart as well?"

"I thought so. Now I'm not entirely sure."

She took a leisurely bite of her scone, watching him with no appearance of earnestness or impatience. The unhurried scrutiny only added to his growing feelings of guilt. He had not afforded the woman he loved the patience he was being shown now.

Grant needed time to think, to sort all of this out. Yet he'd not come on this matter, neither could he leave without addressing the actual reason for his visit.

"You said something last night that weighs on me. You mentioned Mr. Baskon."

She nodded but did not speak.

"I knew a Mr. Baskon during my years in Rafton. I have come on the hope, the prayer, that the man you spoke of, who has been given the Herricks' blessing in pursuing their daughter's hand, is not the same Mr. Baskon I remember."

"And if he is?"

He leaned forward, pleading. "You must do all you can to convince her not to accept him. He is the worst sort of person—terrible in a way that defies polite explanation. I cannot imagine she does not know some aspect of this."

Miss Chadwick took a slow sip of tea. By all appearances, she did not intend to answer his inquiry.

"Please. If you have any influence with her, please attempt to turn her from this course. I cannot bear to think of the misery that awaits her if she goes through with this."

"She has passed through a great deal of misery already."

Grant was beginning to realize how true that was, and how much of that misery could be laid at his feet. Yet this matter went beyond him and his regrets. "Mr. Baskon will destroy her spirit, Miss Chadwick. He will drain the very life from her. And hers is a life worth saving."

"What of treasuring, Mr. Ambrose? Is hers a life worth treasuring?"

The question bordered on the absurd. "Of course it is. She is wonderful and dear and kind and clever and so many other glorious things. How could anyone not treasure her?"

She nodded slowly. "Ponder on that, sir. Ponder."

He was dismissed on that declaration, which he carried with him the remainder of the day. How could anyone not treasure her? Yet he had not cherished her as he ought. And he had lost her.

Though he'd come to terms with that years earlier, Grant found the pain of it pricking at him anew. She'd slipped away, not because she'd lost interest, but because he had misunderstood and had been unwilling to risk rejection in order to know, for certain, her feelings.

Did any of her tenderness for him yet remain? And did he have the courage to find out?

Chapter Eight

Carina eyed the gathering of people on the back lawn of the Garold home with growing trepidation. "The first time we met Mrs. Garold, I thought you didn't like her."

"I don't." Her aunt's dancing eyes told another story. "I'm keeping my enemies close, as they say. And, seeing Miss Beaumont ahead, I'm assuming you are adhering to the same adage."

"Miss Beaumont is not my enemy," Carina said.

"Isn't she? I saw how adamant she was in preventing Mr. Ambrose from returning to our corner of their music room a few nights ago."

Carina had noticed that as well, but she had no claim on Grant's attention. Truth be told, she wasn't certain she would have wanted his company had she been given it.

He'd been kind and generous that evening, and when her aunt hinted that Mr. Baskon had successfully petitioned for her hand, he'd shown genuine concern. Yet he still had not openly acknowledged their connection. He still treated her in many ways like a stranger. The Grant she once knew would not have done that.

She didn't know what to think of him anymore.

Aunt Chadwick adjusted her parasol, shading herself from the late afternoon sun. "Would you care to place a wager on how long after Mr. Ambrose's arrival"—she motioned just ahead of them to Grant's approach—"Miss Beaumont will come claim him?"

"Perhaps Mr. Ambrose is not actually intending to join *us*."

"Of course he is. And you might as well call him Grant. I know that is how you think of him."

She turned shocked eyes on her aunt and received a grin in return. The grumpy, disagreeable lady Carina had been told to expect had proven anything but.

"Ladies." Grant reached them in the next moment and offered a quick, eager bow. "Forgive me for the precipitous dive past the expected pleasantries, but there is something I simply must show Car—Miss Herrick."

Aunt Chadwick hmphed. "The two of you. I am absolutely certain you'll be the death of me."

Grant most certainly heard the comment, but he did not acknowledge it. His eyes had not left Carina. "Will you come with me?"

Oh, the ache of hearing those five words five years too late. "To where, exactly?"

"Not far. Just to the end of the lawn."

Aunt Chadwick shook her head. "I'll stay here if it's all the same to you. These old bones of mine don't wander about for no reason."

"My *young* bones don't either," Carina said firmly.

"There is a reason." Grant still had not looked away. "I believe you will be happy to have made the short journey."

Heaven help her, she wanted to go. She did not yet fully trust him; she knew perfectly well how easily he could break her heart. Yet that same heart urged her to accept, to have one more walk with him, to enjoy a moment that echoed so many in which she'd been happy.

"I suppose if it is only across the way." She tried to hide the wariness she felt. "Provided, of course, my aunt sees nothing improper in the undertaking."

Aunt Chadwick waved off the concern. "I suspect he'll behave himself with the entire garden party privy to his every movement."

"I would behave myself regardless," Grant replied.

They were motioned away. Grant offered his arm. With a quick intake of breath, Carina accepted it. How familiar the arrangement was. The passage of half a decade had not erased the memory.

"Am I permitted to ask what I am to anticipate at the end of this walk?"

"That would spoil the surprise, don't you think?"

Walking with him was rendering her tenser than she might have expected. Her heart beat out a rhythm of remembered hurt. "I am not so fond of surprises as I once was."

"But I suspect you are still fond of a breathtaking vista."

Though she did not want to admit it, he had piqued her curiosity.

"I never knew anyone who loved trees and gardens and nature the way you did—*do*." He glanced at her, clearly searching for the answer.

"Yes," she said. "I do still love nature."

"I am pleased to hear that."

"Why? Do you fear I have changed as much as you have?"

"I have not changed as much as you think. And no, I am

pleased because I always liked that about you and because the surprise I have planned would be a failure otherwise."

She searched the area ahead of them but could not figure out what he wanted her to see. The lawn and surrounding trees and shrubbery were lovely, but she saw that from where she had been standing. There had to be something else.

"What is it?"

He smiled at her. Heavens, he smiled at her. "Something special."

They reached the edge of the garden. He motioned ahead of them, beyond the shrubbery. Below them sprawled a valley. The town of Wilkington didn't entirely fill it. At the edges were fields and clusters of trees.

Carina pressed a hand to her heart. "It's like our spot used to be."

"Yes. Precisely. The city being there changes it, but I thought of our spot the moment I saw the view."

She looked up at him. "You do remember it, then?"

He met her gaze. "Of course I do. My happiest memories were made there."

She returned her attention to the view, hoping it would soothe the growing ache she felt. "One of my *worst* was made there."

"Carina, I—"

"There you are, Mr. Ambrose." Miss Beaumont arrived a little out of breath, as if she'd rushed over.

Carina should have taken Aunt Chadwick's wager.

"The other guests are anxious for your company, Mr. Ambrose. It would not do to keep them waiting."

Carina returned her gaze to the valley below. It really was beautiful. She could stay there and enjoy it, allowing the serenity to lighten her heavy heart. That particular approach had worked before. It had seen her through Grant's departure, the change in his letters, the realization that he would not be coming back. She'd also retreated to the comfort of nature when her parents lost patience with her, when Mr. Baskon focused his unwanted attention on her, and when she'd been sentenced to a summer spent with an aunt she expected to be a terror.

But Carina was done hiding from difficulties and waiting for them to pass. Living with Aunt Chadwick the past two weeks had taught her to be stronger than that.

She offered Grant and Miss Beaumont a quick dip of her head. "I, too, have acquaintances here today. I will go greet them and leave you two to do the same."

"Don't go, Carina. Please."

Miss Beaumont's eyes widened. "Carina? That is very . . . personal for a fortnight's acquaintance."

Carina glanced at Grant. Would he continue to tiptoe around their history and the role she'd once played in his life?

He didn't hesitate. "We have known one another far longer than a fortnight. For seven years, in fact."

"Seven—?" Miss Beaumont's amazed gaze darted between them.

"Miss Herrick hails from Rafton," Grant said.

"Your Rafton?"

His lips turned up in a small, subtle smile. "*Her* Rafton, where I was fortunate enough to live for a time."

"You did not mention this before." Miss Beaumont's attention was now fully on Grant.

"At first I was too shocked to think clearly, then I was simply too thickheaded."

"I don't understand."

Carina silently excused herself, making her way toward the gathered guests and leaving Grant to make what further explanation he chose. But he didn't remain behind long. He caught up to her before she'd reached the others.

"You have abandoned Miss Beaumont?" she asked.

"She abandoned me."

Carina looked back. Sure enough, Miss Beaumont was cutting her own path to the Garolds' guests. Grant kept close to Carina's side.

"You told her that we knew each other," Carina said. "Does that mean you are no longer ashamed of our one-time connection?"

"I was never ashamed."

"I have a difficult time believing that."

His hand brushed against hers as they walked, though he made no move to claim hold of it. "Seeing you after so long was overwhelming and confusing."

"As was your silence five years ago."

When he spoke again, his voice was quieter, softer. "I thought your feelings for me had changed."

"Why would—Why would you think that? I wrote to you faithfully, eagerly."

"Impersonally," he said. "Or so it seemed to me. I mistook your questions as an attempt to avoid more personal topics."

"I was meant to share your life with you. Asking about that life could not have been *less* impersonal." Sharpness edged her words. "Despite the unfairness of your assumption, you never asked, never inquired, never spent the seconds required to simply ask if I loved you still, if my heart had changed. And you never came back. You simply gave up and tossed me aside."

"I was a coward."

She watched him closely, her mind spinning with his words.

"I knew if I went back to Rafton and saw with my own eyes that you had grown indifferent, I would have to accept that it was true. I couldn't face it."

No. Her heartbreak could not have hinged on something so minute, something so easily fixed as a misunderstanding. "So you left me to pick up the pieces, to endure the pity and amusement of an entire town who knew of my disappointment? You resigned me to that fate in order to save yourself discomfort?"

"I do not expect or deserve your forgiveness," he said firmly. "I simply thought you deserved to know the truth."

"I would have gone to Preston." She made the admission without forethought, without any real understanding of why she was confessing so much to him. "When your letters turned colder and you did not return home, I thought often about going there and seeing if I could sort out what had changed. As a young, unmarried lady, I hadn't that freedom. *Everything* rested on you."

"And I let you down." The sadness in his tone and expression surprised her. "I was a fool, Carina. An utter fool."

"And I learned not to be one." She set her chin at a determined angle. "So I thank you for that life lesson, Mr. Ambrose. Our association taught me to be strong."

She turned and walked away, telling herself she had nothing more to say to him, that the demons of her past had been laid to rest. Yet she thought on the matter as the day wore on. In conversation with others, sitting beside her aunt, joining in the afternoon meal, she thought on it. Lying in her bed late that night, her mind returned again to Grant's words, to why she had lost so much five years earlier. All for a misunderstanding made worse by fear and cowardice.

Despite her show of strength and resolve, her mind was far from at ease, plagued by two words: *What if?*

Chapter Nine

Grant sat in his office two days after the Garolds' garden party, attempting to focus on his work. Confessing to Carina what a mull he'd made of their courtship left his mind heavier instead of lighter.

His thoughts swirled around a list of unanswerable questions. What if he had understood the tone of her letters all those years ago? What if, once he'd begun to worry that her affections waned, he had faced his uncertainties and returned to Rafton to see her again? What if he had simply written to her and asked?

He wouldn't have lost her.

Harold Brown, a bookkeeper at the mill, poked his head inside the office. "Sir, you've a Miss Herrick here to see you."

Grant jerked to his feet, ramming his legs into the desk. The inkwell shifted precariously. Pen nibs spun about. His stack of papers slid across the desktop.

"Should I show her in, sir?"

Grant snatched at the items chaotically spread on the desk. "Yes. Of course." He had only just put his desk to rights when she stepped through the doorway. "Carina." He really ought not to use her Christian name. He had relinquished that right long ago. "Miss Herrick. What brings you here today?"

"I am on an errand for my aunt." She twisted the drawstring bag hanging from her wrist, looking at him fleetingly. "My aunt wishes to know, on behalf of the Ladies' Aid Society, how the Evans and Post families are faring."

"Of course. Won't you be seated?" Grant motioned to a chair near the desk.

"Thank you." Her discomfort was palpable, yet somehow reassuring. There was no anger in her posture or tone, but neither was there the stark indifference he'd felt in the earliest days of her sojourn in Wilkington.

Something had changed between them. He didn't have a word for it—not yet—but his heart began to hope. Perhaps there was now a foundation upon which he might build a new connection.

His first inclination was to return to his usual seat behind the desk, but he thought better of it. He sat, instead, in the chair beside hers. She didn't object.

"The Evans family is in a new house, one without a leaking roof." The Ladies' Aid Society had been instrumental in that arrangement, so that likely was not what Miss Chadwick had sent her niece to discover. "Mr. Post has been reassigned to an area of the mill that allows him to keep hours that are the same as his daughters'. That has eliminated the difficulty of his little ones being alone so much of the day." He had reported that to Mrs. Garold. "I confess, I'm not certain what to tell you that the Society doesn't already know. I don't wish to waste your time."

She smiled, hesitantly but sincerely. "Outside of this one errand, my time is my own today. Even if I accomplish nothing, I find myself quite pleased at this newfound freedom to choose how I spend my day. I never had that luxury in Rafton."

"Ladies are seldom afforded that luxury anywhere, though the factory towns are less strict about such things."

"My parents would be horrified." Yet amusement lit Carina's face. "They are not in favor of me having any degree of independence."

"Have things been difficult at home? In Rafton, I mean?"

She nodded. "Increasingly so."

"Perhaps—" He was taking a great risk. "Perhaps your aunt would allow you to remain after the summer is out."

"I believe she would." Carina nodded in thought. "I hope she would. I have so enjoyed being here, not merely because I can choose how I spend my days, but also because I like living with her, learning about her life, and becoming a friend of sorts."

Hope expanded quickly and painfully in his chest. "You would consider staying here? In Wilkington, I mean."

"Returning to Rafton would mean living with my parents' unending disapproval or choosing a life with Mr. Baskon—neither of which would be the least pleasant."

She did see Baskon for the cad he was. That was a relief.

"Wilkington is beautiful in the autumn," he said. "It would be a shame if you were not here to see it."

Carina did not look at him. "Miss Beaumont might disagree with you."

"Oh, no. I am certain she feels the same way about autumn."

That earned him a well-loved smile. "You are teasing me." Her dark eyes turned up to him.

"Oh, no, Miss Herrick. I never jest while at the mill."

The stiffness of her posture had given way to greater ease. Her tone softened as well. "You told me in one of your letters that being a man of business required you to be ceaselessly somber. I struggled to even picture it."

"That was a miserable time." He propped his elbow on the arm of his chair, leaning the side of his head against his upturned fist. "My time was not my own. I hadn't the freedom to be the person I truly was. I sometimes felt like I didn't even have *myself* for company."

She offered him a look of commiseration. "We've neither of us had an easy few years, have we?"

"No, we haven't." Grant hoped she could hear his sincerity. "I remember in Rafton, when either of us would be upset or struggling with something, the other would listen and offer support and empathy. How I've missed that. There is such hope in simply knowing one is not suffering entirely alone."

"I have missed that as well." There was yet some hesitancy in her eyes, but less of it. Less wariness. Less uncertainty.

Still, instinct told him to tread lightly. "I wish I had something more for you to report to the Ladies' Aid Society. My role in the two families' recovery has been minimal."

Grant kept his gaze and posture more casual than he felt, afraid if he pressed the matter at all, she'd pull away again.

"Perhaps my aunt sent me as a spy." Carina smiled at her own suggestion. "She invests in businesses, you know."

"I do know that." He shifted in his chair, closing the gap between them conspiratorially. "Perhaps I should recruit you as a spy for your aunt. You could tell her how impressed you are with the way everything is run here, that the bookkeeper— the man who showed you in—is very efficient."

Amusement tugged at her features. "I did not see any of his books."

"He showed you in efficiently. You needn't elaborate."

"What else am I to tell my aunt?" Laughter touched her words.

He'd begun this bit of distraction as a means of having a light conversation but took it up in greater earnest. It was not her aunt's approval he found himself wishing for, but hers.

"You could tell her that we are turning a profit, though not an enormous one. Further, that I recognize most workers do not enjoy their employment in a factory, but I have done what I can to ensure their safety and well-being. I have installed the most recent developments in air circulation to make the heat and fibrousness of the air bearable. I invest in the upkeep of the machines and engines so they are as safe as possible. I have limited the hours children are permitted to work. I provide a meal for the workers during the day; it isn't elaborate, but it is filling and, in far too many instances, very much needed."

"Do not all factory owners do as much?" It was precisely the sort of question he had so fully misunderstood five years earlier. She was not dismissing his information or brushing it off with only vague interest. Her voice rang with curiosity. If only he'd been able to hear her ask these things in person.

"No, they do not," he answered. "My uncle is not entirely convinced that my approach is a good one. It does cut in to the factory's profits."

"Why pursue it, then?"

He adjusted his position, facing her more fully. "From a strictly business viewpoint, there is economic benefit to workers who are healthy and not resentful of the work they do. They work more efficiently, and we retain workers, which saves us the cost and inconvenience of finding and training replacements."

Carina did not appear fully satisfied with the answer.

"From a more personal viewpoint, however," he

continued, "I think of families like the Evanses and Posts, and, though I have never lived in the degree of want and struggle that they do, I cannot escape the fact that they are every bit as human as I am. Were I in their shoes, I would want the man I worked for to make my working conditions bearable. I cannot do everything that they might wish me to, but I can do something."

"I have heard a rumor that you are not an ogre," she said. "I find the rumor a little suspect, though, considering you are the one who started it."

"My being the source of the story does not make it untrue."

"Indeed." Her gaze dropped to her hands folded in her lap. "I find myself suspecting the story is true."

If ever he'd received a welcomer compliment, he could not recall it. "You, then, will be making a favorable report of me?"

"I suspect I will." She looked at him once more, her gaze uncertain, but hopeful.

"I cannot tell you how pleased I am to hear that," he said.

Color stained her cheeks. She stood.

He rose as well. "Until we meet again, Miss Herrick."

"I look forward to it."

For his part, Grant more than looked forward to seeing her again. He meant to plan for it and be ready. She would, at the very least, be staying through the summer. He, then, had mere weeks to show her that all was not lost between them, that Wilkington could offer her more than just the beauty of nature and the pleasure of her aunt's company.

He had mere weeks to attempt to find a place once more in her heart.

Grant arrived at Chadwick House the next evening with a small handful of wildflowers and a growing nervousness. He had no idea how he would be received. He did not know at what time the ladies of the house took their evening meal, but, with his responsibilities at the mill, he could not possibly have come sooner. He only hoped his timing proved appropriate.

The butler eyed Grant's flowers, then offered a knowing smile. The staff had been surprisingly personable on his last visit as well. It seemed to simply be their way.

"Miss Chadwick is just in here," the butler said, motioning to the drawing room.

Grant stepped inside. He offered a bow to Miss Chadwick.

He'd not said a single word when Miss Chadwick spoke. "She's in the east garden."

"I am so transparent, am I?"

"Yes. Quite." Miss Chadwick eyed his flowers. "I believe she will appreciate your offering."

"I do hope so."

"She told me you confessed to the stupidity that led to your separation, that you misunderstood her letters and had not the fortitude to approach her in person." The observation was not a flattering one, yet her tone spoke of approval. "I like that you admitted your mistakes, that you didn't try to reassign the blame or wriggle out of it. She deserves to know that she didn't do anything wrong."

"For too many years, I let myself think she had. That was easier than admitting to myself that I'd ruined everything."

Miss Chadwick's expression turned almost maternal. "Misunderstandings occur often enough, and fate does not always allow us to see them in time. You, however, have a chance."

He squared his shoulders. "One I do not mean to waste."

"Very good." She pointed a slightly crooked finger in his direction. "She's less jumpy when you're about than she was when she first arrived, and she no longer wears that look of worry whenever you're mentioned. Now's the time to build on that thin foundation. Show her you've grown. Show her you're to be trusted."

"I will try."

"And, whatever you do, show her you care, that your feelings are tender. A lady needs to know that, or she will never feel safe embracing those same feelings in herself."

"We are both taking a risk pursuing this possibility," he acknowledged. "But it's one I ought to have taken five years ago."

She smiled, her face tucking into pleasant and happy wrinkles. "And one you ought not put off. The east garden. Off with you."

He sketched a quick bow and hurried away. If he had even the smallest chance of regaining Carina's favor, he would not waste a single moment.

Chapter Ten

Carina had developed a particular fondness for the small pond on the east end of the Chadwick House grounds. The trickle of water and chatter of distant songbirds, coupled with the pleasant shade of tall oak trees rendered the spot nearly perfect. It was her place of solace and peace. She stood there as the evening wore on, her mind returning to her visit with Grant the previous morning.

She had been fairly quaking with nervousness when her aunt had sent her to receive the report. How was she to endure the undertaking, she asked herself, if Grant proved unkind or angry at her sharp words at the Garolds' garden party? What if he returned to his earlier indifference?

But he had, instead, been attentive and kind and charming. She saw in him the Grant she remembered from those idyllic months five years earlier, the Grant she could so easily love again, the Grant who broke her heart.

Did she dare trust him?

As if fate meant to require an answer of her, she spied him walking up the path toward her. The moment painfully paralleled his last afternoon in Rafton when she stood in their spot, watching him approach, heart soaring with possibilities. This time, she watched him with uncertainty and a fragile thread of hope.

The years had changed his stride. He'd once trod the streets of Rafton and the footpaths of the surrounding countryside with a bouncy, jaunty step. He now moved with focus and purpose. Truth be told, she sensed the same change in herself. Maturity and experience had exercised their mutual influence to ground her a bit more, but she was not unhappy or pessimistic. She hoped the same could be said of him.

"Carina." He offered a friendly bow as he reached her. "Your aunt told me I could find you here. I hope you do not mind the interruption."

She eyed the wildflowers in his hand—yellow and orange blooms. "Tell me the flowers are for me and I might forgive you."

Oh, his laugh. That had not changed. Neither had her heart's warm response to hearing it. "They are, indeed, for you. I hoped you might appreciate them."

He held the bouquet out to her, and she accepted it. "I believe wildflowers are my favorite thing about summer." The flowers held only the lightest fragrance, yet she liked them better for it. The subtlety of their scent only enhanced the intensity of their color.

"Living in Wilkington has taught me to value berries as part of summer," he said. "The townspeople hold a festival each year celebrating the berry harvest. It was one of my earliest introductions to the place upon arriving a year ago. I look forward to it again this year."

"That sounds wonderful."

"I hope—" He swallowed audibly. "I wonder if I might be permitted to accompany you to the various vendors' booths during the festival. If you would like to, of course."

Her pulse pounded in her neck. Heavens, she was nervous. "I would appreciate an experienced guide during the festival." She meant the remark to be witty, but it emerged nothing short of awkward.

His countenance fell. "Your aunt has greater experience with the festival than I do."

"Yes, but she did not bring me flowers."

That brought his eyes back to hers and a hint of a smile back to his face. "No, she didn't."

"Would you mind if we walked for a bit?" She hoped moving would make her fretting less obvious.

"I would not mind in the least," he said. "I have always enjoyed outings with you."

Her mind flooded with memories. "We did a great deal of walking, didn't we? The way I talked your ear off about plants and trees and vistas. You no doubt longed for winter simply to stop my ceaseless prattle."

"I thought nothing of the sort." He spoke gently, fondly. "I would have walked through a blizzard for the joy of your company."

She felt heat steal over her cheeks. "I take leave to doubt that."

"And I take leave to prove the truth of my statement. The next time we have a blizzard, you and I are going for a walk."

They slowly meandered along the edge of the pond, a light breeze rustling branches and flower stems. Summer was winding to its conclusion, yet autumn had not yet claimed the landscape. The air was cool without being cold. The sky was soft. The birds were singing lightly in the distance. Everything about the setting evening was perfect for a leisurely walk.

"Chadwick House boasts a great many gardens," Grant

said. "That must please you to no end."

She smiled at that. "You, of all people, know the depths of my love for flora."

"I worried about that when I first reached Preston," he said. "The only accommodation I could afford was a small flat tucked into the most crowded part of the city. Hardly a blade of grass to be seen for miles, let alone trees and shrubs. I couldn't imagine you being anything but disappointed by that."

He must not have given up on her too quickly for him to think of such specific concerns.

"So much about my situation then was not at all what we dreamed of," he continued. "You would likely have been miserable."

"You mistook my priorities, Grant Ambrose," she said, but not unkindly. His concern for her was touching. "I had all the trees and meadows and open spaces I could possibly have hoped for in Rafton, but it was not what I wished for most."

"And I had every opportunity to grow as a man of business and a future captain of industry, but it was not what I wished for most."

They had both suffered needlessly. The misunderstanding that kept them apart could have been avoided so easily. A visit. A letter. A single question.

Grant stopped walking and took a deep breath. His eyes met and held hers, a plea in their depths, hope and fear.

"Have I any chance, Carina, of beginning again? I do not presume to be in a position of reclaiming your affections to the degree I once had them—heaven knows I forfeited that right—but not having you in my life has left a void nothing has been able to fill. To have even your friendship would be a blessing beyond anything I've let myself hope for these past five years."

A void. How well she knew that feeling, yet the idea of fully loving him again worried her. Could she trust him enough to allow the possibility of a friendship between them? There was still a risk there, but a far more calculated one.

"I—" Her courage almost failed her, but she rallied. "I would like to try being friends."

A look of palpable relief slid over his features. She hadn't realized how much tension filled his frame until it dissipated.

"Thank you, Carina," he said. "Thank you for having faith in me—the first vestiges of it, at least."

The idea of treading this slippery slope with him ought to have caused her more consternation than it did. Instead, she felt . . . hopeful.

Chapter Eleven

Carina found herself anxiously anticipating Wilkington's festival at the beginning of July to mark the berry harvest. Though industrialization had ended much of the agricultural pursuits thereabout, most homes still grew berries of one kind of another, and the tradition lived on. She accompanied Aunt Chadwick to the celebration, eager to be part of something so important to the people in this town of which she was growing so fond.

  The finer families in the surrounding area were afforded tables at which to enjoy the tarts, pies, and various berry-laden treats. The population in general made quick work of their victuals under the shade of obliging trees or walking about the various booths and vendors. It reminded Carina of the late-summer hiring fair held outside Rafton each year. Did Wilkington hold one of those as well? Two festivals each summer sounded lovely. She had always been fond of gatherings, especially when punctuated by such cheerful voices as were heard here.

  Aunt Chadwick, who often insisted her "old bones"

required resting, despite being one of the most indefatigable people Carina had ever met, remained at the table with Mrs. Garold but insisted Carina seek out a friend or diversion. The independence Aunt Chadwick regularly granted her often took her by surprise, so unaccustomed was she to it. Truth be told, she wasn't certain it was entirely proper.

Still, the festival was showing itself to be a peaceful one, lacking the more questionable entertainments the hiring fairs often included. It would not be truly unacceptable to walk about a little on her own. She was fond of walking, after all. More so of late.

Grant had walked with her in the Chadwick House gardens every evening for the past fortnight. Though the initial excursions had been rather awkward undertakings, they had swiftly transformed into the pleasant and personal interludes they had once shared in Rafton. He spoke of the mill and other investments he was involved in. He told her of ventures he hoped to take up in the future. She spoke of friends she'd made in Wilkington, of her aunt's activities and stories, and, as she'd once done easily and without hesitation, she began telling him of the dreams she had for her future. As before, he didn't mock or dismiss her. He listened and encouraged. Perhaps he hadn't changed as much these past years as she'd feared.

Her heart had ceased aching when she thought of him. Instead, it warmed and expanded in anticipation of his company. That, she felt certain, was a good sign. Her cautious nature—an aspect of her personality that had developed over the past half-decade—kept her from fully embracing these growing feelings, but neither did she dismiss them entirely.

Aunt Chadwick assured her she was welcome to remain at Chadwick House as long as she chose. Carina meant to use that time to sort out her past, her future, and the mess of emotions tied to both. And, despite the uncertainty attached to it all, she was optimistic.

She had perused not more than a half-dozen vendors' offerings when she spied Grant ahead. His attention was on Mr. Beaumont, and he'd not yet seen her. Not wishing to interrupt, Carina approached quietly and slowly. She would simply wait until an opportunity presented itself.

"Has Miss Chadwick decided to invest in the expansion?" Mr. Beaumont asked Grant.

"I honestly do not know," Grant said.

"You are at Chadwick House every night." Mr. Beaumont eyed him in disbelief.

But Grant only laughed. "I am not there on business, sir."

Warmth spread through Carina's chest. She knew perfectly well why he came to Chadwick House. He came to see *her*.

"You are courting her niece, aren't you?"

Carina held her breath, awaiting the answer. She felt certain he was, in fact, courting her, despite their stated intention of building a friendship. But he had not said as much outright. To hear the words . . . So many of their difficulties five years earlier had arisen from words left unsaid.

"I am doing my utmost," Grant said. "Ours is a difficult history."

"Yes, my daughter said as much." Nothing in Mr. Beaumont's posture or tone spoke of disappointed hopes. Perhaps Miss Beaumont hadn't set her sights as firmly on Grant as Carina thought when they first met. "Are you making any progress?"

"I believe so. Regardless of the outcome, I consider myself the most fortunate of men to have her in my life again, in whatever way she will permit."

She stepped away, finding a quiet spot despite the

bustling crowd. *The most fortunate of men.* What a perfectly lovely thing to say. He was truly happy to have her in his life again. The sentiment was mutual. Indeed, over the past two weeks, he had become an integral part of her life once more. And the prospect did not terrify her.

"Good afternoon, Miss Herrick."

She smiled at the sound of Grant's voice. "Mr. Ambrose. You are just in time."

"Am I?"

She looked up at him. "I have been forced to wander this festival all alone."

He held his hand out to her. "Wander alone no more, my dear."

She slipped her hand into his.

He raised her hand to his lips and kissed it tenderly. "My darling, dearest Carina."

At the warmth of his touch and the tenderness of the endearment, joy took wing in her heart.

"I do not believe one generally kisses a person one considers merely a friend." She meant the remark to be teasing, but the words quavered.

He brushed the thumb of his free hand along her cheek. "No, one does not."

"Grant?" She could manage no more than that.

He simply smiled and put her arm through his. "The festival is yours to explore. What would you like to do first?"

She rested her head against his shoulder as they walked. "Everything."

Chapter Twelve

Grant felt the shortening of days acutely as the summer wound to its inevitable conclusion. Carina had not said what she intended to do. Did she have reason enough to remain in Wilkington? Her efforts in the Ladies' Aid Society would be greatly missed by the people she'd helped over the past months. Miss Chadwick would sorely miss her; the two ladies had become dear to each other. The area's many gardens and vistas would be the lonelier were she to leave.

None of that pressed on Grant's heart as he made his way along the pond in the east garden of Chadwick House. Many people would miss her, but Grant would be devastated, broken. He knew what it was to lose her; he could not bear it again.

She stood precisely where she always did before their evening walks in the gardens. Here in Wilkington, they'd claimed a spot as their own, just as they had in Rafton. When he last met her in their designated place five years earlier, he ran to her, spinning her about with unfettered excitement. He'd been so certain of the future then.

This time, he was the one facing the possibility of *her* departure. The prospect tore at him. He'd tried so hard over the past weeks to win back her regard. He felt he'd succeeded to a degree. But was it enough? Would it ever be?

"Good evening," he said.

She smiled softly. Uncertainty tore at Grant's nerves. He meant to ask her about her plans, her future. Their future. Though the answer might break his heart, he had to know.

"I have something for you." He swallowed against the sudden lump in his throat.

"Have you?"

He pulled from his jacket pocket a folded and sealed letter and held it out to her.

"A letter?" She eyed it with obvious confusion.

"The letter I ought to have sent you five years ago."

She took it but didn't immediately open it.

Grant took a fortifying breath. "The summer is all but over, and I know full well you might be leaving. Too much was left unsaid a half-decade ago; I cannot let that happen again."

Her hands shook a little as she flipped the letter over and broke the seal. The wind tugged hard at them both, whipping the tree branches and bushes nearby, not unlike the day they'd parted in Rafton. How he hoped this evening would bring greater happiness than that day.

She did not read his words aloud. She didn't have to. Grant knew the short missive by heart.

My darling Carina,

I love you. I know there are more elegant and poetic ways of expressing what is in my heart, but urgency compels me to unromantic frankness. I have loved you all these years. Losing you left a hole in my very heart—one that you and you alone can fill. Whatever you choose to do, wherever you choose to go, know that I love you with all my soul and will do everything in my power to make certain you never doubt that.

Your affectionate and loving,
Grant

She did not look up for several long moments, far longer than was required to read the single paragraph. Her wide-brimmed bonnet hid her face, rendering him unable to see, let alone interpret, her expression. Had he said too much? Too little?

"Do you wish for me to remain?" She spoke quietly without looking at him.

"I wish for you to be happy."

"That is not what I asked." She met his gaze at last. She watched him so intently he wasn't even certain she was breathing. "Do you wish for me to remain?"

He took her hands in his. "My darling, I walked away from you—from us—five years ago. I lost everything that mattered to me. Second chances are rare in this world. I doubt fate will give us a third."

Worry pulled at her brow and the corners of her mouth.

"Allow us a chance to grow closer and find each other again." He closed his eyes as he tenderly kissed her fingers. "Please stay, my beloved. Please stay."

"Your letter says that you love me."

He looked at her once more, hoping she could see and feel the sincerity of his words. "Of course I do. I love you, Carina Herrick. I love you with every breath, with every thought."

Her smile blossomed once more. "I've waited years to hear you say that."

"I should never have left it unsaid so long. I never will

again. Not ever." He wrapped his arms around her and pulled her close. "Will you stay?"

"I would not wish to be anywhere else."

He bent and brushed a kiss to her cheek.

She set her hands on his chest, gazing into his eyes, then slipped her arms about his neck. "I love you, Grant Ambrose."

He kissed her as the sun set. Fate had, indeed, been kind. He'd lost the love of his life, and the heavens had crossed their paths once more. Life would, no doubt, bring difficulties and worries in the years to come, but neither of them would face those challenges alone again.

About Sarah M. Eden

Sarah M. Eden is the author of multiple historical romances, including the two-time Whitney Award Winner *Longing for Home* and Whitney Award finalists *Seeking Persephone* and *Courting Miss Lancaster*. Combining her obsession with history and affinity for tender love stories, Sarah loves crafting witty characters and heartfelt romances. She has twice served as the Master of Ceremonies for the LDStorymakers Writers Conference and acted as the Writer in Residence at the Northwest Writers Retreat. Sarah is represented by Pam Victorio at D4EO Literary Agency.

Visit Sarah on-line:
Twitter: @SarahMEden
Facebook: Author Sarah M. Eden
Website: SarahMEden.com

Other Books by Sarah M. Eden

HOPE SPRINGS SERIES
Longing for Home
Hope Springs
Love Remains
My Dearest Love
Long Journey Home

REGENCY ROMANCES
The Kiss of a Stranger
Glimmer of Hope
An Unlikely Match
For Elise
All Regency Collection
British Isles Collection

THE JONQUIL BROTHERS SERIES
Friends and Foes
Drops of Gold
As You Are
A Fine Gentleman

THE LANCASTER FAMILY SERIES
Seeking Persephone
Courting Miss Lancaster
Romancing Daphne
Loving Lieutenant Lancaster

TIMELESS ROMANCE ANTHOLOGIES
Winter Collection
Spring Vacation Collection
European Collection

Annette Lyon

Chapter One

Not a year had passed since Sarah last traversed this section of road between the village of Wilshire and London. As usual, she rode in the servants' carriage with Mrs. Roach, the housekeeper, and Betsy, the cook. Together, the three of them would join the small staff at Ivy House, the family's London town house, which had a cook—who also served as scullery maid—a servant, and Mrs. Jones as housekeeper—who also filled any other job that might be required. They ran Ivy House the rest of the year, which was plenty for the few days at a time that Mr. Millington visited the city on business.

During the summer months, when his wife and children joined him for three months, more help was definitely needed. As was the case every year, the rest of the staff stayed at Rosemount, maintaining the estate until the family's return.

The servants' carriage had room for one more, but the two other servants going to London didn't ride with the others. The first, Miss Leavey, was the children's governess, and the other was Mrs. Heap, lady's maid to Mrs. Millington. Due to business obligations, Mr. Millington and his valet had gone ahead to London and awaited them there.

For her part, Sarah came along as additional maid. At Ivy House, she typically spent her days cleaning rooms, scrubbing dishes, and doing anything else Mrs. Roach or Betsy ordered her to do, which at Ivy House tended to be a significant amount of work.

Sarah often wondered if the entire family would have still gone to London every summer if more of the seven babes Mrs. Millington had borne yet lived. Not for the first time, she felt grateful on her mistress's behalf that another child hadn't come along after Nathaniel, who'd passed his third birthday during the winter. The poor woman's constitution couldn't have tolerated the strain. Her temperament, which had become abrasive and easily provoked, already suffered.

Sliding her fingers between the curtain and the glass, Sarah peered outside. A bend in the road showed the family carriage moving smoothly across the rolling emerald countryside. She'd never ridden in one of the family carriages, only in the older ones, which bumped and jolted with every pebble and divot on the road. She'd seen glimpses inside Mrs. Millington's favorite carriage: padded benches and silky pillows. And it had a smooth ride. One could only dream of how much more comfortable a journey would be within such a conveyance.

When the carriage turned suddenly, Sarah instinctively tried to brace herself by holding tighter to the carriage door. She needn't have, of course; next to her, the cook's ample figure filled their shared bench entirely. Indeed, a vise could not have held Sarah any tighter to her spot than the combination of the carriage on her left and Betsy's girth on the right.

Unaware of the sudden turn, Betsy snored away, head down, which emphasized her chins. When the careening ended and the carriage was solidly upright again, Sarah wrapped her cloak around herself against the damp cold.

Mrs. Roach sat on the bench across from Betsy and Sarah, with plenty of room on either side. She sat square in the middle of it, owning the space as if it were a throne. Due to her station, she had benefits other servants lacked. Even so, Sarah wished she could ride on Mrs. Roach's bench. Betsy sampled her own cooking so often that she'd acquired a significant girth. The ride to town had never been comfortable, but Betsy must have indulged more than usual, as the space left for Sarah this year had become so tight as to be almost unbearable.

Sarah eyed Betsy and wondered if she could make the cook move without waking her. Perhaps if she leaned to the side, pushing slightly against Betsy, the cook would shift for her own comfort and—hopefully—make more room for Sarah. Right then, Mrs. Roach lowered the ledger she'd been reviewing and peered over the top of her glasses right at Sarah, her arched brows questioning.

The woman must read minds. Sarah smiled innocently and folded her hands in her lap, looking to the window again, despite the view being once more blocked by the curtain. *She thinks of me as a child of ten, in need of discipline and correction*, she thought, then quickly prayed to the saints that Mrs. Roach couldn't read minds after all.

Mrs. Roach returned her attention to the ledger, which contained lists and notes she'd prepared and consulted many times over the last month as she'd made preparations to ensure a smooth and successful Season.

For her part, Sarah could hardly contain her excitement at knowing that she'd be in London again. Feeling jittery from anticipation as well as from Mrs. Roach's gaze, Sarah moved the curtain aside again. This time, she looked through the slightly warped glass as the landscape passed by. The rain had ended, and the sun had come out, leaving a damp road but plenty of warmth coming from above. When they'd left Rosemount early that morning, a mist of pale gray clouds had stretched across the sky, barely visible as dawn approached. Now shafts of golden light shot through the remaining clouds down to the green hills and valleys.

She peered as far ahead on the road as she could—scarcely farther than a stone's throw—eager to spot the telltale signs of the approaching city. The road would be smoother because it was better cared for, due to having so much more traffic than country roads. Sheep and farmland would become scarce. More buildings would appear, closer together and taller. Many streets had buildings four stories high, so one couldn't see far into the distance at all.

Ivy House also stood four stories, but the street didn't feel as crowded as so many did. That was likely because it was wider than poorer areas of town, where the streets were so narrow that two young women could stand side by side, holding hands, and each could touch a building on the other side of the cobbled way.

While one side of Ivy House's street was lined by a long building of town houses, the other side held a groomed park. Miss Leavey often took her charges there on warm days, always locking the gate behind them to ensure that no undesirables—those who weren't residents of the town houses and therefore didn't pay for the upkeep or right to use the park—came in.

The town houses themselves made the street feel even broader. A short flight of steps set the doors back from the sidewalk. Sarah thought the town houses were beautiful, yes, but some could also seem cold and unfriendly, as if they deliberately stood higher than other dwellings and apart from the street as a sign of aloofness and superiority.

As if buildings have personalities. Sarah smiled softly at the thought. She'd always ascribed feelings to places, though she told few people about it because she knew from experience that many people thought such ideas were silly. So while Ivy House and its neighbors were beautiful in their own grand way, she preferred the parts of the city where doors opened right to the sidewalk. Those doors seemed welcome and inviting, never holding themselves higher than others. Instead, whenever she walked past some, she felt as if a dear friend she'd never before met might open a door at any moment and introduce themselves.

The Millingtons had bought two town houses, then had the interior wall between them torn down to make the house twice the size. It was a lavish thing to do—something only a rich tea merchant could afford—but it was also something Sarah felt grateful for.

Servants always worked and slept in basements, of course, and the lower floors of other town houses were so small that only the housekeeper had a room with a lock. The other servants had to make do, sleeping in the small kitchen or the even smaller scullery, usually without beds. But with twice the basement space, Betsy got a room of her own, and Sarah slept in the second scullery. While a room with a door, like she had at Rosemount, would have been welcome, she was grateful to have a space to herself at Ivy House.

Sarah had been so deep in thought about Ivy House, the servants' quarters, the parks, and simply thinking of London in such vivid detail that her attention had drifted from the view out the window. When she blinked and focused her eyes through the glass again, she found none of the signs of city life she'd hoped for. She let the curtain fall back into place and sighed as she sat back on the bench.

Again, Mrs. Roach looked up at her from over the top of her spectacles. "Why are we sighing?" she asked in a tone implying that Sarah had released not an audible breath but a speech containing a litany of complaints. But Sarah wasn't about to be cowed by the older woman; she knew Mrs. Roach had a softer inside than she let on. Sarah hadn't seen it often, but it had appeared enough times over the five years she'd worked for the Millingtons for there to be proof of its existence. Yet complaining about how the journey had been hard on Sarah's much younger body would seem disrespectful to Mrs. Roach, who didn't utter a word of complaint despite her aging body and rheumatism.

Sarah didn't know how to answer the simple question, because the other reason she was sighing was from missing Jacob and anticipating a reunion with him after almost a year.

Jacob.

Just thinking his name sent a thrill up her back. She felt the corners of her mouth curve, and before Mrs. Roach could interrogate her about it, she bit her lower lip to stop the smile. When she felt certain she could keep herself from smiling—an act that required a level of acting skill known to few—she shrugged. "I'm eager to arrive, is all."

"I'll second that," Mrs. Roach said, turning a ledger page and peering through her glasses at the writing. "My bones are getting too old for traveling in such a contraption."

Sarah lifted an eyebrow in surprise. She'd never once heard Mrs. Roach say an untoward word about her circumstances, not so much as the slightest implication of a complaint, and certainly not about the satisfactory—or unsatisfactory—nature of anything the Millingtons provided.

Mrs. Roach made a notation with a pencil. "It's been a long time since a young woman of marriageable age in this household spent a Season in London. The last was Mrs. Millington herself."

"Have you been with her that long?" Sarah asked, suddenly intrigued at the idea that Mrs. Roach might have been in the service of Mrs. Millington since before she'd wed. How long had Mrs. Roach worked for that family, and had she left their employ to follow their youngest daughter and her husband?

She had so many questions, but none appropriate for a maid to be asking.

"I've seen many young women find a husband during my years of service," Mrs. Roach went on. Her mouth relaxed, and the normally thin line might have even curved slightly. "Not all of them have been those who attended balls and had large dowries to attract a man." Another look at Sarah, equally pointed as before, but this time with a glint of amusement in her eye.

Now this was a wholly unexpected turn in the conversation. Was Mrs. Roach toying with her?

Mrs. Roach never toys with anyone about anything, Sarah reminded herself. She'd long wanted to make a better life for herself, but that meant book learning so she could perhaps become a teacher or governess, something other than a housemaid. A better life would also require the Millingtons to write her a letter recommending her to future employers.

In her heart of hearts, however, Sarah couldn't imagine herself twenty years hence as a governess. Not that she didn't believe in herself. Had she been born to privilege and money, she would have received an excellent education—one, ironically, she wouldn't need to better her life because she would have had a dowry and marriage prospects. A wealthy young woman used her education to read books and quote scholars as a way to impress men during her own Season.

Which, she realized with a start, would likely have been this very summer. Girls her age would be attending the balls, looking for a husband to care for them over the course of their lives. Girls like Sarah, however, would be serving their families, hoping to keep their positions and be taken care of somehow, in some way, for a few years yet. In her nightly prayers, Sarah often expressed gratitude for finding employment with a kind family, even if Mrs. Millington had a temper. Rumors flew rampant about maids and even governesses who'd lost their position because of a forward husband pushing his will on her or being blamed for wrongdoing they were innocent of.

There was no telling what her future held, of course, but in the quiet corners of her heart, Sarah had long wished—nay, hoped—that someday, she and Jacob, the sole male servant who lived at Ivy House all year long, would marry.

He was the main reason Sarah felt jittery at the thought of her upcoming summer in London. He was the reason she looked for signs of the city approaching. He was the handsome boy she'd known for five years, who grew handsomer every year. He was the one she'd exchanged letters with throughout the year. And he was the one who, last Season, had almost kissed her in the scullery in a rare moment when they'd been alone.

Mrs. Roach had long since returned to her ledger and had even turned the page, but her words still burned through Sarah. She looked askance at Betsy and watched her chest rising and falling, hoping that with each breath, the snoring would remain at a high volume, because that would mean she was deeply asleep and wouldn't hear what Sarah was about to ask. Her insides felt like jelly as she leaned forward.

"Mrs. Roach?" The name came out as little more than an awkward croak.

"Mm?" the housekeeper looked up and startled when she saw Sarah's face so close to hers. She removed her spectacles and waited for Sarah to continue.

She wasn't sure she could. After one more look over her shoulder at Betsy, she girded up her courage. She spoke just loud enough to be heard over the creaking wheels, clop of hooves, and snoring cook. "Do you mean that you've seen servant girls who have found husbands of their own during the Season?"

The thin line curved again. This time it was most definitely a smile. "That is precisely what I mean." Mrs. Roach settled the spectacles in place again, lifted the ledger, and added, "You're of an age. I thought the information might be useful to you this year."

Sarah sat back, astonished into silence. Mrs. Roach's smile remained. Now Sarah bit her lip, not to hide her smile, but out of a new sense of excitement. Mrs. Roach didn't know about Sarah's hopes for going to school, and she couldn't possibly know about how Sarah felt about Jacob, yet the housekeeper hadn't assumed that Sarah's future consisted of decades in service.

Please be right, Sarah prayed silently as she raised her fingers to her lips and smiled so broadly that her cheeks hurt. *Please be the summer he kisses me.*

Chapter Two

Little Ellie had her arms tight around Jacob's neck as he carried her back to the orphanage after a brief excursion together. It hadn't been long—only thirty minutes—and the outing didn't end with treats like a penny candy, something he did for her as often as he could. But this week, Jacob didn't have the money, nor could he spare more than half an hour with her, not when he had Mrs. Millington and the children arriving at Ivy House today.

Her husband had left for a business meeting early that morning and wouldn't return until after dark. He had been in town for nearly a week and, as always, proved himself to be easy to serve. He preferred to dine simply when alone, and on days he left the town house for business meetings or social engagements, he often had sustenance provided for him, leaving the servants free to enjoy a simple cold supper of apples, bread, and cheese, or, in the winter, some warmed-up soup.

His wife, on the other hand, expected—nay, required—the servants of Ivy House to greet her the moment her carriage rolled to a stop on the street. Every day of every Season, she demanded far more attention, from meals to clothing to chores and visits. The children were growing, which likely would increase the burden on the servants. Keeping energetic wee ones occupied—and quiet—upstairs until their parents wished them to be trotted out for guests required great efforts of everyone, not only the governess. Of course, Miss Leavey would take great pains to ensure that they weren't underfoot as best she could.

Mary, the regular cook at Ivy House, had been preparing food since morning—her last day for three months that she'd be the captain of the kitchen as Betsy would take over tomorrow.

Jacob and Mrs. Jones, the housekeeper for Ivy House when the family wasn't in residence, had together made sure the place was dusted, swept, warmed, and otherwise in order. This was for both Mrs. Millington's sake, as well as Mrs. Roach's. Mrs. Jones would *not* have another housekeeper coming in and finding fault with the way she managed Ivy House during three seasons of the year. Mrs. Jones didn't stay in the city during the summer; she stayed with her sister's family in the country, which was just as well. Two housekeepers under the same roof wouldn't bode well for anyone.

Jacob hugged Ellie tighter as he crossed an intersection, hurrying across the slanted street to avoid buggies and other vehicles. Not for the first time, he wondered why the Millingtons didn't hire another male servant for the summer. He did the jobs of butler, under-butler, footman, and any other office more proper for a male servant to perform than a female one. And while he was grateful for the position, with the extra work he did during the warmer months, perhaps he deserved a higher wage.

Granted, during more than half the year, he didn't wear so many hats, and he had many days to himself to borrow and read books, visit his favorite pubs for singing and camaraderie, and spend time with Ellie. Seeing as Mr. Millington's business trips were often separated by weeks, Jacob had quite a good life. He had a roof over his head, a fire to keep him warm, and food in his belly.

In the five years he'd held this position, he hadn't felt any manner of discontent, not even with his wages, until the last few months. Ellie squeezed her little arms around his neck as hard as she could, her eyes squinching with the effort before she planted a kiss on his stubbly cheek.

"I love you, Jacob!" she cried and hugged him once more. When his step slowed, she released her grip and twisted to look where they were headed. She must have recognized the pale-yellow door with the diamond-shaped, bronze handle in the center because she quickly turned her back to it and buried her face into his neck. "Please don't take me back. Not yet. That was too short."

"I know, love." Jacob patted her back, trying to mask his own emotions. The sadness of leaving Ellie behind always lurked in the shadows, ready to pounce at any moment. If he had only himself to think of, he wouldn't have been so concerned with his wages, but all that had changed in January when Oona died and Ellie was sent here—to Cloverfield Orphanage. "I want to spend as much time with you as I can. You know how much I enjoy our afternoons together, but I haven't much time today."

He could try to explain that he was cutting the visit short for her sake, but she wouldn't understand the complicated realities of employment and how his wages supported her. No matter how she pleaded with her sad, little eyes and pushed out lip, he would stay firm. He had Ellie's welfare to think of over that of anyone else, himself included.

Including Sarah, he thought grimly as he set Ellie onto the cobbled sidewalk before the door.

"But we didn't buy penny candy," Ellie protested. She planted her chubby little fist on one hip and tilted her chin up to look at Jacob. He did a remarkable job, if he said so himself, of hiding his amusement. "And Jacob, we *always* get penny candy."

"Not always, love," Jacob said, attempting to hide the wistfulness he felt. "We haven't the time to stop for any today."

"But—"

"I'll make it up to you another day. Promise."

With her fist still on her hip, Ellie stuck out her lower lip and tilted her head in challenge. "How?"

"The family is coming to town for the Season." He didn't need to say which family. "And that means—"

"The fancy cook's cranberry tarts!" Ellie's mouth rounded into a big O. "Will you bring me some?"

"Of course I will."

"They're even better than penny candy," Ellie said, hopping up and down.

Jacob laughed, from both her excitement and his own relief that she wouldn't be leaving his side in tears. "I'll bring as many as I can fit in my pockets."

"How many is that?" Ellie's eyes were bright as she held her arms out like a fisherman bragging about the length of a prized catch. "This many?"

"Hmm," Jacob said, pretending to study the breadth of her reach and ponder her question. "Maybe not *quite* so many as that. A pile of tarts bigger than your head would be awfully hard to eat all at once. They wouldn't fit inside ya!" He tickled her ribs.

She giggled wildly, and when she caught her breath, she held her hands over her middle, forming a circle. "Then it must be as many as can fit here," she said in a matter-of-fact tone.

"As you wish," Jacob said with a slight bow.

"A smaller pile would be easier to hide from the others anyway," Ellie added as she turned to the door.

A familiar ache tugged at Jacob's heart. Every visit to Ellie revealed a part of orphanage life he hadn't known about before, and he couldn't bear the thought of his own flesh and blood living such a life—of his sister's child accepting such a life as normal. Of Ellie having no chance for school or a future beyond that of a factory worker or, if she happened to be lucky, a servant in a middle-class household.

He tried to cover a sigh as they went through the yellow door. Ellie rushed inside ahead of him to the base of the stairs, where her pace slowed; her legs were barely long enough to reach from one step to the next. She kept her balance with one hand on the wall, her tongue sticking out with concentration as she climbed.

Jacob followed her up. He didn't urge her to hurry or swoop her into his arms again to carry her to the second floor. He took the steps slowly as he mulled over what the next weeks would hold now that the Millingtons were back in town, and therefore how much less often he'd be able to slip away undetected to visit Ellie.

As it was, he'd have to run back to the town house. He checked the clock on the wall ahead and shook his head worriedly. Their brief visit to the public park had taken longer than intended. No matter how fast he ran, he might not return in time.

When Mrs. Millington arrived, all of the servants were expected to be awaiting her, lining the steps to the door and dressed in clean, pressed uniforms. As the sole full-time male servant of the town house, his absence would most certainly be noticed. If he arrived in time, an unshaven face would be almost as bad as not appearing at all. Either way, displeasing the missus could mean harsh consequences.

Travel always wore out Mrs. Millington, and after her arrival from the country house, she often flew into a fatigue-induced rage, during which she might insult everyone in sight, make odd demands, or threaten to dismiss someone. Three years ago, she'd done more than threaten; Bertha, the scullery maid, had been dismissed quite suddenly upon the missus's arrival—as far as anyone could tell, due entirely to a stained apron. If they were lucky, the lady of the house would skip the irritable rage and instead collapse on her bed for a nap to sleep off one of her headaches.

He could hope as much, but he couldn't assume that his position would be safe if he wasn't at his station, properly dressed, in time for the carriage to pull up. Not so long ago, Jacob might have been foolhardy enough to flirt with danger by being a few minutes late. But that had been before his modest monthly pay supported more than himself. He'd seen Mrs. Millington dismiss servants before; she never did so with the promise of a letter of recommendation. Such a deliberate act of omission all but guaranteed that the former servants would never find a position equal to the one they'd been cut off from—if they found any position at all.

He simply could not take such chances, not with Ellie relying on him.

He took her chubby, little hand in his—a feeling he was most grateful for, as it testified to the fact that she had enough to eat. It was a sign that he'd done right by allowing her to be sent to the orphanage—not that he'd had much choice in the matter. If he'd tried to care for her on his own, he would have needed to find work elsewhere, and they'd have likely ended up destitute and living on the streets.

He followed Ellie into a large room where Miss Gibbon supervised the orphans as they worked in silence on some craft or another. When they walked through the door, Ellie held his hand even tighter and turned to him, her face uplifted in pleading.

"Don't go, not yet," she said, her forehead drawn, creating little wrinkles that made Jacob's heart melt. "I hate practicing my stitches. I'm so poor at them, and Miss Gibbon insists we girls practice on samplers, over and over again until we get our stitches perfectly even." She looked over the room with a forlorn expression before turning back to Jacob. "It's *awful.*" The last was added in a tone hinting that embroidering samplers came close to the misery of the lion's den.

Once more, Jacob prevented a smile from showing his amusement. He dropped to one knee. "I really must go now."

Ellie clung to one of his hands with both of hers and hopped twice. "But—"

"I must," Jacob repeated, stopping her. He took both of her hands between his, shaking his head sadly. He surreptitiously glanced at the wall clock behind Miss Gibbon's desk, and on the instant was unnerved to see how quickly the minute hand made its way around the circle. He focused on Ellie once more. "I'll come again as soon as I can. I promise."

"But when will that be?"

"I don't rightly know," he said, hedging. "As soon as I'm able."

The little girl sighed. "Will you be away a long time?"

How much time did a four-year-old consider to be "long"? At that age, a fortnight could feel like an eternity.

Jacob looked her straight in the eyes, which were glassy with tears she was clearly trying to be brave by not shedding. Her lower lip trembled, but she was trying to hide that as well. He reached out and smoothed her strawberry-blond waves, fighting to be as brave as she. "I won't be gone long. I can't say for sure how many days will pass. It may be quite soon, even."

He had yet to puzzle out a way to explain to the Millingtons—or the staff—about the situation and his responsibility to Ellie. How could he possibly find a way to explain to a young girl that she was a bastard child, and that therefore his connection to her wouldn't be looked upon kindly if word reached his employers?

"The family is coming today—any moment, perhaps—and I must be there when they arrive." He licked his lips, forcing himself to go on. "And while they are here, I won't have as much time to come visit."

Ellie opened her mouth to protest, but Jacob shook his head and cut her off. "No, I don't know what their plans or schedules will be like. But I promise"—he tapped her button nose—"that I'll come ever so often as I possibly can."

"Very well." She sighed with her whole body, making her hair bob and her dress sway as her arms plopped to her sides. The gesture reminded him of the quilt his mother made him when he was but a wee boy, and how, if he grew afraid at night, he rubbed the layers of fabric between his fingers. It wasn't as effective as being rocked by his Ma, but his quilt offered a comfort that was the next best thing. Now he hoped that the texture of his linen shirt might offer little Ellie some measure of comfort as well.

"Do you think," Ellie said slowly, still fingering his sleeve, "cook will make her cranberry tarts soon?"

"I'm sure she'll make something delicious every day. How about this: I'll bring you some treats every time I visit."

"Truly?" she said the word soberly, as if determining the veracity of his promise.

"You have my word as a gentleman," Jacob said with a nod of his head, as if he were a nobleman and she a high-ranking lady.

Ellie grinned broadly, then threw her arms around his neck and squeezed so hard he could scarcely breathe. He didn't mind the lack of air at all, however; he'd have been happy to die in the embrace of sweet little Ellie, who was as dear to him as anything and anyone.

A surprise, that, he thought as he embraced her in return. He never imagined that a child could own his heart so entirely, that he would sacrifice so much for her based entirely on the simple fact that they shared the same blood.

I must keep her a secret, he thought, not for the first—nor the hundredth—time. *If the family learns of her, what will happen to me? To Ellie? How will I pay for her care?*

The little girl released his neck, placed a peck on his cheek, and went to Miss Gibbon, who'd called her over.

If word reaches Ivy House, Jacob thought as he watched the supervisor hand Ellie an embroidery swatch, *will I lose Sarah?* He couldn't bear to imagine the confusion, and possibly disdain, on her face. Worry over Sarah's opinion of him, and whether she'd still cared for him, dogged him almost as much as his concerns for Ellie.

Five years ago, when he'd entered the gangly years that straddled boyhood and manhood, he and Sarah had shared a sibling-like affection. They were both too young then to think of matters like boys and girls making eyes at one another. Then, two summers ago, he noticed her as someone more than a peer who wore dresses. And ever since last summer, his feelings for Sarah had blossomed into full-fledged love.

Since her return to the country, she had corresponded

regularly with long letters, ones he read and reread often. His letters in return were much shorter, as he didn't have as much practice learning to write. She had far more experience in both reading and writing, thanks to Mrs. Roach teaching her over the years. He worried that his letters, painstakingly written one misspelled word at a time, were awkward and stilted and that his script was illegible.

Many times, he'd wanted to write about how he felt about her, but he never found the words or the courage.

The same applied to telling her about Ellie. He hadn't dared breathe—or write—a word on either subject. He suspected—hoped—that Sarah returned his feelings, but would she still view him the same way if she knew about Ellie?

And if the Millingtons discovered the information, and learned that Sarah knew but hadn't told them of it, he wouldn't be the only one losing a position. He couldn't risk telling Sarah—for her sake as much as anyone's.

As the date of her arrival had approached, he'd done everything in his power to convince himself that protecting Sarah was the one and only reason he didn't mention his niece. Until his sister Oona's tragic pregnancy, and more recently, her death, he would have thought poorly of someone in the very situation he now found himself in.

I cannot bear the idea of Sarah looking at me differently.

From the door, he watched Ellie walk slowly and deliberately to a chair across the room. She sat and scowled at her sampler before taking the needle and beginning to stitch, her lips screwed up to one side as she concentrated.

In the distance, he heard cathedral bells ringing, and he was jolted out of his reverie back to the urgency of the moment. He raised an arm and caught Ellie's eye, waving his goodbye before hurrying out of the room, down the stairs, and outside. Once on the sidewalk, he gripped his hat in one hand so it wouldn't fly off and then ran as fast as he could, dodging buggies and horses—nearly getting trampled a few times—as he prayed he'd get back to Ivy House before Mrs. Millington and her entourage did.

Chapter Three

Sarah never failed to be surprised by her own reaction to the journey. Without fail, Mrs. Millington insisted on a punishing pace, one that jostled Sarah and made even her young bones and joints ache. A trip that would take most people two easy days was therefore accomplished in one. Sarah often wondered where the eagerness to arrive stemmed from, seeing as Ivy House was so much smaller than Rosemount. She guessed the eagerness might be the anticipation of balls and other social events that, by virtue of living in the country, one didn't have access to during the cooler months. Every year, Sarah silently pleaded with the heavens that Mrs. Millington would take more stops, perhaps spend a night at an inn instead of merely switching horses at one. At the very least, she wished they'd slow down so the servants weren't bruised and aching by the time they arrived.

Yet in spite of the miserable journey, the moment they entered the city proper, any wish for a slower trip vanished for Sarah, along with complaints of aches and fatigue. A thrill replaced all of that. Curtain pulled aside once more, she took in every sight and sound. Even with the window closed, the smells of the city surrounded her—so different from the countryside. Others turned their noses up at the smells, saying they were from factory smoke and such, but she spent plenty of time around grass and trees and flowers during the rest of the year. These smells meant she'd arrived in the city.

Though her time here would largely be spent cleaning and scrubbing, it would also include strolls in the city and visits to pubs, where she would be able to catch up with summer friends, sing songs, and have bread pudding that was considered too simplistic for Betsy to make for the Millingtons, but which Sarah found divine. It was probably too common to be served to the family, but the sweetness of each bite made Sarah's heart happy. It was the taste of London—a city bustling with more people than she could count, living their lives and doing things she could only dream of.

Such a change from the country, where they lived in relative isolation. When she did see others, they mostly consisted of other rich families, and if she was fortunate, their servants.

But here, one could find people of all classes and backgrounds. Sometimes she meandered the narrow cobbled streets, imagining what it would be like to go into the shops and buy pretty hats, dresses, shoes, and jewelry. She hadn't much money, so if she spent any, it was generally at a bakery, buying an inexpensive sweet bun or pastry. Other times, she walked across one of the bridges spanning the Thames, stopping at the midpoint to lean over and watch the water rushing by or leaning back against the railing to watch people as she ate her treat. She loved watching mothers pushing prams. Newspaper boys. Workers going to or coming from the factories. A small girl selling flowers. Street musicians. Children heading to school. And so much more.

The driver turned a corner, and there, at the end of a long row of town houses, stood one with stately stairs, a bright blue door, and a polished bronze knocker. Lining the steps on either side were servants awaiting their arrival. A zip of nervousness shot through Sarah's stomach. Her hand went to her middle as her heart seemed to leap into her throat. She let the curtain fall, closed her eyes, and tried to breathe.

In another moment, I'll see Jacob.

That should have been a happy thought. And it was, but mingled with that happiness were also a number of other emotions, tying her middle in knots. Would Jacob still care for her only in the way they'd confessed last summer? Through their correspondence, her admiration had moved far beyond what she'd felt in August. She loved Jacob now.

But what if he no longer cared for her in the small way he had before, and instead had moved on to admiring other, prettier girls? She'd enjoyed his letters and writing her own in return, but his missives tended to be shorter than hers, and, of course, they lacked the kinds of things that typically said what he thought and felt—the tone of his voice, the quirk in his smile, the sparkle in his eye when he teased her. His scrawl never could have conveyed any of those things, no matter how eloquent a writer he was. And he was certainly not an eloquent writer. All the more reason for her eagerness to see him—talk to him again. Finally, they would be able to converse in person about more than books and newspapers. Perhaps pick up where they'd left off.

Over the last several months, they'd avoided the topic of their feelings for each other, save for a brief mention in his last letter: *It will be so good to see you again.*

That was all he'd written about her impending arrival.

Sarah would have given her eyeteeth to see and hear him speak those words so she'd know what they meant.

Please be more than brotherly kindness.

He'd long since lost any aura of being a brother for her.

The driver called to the horses. The clip-clop of their hooves slowed, and the carriage gradually rolled to a stop. Sarah took a deep breath to brace herself. The driver opened their carriage door, completely blocking her view. All she could see was Mrs. Millington, already alighted from her carriage, the governess following behind, struggling to comfort and cajole the children into behaving for their mother just a moment longer.

"Be very good," she told them in a high-pitched voice, "and when we're upstairs in the nursery, I'll show you a special toy that's waiting for you there."

"What kind of toy?" young Caroline asked doubtfully. Her little brother sucked on his thumb, then pulled it out when Miss Leavey gave him a chastising look.

"It's a surprise. You must behave to find out." The governess glanced at Mrs. Millington, who didn't seem to notice her children's words or behavior. Miss Leavey visibly relaxed.

When Mrs. Millington reached the base of the stairs, Sarah could no longer avoid noting the servants of Ivy House lining the sides. They were all wearing clean, freshly pressed clothes as they stood at attention, ready to welcome their mistress and accommodate any request. On one side stood Mrs. Jones, the housekeeper. On the other were Mary, the cook, and a stair above her, Mr. Lunceford, who served as Mr. Millington's valet.

No Jacob. As the only full-time male servant at Ivy House, his absence would be glaring. Why would he miss one of the most important moments of the year?

The Last Summer at Ivy House

Mrs. Roach had already exited the carriage, and now Betsy blocked the view, straining to move her ample self from the bench through the door. Sarah couldn't bear to have the sight of the servants withheld from her any longer. Every second Betsy took, Sarah held in a cry of impatience.

Had she seen correctly? Was Jacob not on the stairs at all? Had he raced out to his spot during the few seconds she couldn't see the steps? If not, where was he? He couldn't have been dismissed unless it had happened in the last week, since he posted his last letter.

At long last, Betsy pushed through the door and reached the ground. Sarah could see again. She removed herself from the bench, took the driver's offered hand, and alighted as quickly as possible. Her lower back and knees ached from standing so suddenly, but she paid them no heed, instead craning her neck around those ahead of her and counted the servants on the steps.

Mrs. Jones, one. Mary, two. Mr. Lunceford, three. Where was Jacob? Could he be out on an errand for Mr. Millington? That seemed unlikely; the tradition of all servants being present to welcome the missus wouldn't be abandoned based on the need to fetch the bootblacking or some such.

A thread of worry wove through her chest. Jacob could be ill. He could have gotten into an accident of some kind. He could have fallen into the Thames and drowned.

A movement at the next cross street, just past the town house, caught Sarah's eye. A figure darted across the street, hunched over as if trying to hide. Someone male—aside from a swiftness that wasn't possible in skirts, the figure clearly wore trousers. The moment was over before she'd comprehended that, but now she studied the person crouched behind a shrub. She could just make out the top of his head, which appeared to have dark hair, though with the shadows of the waning day, she couldn't be sure. She felt fairly confident that he wore a pale shirt and dark trousers.

"Sarah, are you well?" Betsy's voice broke into her thoughts. "You look peaked. Do you need to lie down for a spell? I'm sure I can warm up some broth for you."

"Thank you," Sarah said with a smile. "But I'm quite well, or as well as anyone can be after a long day's drive."

Mrs. Roach noticed the interchange and turned back, one eyebrow arched. "Are you feverish? Does your head ache?" Her tone might have sounded terse to an outsider, but Sarah knew her well enough to recognize genuine concern.

"Neither, but thank you, Mrs. Roach. I'm just a little tired, is all."

With both Mrs. Roach and Betsy satisfied, they headed for the town house, and Sarah followed. The drivers unloaded the trunks, and soon they would be taking the carriages to the stable house, where the horses would be unhitched.

Out of the corner of her eye, Sarah couldn't help but pay close to attention the mysterious person behind the shrub. He lifted his head just enough to see over the top—and Sarah stifled a gasp.

Jacob! What was he doing hiding behind a hedge of boxwood?

He caught her eye, and his own widened a bit. He lifted a finger to his lips, then ducked into his hiding place once more.

"Are you *sure* you're quite well?" Mrs. Roach said again. "You're even paler than a moment ago."

Everyone turned to stare at her now, including Mrs. Millington—something Sarah was suddenly grateful for, as it meant no one would see the hedge or the person hiding behind it. She'd never before sought attention from the family—rather, the opposite. Most of the time, if someone had cause to think of her at all, it was because she'd failed to adequately sweep the cinders from yesterday's fires or forgotten a chore altogether.

But now, Sarah hoped everyone would notice her and her alone so Jacob could safely escape detection. She prayed that Mrs. Millington wouldn't notice his absence on the stairs at all, and instead simply march up them, climb the stairs to her quarters, and collapse on her bed with a list of complaints. Sarah would be happy to endure a solid day of such demands if it meant no complaints were leveled at him.

When Sarah didn't answer immediately, her mind caught up in a confusing mix of thoughts and emotions, like two storms colliding over a field, Mrs. Millington lifted her chin and walked toward Sarah. The act was both a relief and terrifying. Sarah clasped her hands together to keep their trembling unnoticed.

"You look peaked," Mrs. Millington said as if she were the first to voice the opinion. With a highly unprecedented act, she reached out and pressed the back of her hand to Sarah's forehead. "No fever. Take a short nap and some cod liver oil, and then report to Mrs. Roach."

Sarah dipped her head and bobbed at the knee. "Yes, ma'am."

A blur to the side moved from the shrub, crossed the street, and disappeared from view to the rear of Ivy House. Sarah breathed out with relief. Jacob could easily get inside through the servants' entrance and quickly get himself presentable. Almost on the instant he'd vanished from view, Mrs. Millington turned to the stairs again.

Jacob must have a good reason to be late, she thought. He wasn't the kind to foolishly lose track of time. She not only knew Jacob; she loved him.

Mrs. Millington tested her own forehead with the back of her hand. "Perhaps I've caught a touch of something from the exposure to the air today." She closed her eyes and shook her head slowly. "I must lie down. Mrs. Roach, please bring my supper to me in my room. I haven't the strength to go down to the dining room."

"Of course, Mrs. Millington."

With that, the missus climbed the steps, only half acknowledging the staff as she went—nodding ever so slightly to her left at Mrs. Jones, then her right at Mary and Mr. Lunceford—until she reached the door, which was held by one of the drivers. She walked right inside without another word. Whatever ailment she had, it had distracted her enough to forget that an even number of servants—and *two* male ones—should have been on the steps.

Mrs. Millington beckoned for her lady's maid to follow her inside and up the flight of stairs to her quarters. Sarah held her breath until the women were out of sight and the driver allowed the door to close. She released the breath she was holding, turned about, and sat on a step. The other servants were descending the staircase as well, no doubt to enter around back to the basement.

Mrs. Roach paused beside Sarah. "Do come in and lie down."

"Yes, Mrs. Roach. I'll be right in." Sarah sat straighter and smoothed back some wisps of hair that had escaped her bun. After another steadying breath, she stood and ran her hands over her travel-rumpled skirts in an attempt to get rid of the worst wrinkles. Her nerves were alive and well again, jumping about her middle like jackrabbits.

And if she'd seen correctly, Jacob was in the basement. In a few moments, she'd see him again. Speak to him again.

She followed slowly, but the servants' entrance arrived all too soon anyway. She hesitated before going down the steps. Summer had officially arrived. What her future held at the end of the Season remained a mystery. Opening that door would be a step into whatever her future might hold.

After one more effort at smoothing back her hair, Sarah went down the stairs, crossed to the door, and went inside.

Chapter Four

Jacob practically tore off his common-day clothing and dressed in the black suit that was the proper attire of one serving an influential family. His heart raced at how close he'd come to being found out and how lucky he was to have escaped Mrs. Millington's notice. He'd almost arrived in time, but instead had gotten far too close to being discovered.

I will never again put Ellie at such risk, he vowed as he faced the warped looking glass above his chest of drawers, trying to make his nervous fingers create a proper bow tie.

Ellie had been his charge for only a matter of months, and in that time, he'd racked his brain for some way to get her out of the orphanage—better yet, to get her living with him. She should be with family. Cloverfield wasn't horrible compared to some nightmarish places he'd heard of, but it still had its shabby parts and too many children for the number of adults. While Ellie didn't go hungry, he wondered whether the food she was given had any value for helping her grow and be healthy.

He hadn't found a viable way to take her into his own

care, and the longer she remained at Cloverfield, the greater the chance of someone adopting her. What if someone came and took her to Scotland, one of the African colonies, or even India? Her surname would be changed—possibly her Christian name too.

More likely than not, he'd never see her again.

I cannot allow that to happen, he thought, reaching for his suit coat and sliding his arms inside. He prayed that the servants from Rosemount wouldn't say anything to the Millingtons about the neglect of his post today. He didn't think they would, as none of them would benefit if Jacob were dismissed.

Sarah would never tell, he thought as he reached for the knob on his bedroom door. *It's thanks to her distracting everyone that no one saw me.*

With his hand outstretched toward the doorknob, he thought of how Sarah and the others awaited him on the other side. How later, if they managed to find some privacy, he'd thank her for what she did out front a moment ago. Thoughts of Sarah send a renewed spike in his heart rate. He always looked forward to summertime, but this year was different.

Last summer, they'd moved beyond a childhood friendship, and their regard had grown until he found himself unable to picture his future without Sarah in it. The intervening months of letters had been both glorious and tortuous for him. He'd eagerly watched for the post, waiting for her next letter, and when each arrived, he always read it in private for the first time. He carried her letters about with him and reread portions, memorizing the whole until the next one came, and the cycle repeated.

But what if she no longer cared for him that way? He'd be able to tell simply by looking into her eyes. Sarah had many talents, but telling lies—even silent ones—was not one of them. While he stayed in this room, his fantasy and hopes could remain aloft.

I can't move, he thought, staring at his hand on the doorknob.

"Where's Jacob?" someone called. The authoritative voice easily carried through the thick wood door—Mrs. Roach.

Friend today or foe?

"Likely in his quarters," Mary said between chopping sounds; dinner preparations were already underway. "What d'ya need him for?"

"The trunks need to be carried inside," Mrs. Roach said. "I'll go find him." A set of firm, heavy footsteps grew louder; she was coming to check his room.

No point in procrastinating further. Jacob opened the door to see the housekeeper before him with her hand raised, ready to knock. "Why, Mrs. Roach, you've arrived," he said in as cheery a tone as he could muster.

"Yes, we have," she said. "Where, pray tell, were you?"

Jacob tugged the hem of his suit coat. "In my room, is all. Wanted to be sure I looked particularly clean and pressed when Mrs. Millington arrived, so I kept my regular clothes on until the very last minute." He cocked his head as if listening to the floor above, then put on an expression of worry. He genuinely *was* concerned about many things, so he didn't have to pretend on that count. "It appears I'm too late to greet Mrs. Millington."

"You are at that," Mrs. Roach said. "Fortunately for you, Mrs. Millington isn't well at the moment, so she seems to have forgotten that you weren't present at her arrival."

"Truly?" He'd hoped as much but suddenly needed the confirmation from someone else.

"Truly." Mrs. Roach took stock of his appearance,

looking him up and down two or three times. "You were getting dressed, you say?" She couldn't know where he'd been or what he'd been doing, but she did know that his excuse was as thin as vellum.

He swallowed in spite of the dryness in his mouth. "Indeed I was." His voice cracked on the last word, though he wasn't telling a falsehood precisely; he *had* been dressing just now.

"Mm-hmm." She clearly didn't believe him, but she didn't demand a better explanation, at least not for the moment.

He decided to change the subject before she could interrogate him. He seized on what he'd heard from his room. "Are there any trunks needing to be brought in?" he asked, heading for the outside door. He was vaguely aware of Mrs. Roach thanking him, but he didn't hear her clearly because the whole world around him narrowed into a small tunnel where outside sights and noises were fuzzy and indistinct.

For there, in the doorway with the fading afternoon light behind her, stood none other than Sarah.

My sweet Sarah.

Was she his, though?

As he neared, his step slowed to a stop. Her cheeks had flushed pink, and her pink lips were curved into a perfect bow, though she hadn't yet raised her gaze to meet his. "Sarah." He wanted to say more, but her name was all that came out. Yet if she cared for him as much as he cared for her, she might hear his love and devotion even in her name.

She blinked once, twice, and then her eyes shifted from the floor and tracked upward to his face. "Jacob." Her smile widened, and her entire face lit up from the inside.

She cares. I'm certain of it.

From behind, Mrs. Roach cleared her throat in an

obvious attempt to get their attention. Jacob glanced over his shoulder at her. "I need to carry in some trunks," he told Sarah.

"I'm happy to help," she said, but quickly leaned to the side to see Mrs. Roach and added, "if that's acceptable to you, of course. If you have other work for me to do, I'll stay inside."

Mrs. Roach's iron line of a mouth softened. "Go," she said. "But don't take long. The basement needs a good scrubbing if we're to survive the summer in it."

"Yes, Mrs. Roach." Sarah turned about and went back out the door.

Jacob followed behind. She had crossed the small courtyard and was heading up the stairs when he caught up and grasped her hand from below. She visibly started and looked back, but then squeezed his hand in response and continued to the sidewalk, the two of them climbing the stairs hand in hand. When Sarah reached the street level, Jacob released her hand. Best if none of the family or servants witnessed affection between them.

Sarah seemed to intuitively know why he'd let go, because she clasped her hands together casually and began talking in an airy tone as they walked to the front of the town house.

"How much rain did you have in the city over the spring?" A flash in her eyes as they locked his said that she was playing a part for the benefit of listening ears.

"We had quite a wet spring, even by English standards."

They continued talking in that vein until they reached the front of the house—a public street where they couldn't be accused of being truly alone. What luck to be with Sarah—just Sarah—for even a few moments so soon. He had so much to tell her, to talk about, to discuss. And when they weren't talking, he wanted to hold her hand, gaze at the stars in silence, and maybe, if he dared, press a kiss to her lips and declare his feelings.

With these thoughts and more rattling about in his head, they reached the trunks. Sarah sat atop one, and he strode up the front steps of the town house and opened the front door so they could carry the trunks through.

As he turned to Sarah, her brows were knit together quizzically. "Where were you coming from before?" She nodded in the direction of the shrub he'd hidden behind.

"I . . ." Jacob worried his lower lip, pressed both lips together into a half-smile, half-scowl, and folded his arms, all the while staring at the shrub in the distance.

"Come now, Jacob," she said with a laugh. She swatted his shoulder playfully. "It's me. I've known you since before you dared that boy to steal Mrs. Millington's key to the tea box."

"You've known me as long as anyone else here," he agreed.

She'd never known Thomas, not really, but she'd heard others talk about the servant boy who'd worked next door until shortly after Sarah arrived as a maid. Thomas and Jacob used to get into quite a bit of mischief.

One summer, they undertook a game wherein one challenged the other to do something they both knew they oughtn't. If the dare was completed, the victor got to choose a new challenge for the other. The dares became more and more outrageous, until Jacob dared Thomas to steal the key to the Millington tea box. The latter rightfully objected; in that box were stored the most expensive tea leaves from India. Once leaves were removed, they were used over and over by the family, until they were too weak to be satisfactory. Then they were then sent downstairs for the servants to use for their tea until they lost all flavor.

Even now, Jacob often wondered just how expensive tea leaves were. The rigor with which the leaves were steeped for every last bit of flavor, along with the intensity with which the key was protected, indicated that tea might be worth its weight in gold.

Thomas had been caught red-handed. He wasn't allowed to plead his case, but from what Jacob knew, he never attempted to implicate his fellow accomplice. The Foster family next door dismissed Thomas the next week, and he was never seen near Ivy House again. Jacob had wondered more than once what happened to Thomas after that and what his own fate would have been if he'd failed at one of Thomas's silly dares instead of the other way around.

Now, standing before Sarah, he almost wished she'd challenged him to a dare rather than what she'd actually asked of him. He loved Sarah, so he couldn't tell her about Ellie.

I can't hurt someone else I care for—someone I love, Jacob thought.

Loving Sarah meant protecting her from harm. Protecting her meant ensuring that her reputation would never be tarnished as his might yet be. Jacob had seen grown women lose their stations and reputations, and with them, any chance for future employment or marriage. He'd seen young women who had no family to turn to, who, to survive, resorted to . . .

No. He would *not* think on that. It was too horrible to contemplate.

"Come, Jacob. Tell me all about your adventures in the big city." Sarah crossed her ankles like a lady in a rather dramatic fashion, looking at him impishly all the while, her head cocked to one side. The effect completely undid any illusion of etiquette.

"Adventures in the city?" Jacob said airily, heading down

the steps toward her. "What silly novels have you been reading to put such stuff and nonsense into your head?"

"You know full well that I'm not talking about books." She leaned toward him, speaking conspiratorially. "You can trust me, of all people. *I* won't be shocked and horrified, no matter what *scandalous* things you've been up to." She waggled her eyebrows and placed one open hand on her chest as if showing the type of shock others might feel. Her teasing tone said so much—that she was happy, but also that she didn't believe for one moment that Jacob could have done anything untoward, let alone nefarious.

Yet the fact remained that he was tied by blood to an illegitimate child, one he'd do everything in his power to care for.

"Very well," Sarah said, hopping off the trunk and smoothing her skirts. "If you weren't returning from an adventure, what run-of-the-mill, tedious errand were you on when you happened to find a shrub standing in your way?"

The more she pressed, the more he didn't want to speak of Cloverfield or Ellie. But he also knew Sarah; a dog would sooner let loose a fresh bone than Sarah would let loose a topic she was bent on hearing about.

He forced nonchalance into his voice. "I will simply have to keep your curiosity piqued," he said, waggling his eyebrows in return. "I understand that keeping ladies guessing is something modern men do." On his way to the far side of the trunk, he added over his shoulder, "Perhaps I'll tell you all about it . . . at the end of summer." With his back to her, he scrubbed one hand down his face. His chin was stubbly; if Mrs. Millington had seen him unshaven, she *would* have noticed and promptly gone into an apoplectic fit.

"Promise?" Sarah asked. "Promise to tell me before summer's end?"

He turned and fully took in the sight of her. The early evening sun glowed from behind, breaking through her hair like a halo. How could he lie to an angel?

"We'll see," he said. Much of the bravado had left his voice, but he tried to summon a portion of it. "Let's get these trunks inside before I find some horrible challenge for you to do." He instantly regretted returning to the topic she'd referred to.

"I'm intrigued." Judging by her tone, Sarah hadn't noticed that the sails of his confidence had gone flat. She leaned down and gripped the leather handle of the trunk. "What kind of *horrible* things would you challenge me to?"

Marry me. Go to America with me, where we can start a new life together. If the two of them had been to this point in their relationship when she'd arrived a year ago, he might have been tempted to playfully state those challenges last summer. But then Oona had died. And he'd been charged with caring for Ellie.

So he wouldn't be challenging Sarah to marry and leave the country. Besides, she had enough of a stubborn streak that she might very well have agreed right away, perhaps pretending she didn't really care. Her beautiful eyes betrayed her—a fact for which he would be forever grateful to the heavens and whatever angels watched over him. She cared, yes. But did she *love* him?

No matter. He couldn't throw down the gauntlet. Not now. Not until he could support Ellie and, he hoped, not lose Sarah in the process.

He reached down for the handle on his side of the trunk. "Ready?"

"No." Sarah released her side and put her hands on her hips. "I'm still waiting to hear about what kinds of challenges you have in mind."

Despite himself, he smiled, and when he looked at her, it widened. A warmth washed over him. Oh, how he loved her.

"I'll think on it," he said, his voice half teasing, half as serious as life and death. "Someone as special as yourself requires a unique kind of challenge."

"I *think* I'm flattered." The statement held a note of question in it. She chuckled, gripped the handle, and together they hefted the trunk up the stairs and into the foyer.

With every step, Jacob felt his very soul at war with itself as his loyalties and his heart were being torn in two by Sarah and Ellie. They both owned his heart, though in different ways.

His future was at the mercy of a young woman and a young girl. What would he do when his loyalties conflicted?

He and Sarah set the trunk down on one side of the hall, then went back outside. They made two more trips with the other trunks. The conversation had quieted, and Jacob didn't try to breathe life back into it. He couldn't, not when he remained mired in worries. With the last trunk inside, Sarah sent him a smile and a wave before heading to the far end of the hall and down the servants' staircase to the basement.

He watched her retreat, wondering how he could possibly navigate the summer months without losing either Ellie or Sarah.

Or, worse, losing both.

Chapter Five

The day after their arrival at Ivy House, Sarah churned butter in the corner of the kitchen when Mrs. Roach entered, a notepad and pencil in hand.

"Anything missing from the pantry?" she asked Betsy.

"Of course," Betsy said, chopping onions at the table. "Every year I send a list ahead, but Mary always forgets something or other." The words were true, though they came out a bit harsh.

Sarah and Mrs. Roach exchanged amused glances. Betsy complained about Mary every year.

With the back of her forearm, Betsy dabbed her forehead, then continued chopping. "We haven't nearly enough meat." She shook her head disdainfully. "And it's as if no one has bothered to replenish the spices in months."

Mrs. Roach raised the notepad. "What is wanting?"

"Chives, to begin with," Betsy said. "Pepper, cinnamon, and cloves. Not to mention that we're abominably low on molasses, sugar, and lard. How could anyone expect me to make pastries and biscuits without the most basic of ingredients? I'm a cook, not a magician." She chopped some more as Mrs. Roach wrote it all down. Betsy raised the thick knife into the air and used the tip to punctuate her next words. "And marmalade. If I'd known the pantry here was clean out, I'd have brought some of my own preserves from Rosemount." She shook her head and returned to work.

"I've made a list," Mrs. Roach said, holding it out to Sarah. "If you think of anything else, Betsy, let me know, and I'll send her out again tomorrow."

Sarah released the plunger and reached for the shopping list in Mrs. Roach's outstretched fingers. Looking from one woman to the next and back again, she asked, "Shall I go now? Or should I finish the butter first?" Both women tended to act as if they were in charge. Betsy ruled the kitchen, and the butter churn was her domain, as was the need to restock the pantry. But Mrs. Roach ruled the household, and her word overruled Betsy's. Yet Sarah knew that one did well to show the utmost respect toward both women.

"*Now*," Betsy said. "I need pepper and beets right away if I'm to make a proper dinner. Add beets to the list." Once again, she gestured at Mrs. Roach with the knife blade for the latter instruction. "If Jacob's got a free minute or two, he can finish up the butter."

Footfalls sounded on the stone hall outside the kitchen, and not a moment later, Jacob poked his head into the kitchen. "Did I hear my name?"

Sarah's hands instinctively grasped the plunger again. The shopping list wrinkled in her palm. She didn't move the plunger, but her knuckles turned white as she did everything in her power to avoid catching his eyes. Their reunion the day before had been odd at best. One moment, he'd been his fun-loving, teasing, and—dared she think it?—flirtatious self.

Yesterday, he'd been everything she remembered from

summer one moment, then stiff and distant the next, as if they were only acquaintances. He'd grown quiet and pensive, which was so unlike him, as was his odd refusal to answer the simple question of where he'd been that made him late.

She'd expected a thigh-slapping story, not a sentence or two spoken in a quiet tone, with knitted brows, followed by several awkward moments of silence. It was as if the young man she once knew had been replaced by someone else altogether. Perhaps in her excitement, she'd spoken too loudly or had otherwise embarrassed him. She tried to remember every word they'd exchanged by the trunks, searching for any hint of word, tone, or expression—his or hers—to explain his changing behavior, but she couldn't puzzle it out. If she'd offended him she could make amends. But she couldn't fix what she didn't know was broken.

More than likely, he's changed his mind about me and doesn't know how to behave now. The thought made her eyes sting. She blinked a few times and looked at the wall to hide her face. She would *not* show such emotion around others, least of all Jacob.

"You heard right," Betsy said to him as she waved him into the room. "You're in your outdoor clothes anyway. You can come on in and finish churning the butter without worrying about mussing up your suit. I need Sarah to go on an errand right away."

"I could take care of the errand, if you like," he offered. Even in his worn shirt and trousers with threadbare knees, he was handsome enough to make Sarah want to stare at him all day. She preferred him in regular clothes to the servant's coat and tie.

"Mr. Millington is out on business. I'm not needed upstairs until supper," Jacob said. "Or . . ." From the corner of her eye, Sarah thought he looked in her direction, but she kept her focus on the wood grain of the butter churn. "I could go with Sarah . . . as a chaperone."

At that, Betsy let out a full-throated laugh, then wiped her eyes with the back of her hand. "Sarah needing a chaperone in the market. Quite the joke. You do beat all, Jacob."

The suggestion of Jacob going with her on the errand made a drum of her chest, with her heart pounding against it. Did he truly want to go to the market with her? If so, perhaps she hadn't offended him or breached some rule of etiquette she was unaware of.

On the other hand, he might be looking for an excuse to leave the house to go wherever he'd been yesterday. Did he assume she'd help him a second time? The thought that he might want to use her as a convenience made her stomach feel heavy and sour.

She wanted Jacob to genuinely wish to spend time with her, just the two of them, as they had many times over the years, moving about the bustling city on errands for the family. Today's errand would be a relatively brief one, but no matter; she'd looked forward to such times for months now. But now that she was here and he'd been acting so strangely, she didn't know what to think.

"Go on," Betsy said, nodding toward the butter churn. "You men can make butter faster than we of the weaker sex can." She tilted her head and raised her eyebrows in challenge and added, "Unless such work is below ya?"

Kitchen work most definitely was beneath most male servants. As valet, Mr. Lunceford wouldn't have stood for such an order, but Jacob was young, and without the status of a butler or valet. He wasn't wearing his black, pressed servant's suit, so if some buttermilk splashed on him, there would be nothing to worry about.

"I'd be happy to," he said, entering the kitchen fully and striding toward Sarah.

Betsy dumped a pile of chopped potatoes into a pot. "Sarah knows the shops I trust. I need her to go right away. Aside from needing the pepper and beets today, I must have cloves for tomorrow's breakfast."

"Indeed," Mrs. Roach said, drawing out the word. Sarah rose from the stool and gave Jacob a tiny smile as he took her spot before the butter churn. Mrs. Roach watched Jacob work the plunger a few times. "Come, Sarah." Mrs. Roach gestured with a quick motion of her hand. "You'll need some money."

Sarah followed the housekeeper down the hall to her room. Mrs. Roach went inside, but Sarah, as always, stayed in the doorway out of respect. This time, however, Mrs. Roach shook her head. "Come in, girl. Come in."

Unsure what this unexpected turn of events meant, Sarah stepped across the threshold, and when she'd cleared the doorway, Mrs. Roach shut the door.

Am I to be punished? For what, Sarah could not fathom—unless Mrs. Roach knew about how Jacob had hidden behind the shrubs and Sarah's part in keeping that fact from Mrs. Millington. The drum of her heart grew heavier, this time with worry.

"What do you think of Jacob?" Mrs. Roach asked, pacing away from Sarah down the length of the narrow room.

"I—I'm not sure what you mean," Sarah managed.

Mrs. Roach reached the end of the rug, turned about, and walked back toward Sarah, one eyebrow lifted. Sarah had been the target of that eyebrow many a time; it drilled into the very center of her soul. Sarah was quite sure that with Mrs. Roach and her eyebrow on his side, Napoleon would have won at Waterloo. Sarah stood there, hardly able to breathe under

Mrs. Roach's piercing gaze. Sarah swallowed against the knot in her throat.

After a few seconds of eying Sarah, the housekeeper walked—still oh, so slowly—to her writing table in the corner and sat down. She gestured to the stool on the other side of the table. "Please, sit."

Sarah pointed behind her as if Betsy and her knife were there. "What about the pepper and beets?"

"We'll take care of that soon enough," Mrs. Roach said. "For now, sit."

"Of course." Sarah meekly crossed to the stool and sat upon it, setting her clasped hands in her lap.

"You and Jacob have known each other for some time now." It was a statement, not a question, of course—Mrs. Roach had known Sarah and Jacob as long as they'd known each other—but it was a statement Sarah had to respond to.

"I've known him for several years, yes."

My actions from yesterday have gotten me in trouble, then.

Mrs. Roach took out her key chain and unlocked a drawer. "What do you think of him?"

How to answer such a query? What did Mrs. Roach mean by it? How much did she know about Jacob's tardiness? Sarah's clasped hands tightened. The drumbeat sped up so much that it felt like a hummingbird fluttered in her chest; Sarah worried she might faint.

Should I confess? Is that what Mrs. Roach wants to hear? She hadn't directly accused Sarah of anything, but this might be a test to see whether Sarah would admit to wrongdoing.

"Well," Sarah said tentatively, "I think he is a hard worker."

Once more, the arched eyebrow made its appearance. "Anything else?" Mrs. Roach asked.

Sarah was grateful to be sitting; her knees might not have withstood that black arch again. "And he's loyal to the family."

"Yes, I believe he is," Mrs. Roach said, studying Sarah. Then she cleared her throat, counted out some money from the desk drawer, and set the coins on top. "That should be enough for today," she said as she locked the drawer and pocketed the key. "Be sure to return any extra."

"Of course." Was that all? Had she passed the test? Unsure, Sarah stood and reached for the money, baffled about the private interview but grateful that it appeared to be over for the moment.

"You know, I believe Jacob sees you in very much the same way you see him," Mrs. Roach said suddenly.

"Pardon?" Sarah's fingers curled around the coins in her palm; they dug into her skin. Something in the housekeeper's tone made it clear that she meant far more than Jacob's opinion on whether Sarah was also a hard worker and loyal servant.

The eyebrow lowered, and Mrs. Roach's mouth softened into one of her rare smiles. "I have eyes, Sarah, and I haven't always been this old. Rest assured, I can keep a secret. But it occurred to me that this summer may be different from your others here. As I said on the way here, this summer could be a Season of sorts for you. That is, if you'd like it to be." The last was spoken as a question, seeming to probe whether Sarah had come to care for Jacob in the way Mrs. Roach clearly suspected.

How had she figured it out? Sarah had never breathed a word about her feelings for Jacob to anyone. Had Mrs. Roach read their letters? That didn't seem likely.

"What do you say to that?" Mrs. Roach said with a satisfied air.

"I think—" Sarah's throat closed up. "That is, I suspect—" Her mind went blank.

"I've seen the way he looks at you," Mrs. Roach said, a knowing glint in her eye. "He no longer sees you as a playmate or little sister. Oh, no."

Sarah hoped as much—how deeply she hoped, no one knew—but after the awkwardness with Jacob yesterday . . .

"He might have felt that way last summer," she finally said. "And perhaps the sentiment continued during our correspondence, but . . ." Sarah shook her head.

"But what?" Mrs. Roach asked in what Sarah guessed was intended to be a gentle tone, though the older woman had likely never had such a word ascribed to her.

"Ever since our arrival, he hasn't behaved as he used to." Sarah lowered her gaze to her fingernails, not wanting to see pity in the eyes of the woman who knew her almost as well as a mother would.

"Has his behavior been improper in some way?" She hmphed and glared at the door, looking ready to march out the door to take a switch to Jacob's hindquarters as if he were a lad of six again.

"No, nothing like that," Sarah hurried to say. "He's simply . . . *distant*, I suppose may be the best way to describe it. We used to be able to slip right back into our old camaraderie and easy conversation, but this time . . ." She shrugged helplessly.

Mrs. Roach didn't retake her seat, but neither did she march to the kitchen to tan Jacob's hide. Instead, she crossed her arms and stared at the far wall. "Hmm."

Sarah instinctively looked over her shoulder, though she knew all she'd see on the wall was cracked plaster.

After a moment of pondering, the housekeeper broke her stare and strode to the door. She opened it wide, then spoke rather loudly, as if she'd been midsentence when she'd opened the door. "So you see, I must insist that you don't go out alone. Not for another week or two at least, until I can be sure that the highwayman and his men have been apprehended."

Sarah followed her into the hallway, her brow wrinkled in confusion. "I don't—"

"No protesting. You must trust that I know best in this matter. I insist that, at least for today's errand, someone accompany you. Mrs. Millington would never forgive me if something happened to her favorite maid." Mrs. Roach called to the kitchen, leaving a dumbfounded Sarah standing in the hall. "Jacob, I'm afraid I need to pull you away from churning."

"Oh?" After the sound of the plunger settling came a few steps, and Jacob appeared in the hall. "What about the butter?" he asked, his thumb gesturing behind him.

"Mary can finish it. Will you please accompany Sarah to the market?"

Clearly, Mrs. Roach, a decades-long spinster, had decided to engage in matchmaking. For Sarah, just the knowledge that someone had guessed her feelings toward Jacob made her want to crawl into the hole of a dead tree and hide until everyone had forgotten her. She flushed with embarrassment. Judging by the heat in her face—so hot her cheeks felt close to bursting into flames—she had to be bright red. And there was Jacob standing only a few feet away, unwittingly being pulled into Mrs. Roach's snare.

Sarah lowered her eyes to the stone floor, but her nerves wouldn't let them stay there. She looked at the wall, Mrs. Roach, and then finally, unable to stop her traitorous eyes from doing their own bidding, Jacob. He returned her gaze with his familiar impish grin—one that historically preceded a wink when the two of them were alone. He wouldn't do such a thing with others like Betsy and Mrs. Roach present. Would she see that wink again this summer?

Perhaps seeing her again had made him realize he didn't care for her in the same way after all. If that was the case, he wouldn't wink at her again ever, no matter the circumstance.

"I'd be delighted to accompany her," he said.

"Good," Mrs. Roach said. "Hurry now. Betsy is liable to get antsy until she has everything she needs for the day's meals."

"Of course," Jacob said. Smiling at Sarah, he jerked his head toward the servants' entrance. "Shall we?"

"Of—course," she repeated, a mite breathless and confused as to what had just happened.

She'd been brought back to Mrs. Roach's room—which the housekeeper had then locked. Typically, that would mean Sarah had done something worthy of a reprimand. Instead, she'd been asked how she felt about Jacob and was told that he likely felt the same toward her.

Sarah hoped so, but the odds of Mrs. Roach being entirely correct in her estimation seemed as remote as the spinster herself winning a steeplechase.

Chapter Six

Face still hot but not quite as fiery as before, Sarah put one foot in front of the other and followed Jacob outside. Every one of her nerves seemed to be alert, ready to notice and study the slightest hint of what he was thinking and feeling. She noted every action, no matter how minute, the tone of every word, the muscles on his face. Oh, if only she could read his mind. Then she could stop guessing and simply *know*.

But do I truly want to know the truth if it isn't a happy one? she thought as she waited for Jacob to close the door. They climbed the steps from the basement entry to the street level, and when she reached the sidewalk, she waited for him again. As he reached the top, she held her breath, not knowing whether to speak first, and if so, what topic to pursue.

Instead of deciding, she busied herself, slipping the coins and shopping list into her apron pocket, purely to have something to do with her hands. That action was followed by smoothing the wrinkles from her apron and feeling her bun for any loose hairpins.

None of that took long, and soon Jacob stood beside her.

If nerves had sound, a veritable shrieking symphony would have been playing from Sarah's middle. Fortunately, he spared her the awkwardness of knowing what to do or say next by holding his arm out to her.

"Miss Jenkins," he said with a sly grin, the kind he used when he was being deliberately facetious. This was the Jacob she knew and had eagerly anticipated being with again.

Thank the heavens above, she thought, slipping her hand through the crook of his arm and resting it by his elbow.

How long this version would stay around, she didn't know, but she'd enjoy every moment for as long as it lasted. She hoped that the evasive, distant version of Jacob from before had been nothing but an anomaly—the result of spoiled liverwurst or a poor night's sleep.

They walked for a block or so and turned a corner, all in companionable silence. At least, she thought so and hoped he didn't think the quiet was strained between them. But perhaps he felt awkward and was waiting for her to speak first. They'd never wanted for conversation, and in past summers, the few times they'd lapsed into silence had been warm and comfortable—and perfectly natural. But she no longer knew whether she could trust her judgment on such things.

After they'd left the affluent part of town, Sarah decided on a topic, something they'd written about extensively over the intervening months: books. "Have you read the other Dickens I mentioned in my letters?"

She'd come to enjoy anything she could find written by Charles Dickens, and she'd mentioned a particular book in her last letter. Not for the first time, she was grateful that they could both read. Neither of them had much education, but knowing how to read and write allowed them to remain in contact over the nine months they were apart. Sarah deliberately worked on improving those skills in the hopes of one day becoming a schoolteacher.

Such a dream might not happen. It would certainly require much more in the way of education than reading and writing—arithmetic, science, and who knew what else. She'd need the funds for her school, as well as a means of support while attending classes. She doubted students could work full time and attend class. Nevertheless, she held the hope, not wanting her future to remain tied to the Millington family's basements.

"I'm still reading *David Copperfield*," Jacob said. "I haven't had time to look for the other."

"*Dombey and Son*," she supplied, in case he'd forgotten. "You may borrow my copy. Ironic title, though, as the story is mostly about Dombey's daughter. It's a beautiful, heartrending book. I think the longer Dickens writes, the sadder he becomes."

"How so?" Jacob asked, sounding sincerely curious.

Sarah gave a slight shrug. "His earlier works are happier and more lighthearted than his later ones. He started writing books like *Oliver Twist* and *A Christmas Carol*—"

Jacob interrupted with a chuckle. "Are you saying that tales of orphans, pickpockets, and ghosts are lighthearted?"

"It's not the topics that are light so much as how he writes about them." Sarah gave his arm a playful swat but fully enjoyed his teasing—a sign that they were returning to their old selves. "Consider the titles," she went on. "*The Adventures of Oliver Twist* and *The Old Curiosity Shop* sound miles more lighthearted than *Bleak House* and *Hard Times*. Not even you could argue otherwise."

Jacob laughed. "Fine. 'Dark-hearted' story or no, I look forward to reading *Dombey and Son*. While we're on the topic of letters, in my last, I mentioned something that, well, I'm not entirely sure came through properly with my poor writing skills."

"You write very well," Sarah said.

"An expected response from a future teacher." He looked over, his eyes dancing, and she blushed, relishing the moment of being with him and feeling so comfortable, even when it meant a swarm of butterflies had taken over her middle. She would willingly give a home to every butterfly in the world if it meant Jacob would always be near her, look at her as he did now.

How rare it was indeed to find a man who valued education—and an intelligent, educated women with aspirations. One more reason she adored the man. She hoped Mrs. Roach would insist on Jacob being her chaperone all summer long. Not one word of complaint would escape her lips.

They reached the park, and he led her to a bench. She didn't ask why they weren't continuing on to make the purchases Betsy would be waiting on. Rather, she happily took a seat, and he settled beside her. Though the arrangement was hardly scandalous, she caught her breath at his nearness. She could feel his warmth through his sleeve on her arm, as well as the weight of his leg pressing against hers. A more proper girl would have created distance between them, but Sarah had no such compunction. They were in full view of passersby, doing nothing untoward, and she intended to enjoy it.

Jacob turned to face her better. His cheeks had twin rosettes. The thought that she might have evoked such a response made her smile. He took her hand in his. "I've been trying to find a way to tell you about something very important." He looked at her hand resting atop both of his, but didn't go on.

"Yes?" she prompted. Was he about to declare his love

for her? She would happily do the same, if only she knew for certain that he felt it too.

"I care deeply for you," he began, head still bowed over her hand.

"And I you," she said softly. "Very much."

His eyes scrunched at the sides as they always did when he smiled. He took a deep breath, let it out, then raised his face to hers. "My life is somewhat complicated right now. I cannot go into details, but I want you to know that no matter how it may seem, I care for you as much as ever."

"Truly?" That was all she cared about at the moment. Whatever complications existed in his life could be overcome.

"You have my word."

Caring nothing for public stares, she threw her arms about his neck. Pulling back, she held his hands. "What happened yesterday... Was that because of the... complications?"

"Yes," he said simply. "I wish I could explain. I hope I can soon."

"When?" Sarah trusted him but disliked the idea of secrets.

"Honestly, I don't know. But you must trust that the reason I cannot speak of it is, in large part, to protect you."

"Protect me?" She withdrew her hands warily. Her mind turned and turned like the gears in a clock, trying to find an explanation. "Are you involved in something" —she lowered her voice to a whisper—"illegal?"

"No, of course not." His look of hurt pierced her to the center.

"I'm sorry," she said with a shake of her head. "Of course not."

"But it is something that, through an association with me, could tarnish your reputation." He gazed into her eyes, his own glassy with unshed emotion. "I could never forgive myself if you lost your position because of me." The more he said, the more questions she had. Nothing made any sense.

"You can trust me."

"Yes. Of course I can. But I don't trust other people. You matter too much for me to gamble with your position or your future." Jacob ran a hand through his hair, mussing it. "I'm sorry for yesterday, even though I can't talk about it yet."

She nodded her understanding of that part, though she hadn't any idea what troubled him.

He slapped his hands on his thighs and stood. "Now, let's get to the market and discuss this another time." He sounded chipper, but the tone was forced. Did he think he could fool her? Or was this his way of changing the topic? She stood too, and when he held out his elbow, she took it as before. Together, they walked to the corner and waited to cross. As they stepped into the street, they heard someone yelling.

"Jacob!" a deep voice called. "Jacob Croft!"

Beneath Sarah's hand, Jacob's arm stiffened. Indeed, his entire frame tensed. After the slightest of hesitations, he kept walking, not looking to either side but straight ahead like a soldier marching in his proper rank and file.

Sarah looked about for the source of the voice. "Someone is calling you."

"My name's not so uncommon. They must mean someone else." He pressed his other hand over hers and increased their pace so much she had to take two steps for every one of his.

"Jacob!" the man called again. "I need a word with you!" Whoever the man was, he'd made it across the intersection. Heavy footsteps approached from behind them. Only then did Jacob slow down, looking strained with worry and defeat.

"What's wrong?" Sarah asked him, her breath coming quickly.

They stopped completely, but he didn't turn around or remove his hand from hers. Breathing hard, Jacob closed his eyes and braced himself, as if waiting to be struck. A thick hand grabbed Jacob's shoulder and turned him about, tearing her hand from his arm.

She expected to see a thug with missing teeth, no hair across a shiny scalp, and a fist the size of a melon. Instead, she found the interloper to be a gentleman with a coat, hat, and gloves. While he wouldn't be mistaken as wealthy, he certainly looked like a proper businessman. Yet Jacob looked every bit as unnerved by this man as she would have expected from a thug demanding a gambling debt. Jacob's face drained of what little color it had.

Sarah reached for his arm, which hung straight and stiff. "Jacob?"

"Miss Jenkins," he said in a painfully formal tone, "would you excuse us for a moment while I speak with Mr. Huntsman?"

She'd never heard him speak so stilted. Jacob didn't so much as glance her way, keeping his stare on the man, as he added, "I must speak with this gentleman." He pried his arm from her weak grasp and stepped forward. "Could we talk in private?"

"By all means." The man's voice sounded decidedly deep compared to his average frame. He gestured to a nearby alley. "Will a moment over here suffice?"

Jacob looked askance at Sarah, who did her best to determine what he was thinking—who was this man, and what did he want? But Jacob's expression, tone, and words said only that he didn't want her to witness or overhear the conversation.

She took a step backward. "I'll go to the market and wait for you by the apple merchant."

A tiny voice in her head whispered that Mrs. Roach would be displeased to learn that Sarah had gone to the market alone after all. She had to remind herself that the bit about highwaymen and chaperones was nonsense.

"I'll meet you there soon," Jacob said. His eyes seemed to say *thank you* and *I'm sorry* before he and the mysterious middle-aged man entered the alleyway and left Sarah alone.

Chapter Seven

Jacob walked to the end of the alley and behind a metal staircase before turning to speak with the director of the orphanage. Even then, he turned back to scan the opening to the street beyond, making sure he found no sign of Sarah. This outing was supposed to be quick and simple. Yet he'd disobeyed Mrs. Roach's one order—to accompany Sarah—but he'd gotten pulled into the one affair he couldn't afford anyone, least of all Sarah, to learn of.

Mr. Huntsman's amused smile was encircled by his trimmed beard. He tugged on one coat sleeve and then the other, then glanced at the street as Jacob still did. "I presume your lady friend knows nothing about your niece, and that is why you wish to discuss the matter in a smelly, disgusting location?" He wrinkled his nose and looked around.

The alley wasn't particularly dirty, and it certainly didn't stink, though surely it didn't resemble a location that a man of higher station and means would choose for a business interaction. Jacob didn't like hearing Ellie being referred to as a "matter," but thought better of saying so. He deliberately ignored the man's question and asked his own.

"What is so urgent?" With his worry about Sarah overhearing no longer at the fore, his mind turned to other worrisome possibilities. "Is Ellie sick? Is she hurt?"

"Nothing is seriously amiss with the lass." The infuriating man's amusement didn't wane at all.

Though relief washed over Jacob, something still had to be wrong, or Mr. Huntsman wouldn't have chased him down the street. Jacob tried to be patient but couldn't wait. "Then what is it? I have the right to know."

"Oh, I wouldn't say that," Mr. Huntsman said in his most exasperating tone. Was the man bound and determined to worry Jacob to death? Mr. Huntsman clasped his hands behind his back. "Some situations have emerged that you would likely want to be made aware of. Seeing as you refuse to allow communications to be sent through the post, I had no option but to seek you out in person."

Then it was a stroke of luck he'd found Jacob on the street rather than at the town house.

"Tell me." Keeping himself in control took every bit of restraint Jacob possessed.

"She did wake this morning with a fever and a cough."

"Has a physician seen her?"

"No. You see, we haven't the funds to call for expensive physicians whenever one of the children has a sniffle."

"You didn't say she had a sniffle," Jacob countered. "You said it was a fever and a cough."

"That I did."

"Do you need money to pay for a doctor?" He had no idea how much that kind of visit would cost, not to mention medication, special foods, or other costs a doctor would demand. And Jacob *had* no extra money, unless he counted the few coins he'd set aside in hopes of buying Ellie some proper-fitting shoes before the weather turned cold.

"The orphanage will need an additional payment to pay for her care," Mr. Huntsman said. "Not to mention other costs."

"Such as?" Jacob asked warily.

"Oh, costs associated with quarantining the others. Can't have the entire place falling to the same illness. You understand."

Jacob grasped the words, but the reality refused to settle into understanding. Ellie was sick and might not get the care she needed unless he magically found more money.

"But I come bearing some additional news that may ease your worries," the man said.

"Oh?" Jacob's head came up sharply. His insides leapt with hope, but he tried to tamp the feeling down. Mr. Huntsman had never been a purveyor of hope.

The man offered his most patronizing smile. "I've a visit from a most delightful couple, a Mr. and Mrs. Greenhalgh, from Liverpool. He is a respected barrister."

"What do they have to do with anything?" Jacob couldn't fathom what, but a cloud of gloom settled over him anyway, one he'd be unable to shake until he knew more.

"Alas, they have been unable to have children of their own. This morning, they came to visit Cloverfield in hopes of finding a suitable child to adopt. One look at little Ellie, and they fell in love with her. Mrs. Greenhalgh couldn't stop talking about her angelic halo of curls."

Jacob might as well have been shot full of lead for as dead as he felt. He felt himself shaking his head. "Don't let anyone have her. Please. The only reason I brought her to you was so she would be cared for until I could do it myself. That was my dying sister's wish—that I become Ellie's guardian. Please, sir, she is the only family I have left, and I am the only family she has. She's already lost her mother. It wouldn't be right to separate us. You can't—"

"Oh, I most certainly can," Mr. Huntsman said. "And I will. When a couple comes forward willing to adopt a child—particularly one who is otherwise a drain on the system—"

Anger bubbled in Jacob's chest. "Ellie is not—"

Mr. Huntsman cut him off with a raised hand and continued as calmly as before. "The Greenhalghs are able to provide a loving, stable home to an orphan. It is my right—nay, it is my *duty*—to see that a child is given the opportunity to better her life." He paused, looking disturbingly gleeful as he anticipated Jacob's reaction.

For his part, Jacob wanted to punch the man in the face. Instead, he clenched his fists, released them, and clenched them again. "Is it done?" he asked, hoping his voice didn't reveal his dread.

"Not yet, no."

"Is there something I can do to stop it?"

"I highly doubt it." Mr. Huntsman tugged on the cuffs of his coat sleeves again. "I met with the Greenhalghs just this morning, and the process isn't quite as fast as all that. I am duty bound to inform the next of kin, if there be any, before an adoption can proceed."

So that was the reason he'd chased Jacob down. To tell him that, very soon, Ellie would be torn from her only living relative to live with strangers. Jacob would never see her again, and in a few years, Ellie wouldn't remember him at all.

"What must I do?"

Besides race to the orphanage, steal Ellie, and hide her at Ivy House without being arrested.

"You must understand," Mr. Huntsman said as if he were explaining the situation to a fool. "Children need stable homes, a safe place to live, with a father and a mother—who are married, of course. The father must have a comfortable living to provide for her. Naturally, the Greenhalghs fit every qualification. If you could suddenly qualify in the same manner, then you could adopt Ellie, but you don't, so—"

"Wait, *I* could adopt her?"

"Of course you could, in theory. But the fact that she's at Cloverfield at all shows that you cannot." He stepped forward and placed a hand on Jacob's shoulder. "You don't have the ability to provide for her. Even if you did, you are a bachelor with no prospects. Neither situation will change anytime soon, if ever, will they?"

Of course, Jacob could say nothing in rebuttal. All he could do was fume.

Mr. Huntsman removed his hand and adjusted his hat. "I must make a recommendation based on the information I have. Surely you understand."

Ellie was slipping through Jacob's fingers. "But—"

"Your lack of resources is precisely why she ended up in our care, correct?"

Jacob sighed miserably. "Yes." He *couldn't* provide a home for Ellie. He had no home to call his own. He owned no property. He had no wife. No education or station or, well, anything. He had hopes for the future, but hopes didn't pay for rent or food. "How soon will she . . ."

The words stuck in his throat. He couldn't bear the thought of saying goodbye to Ellie, let alone saying farewell forever—a moment Ellie wouldn't comprehend. She had a difficult time adjusting to the orphanage even with his regular visits; how much more pain would her little heart go through when faced with going to a new country and not even her uncle to provide a modicum of comfort?

Jacob lifted his chin and asked, "When does she leave Cloverfield?"

"Friday."

Worry gripped his stomach. "So soon?"

"It would have been sooner, but the Greenhalghs wanted to prepare a room for her in their house and such. Friday morning, they will be back to finalize the paperwork and fetch their daughter."

Their daughter. The hackles on Jacob's neck rose. *Never.*

Mr. Huntsman stroked his mustache with all of the compassion of a tiger having eaten its kill. "I suggest you pay a final visit to Ellie on Thursday—for her sake, of course. It would be best to not confuse or upset her the morning of her departure."

"Could someone else still adopt her first?" The desperate question fell out of Jacob's mouth.

"That would be highly irregular," Mr. Huntsman said, "although I suppose it is possible. But don't set your hat on the hope that a family in the city will adopt her so you won't have to say goodbye. I have done my duty by informing you of the fact that your niece will soon be adopted elsewhere. Don't fret. She will have a good life, one far better than you could provide." Mr. Huntsman tipped his hat, turned, and sauntered toward the street.

Jacob remained by the metal staircase, hating that Mr. Huntsman's words were absolutely true. He had no way of suddenly changing his circumstances to provide for Ellie, not when he could barely provide for himself and the costs the orphanage demanded. Ellie would have more advantages and privilege growing up with an adoptive family of means.

But that doesn't mean she should go. Emotion climbed his throat and threatened to come out in a cry. He lifted his face to the sky to hold back the threatening tears. Residents of the flats above him had their laundry drying in the summer sun, hanging from lines strung overhead. In one spot, several white sheets undulated in the breeze. With the sun shining from behind, they almost looked like angels.

How could anything be better for Ellie than being with her family? he demanded of the faux heavenly choir above him. *I'm her only family. But I've failed her.*

He sank to a metal step and dropped his head into his hands. *Oona, forgive me.*

Chapter Eight

Sarah huddled around the corner, head down, until the man left, taking long strides past without noticing her. Keeping her chin low, she looked out of the corner of her eye and watched him head in the direction they'd come from. He crossed the street and turned a corner. She waited for the space of three more breaths to calm her nerves and assure herself that he wouldn't be returning.

Only then did she straighten from her hiding place, but she kept an eye in the direction the director of Cloverfield Orphanage had gone, trying to piece together everything she'd heard. She'd heard all but the beginning of the conversation—enough to understand the situation and fill in several details on her own.

Jacob used to talk about his childhood, which was influenced by his Irish mother. He and his elder sister, Oona, spent days scampering about the very room their mother lay dying in. He'd always insisted that Oona's name came from the Irish word for lamb, *uan*, which meant she was little and soft and weak, even if she was the elder sibling. Oona readily countered that no, she was named after the Queen of the Fairies, which meant she ruled over him, and he should do her bidding.

He'd told the story of how, on one day in that freezing room, his mother had settled the argument—between coughing fits. They were both right. Oona was her given name so she would remember to be as gentle as a lamb, even as she had the power of a queen and should act like one. She told them to care for each other and keep the other's happiness and best interest at heart. For not only was Oona Queen of the Fairies, but Jacob was the father of the twelve tribes of Israel. They were both powerful in their own ways.

Their mother died only days later from an illness he could only speculate as having been consumption. The siblings were split up to live with different relatives, but fortunately, both remained in the city, near enough to remain in contact and, as their mother wished, make sure the other was happy and safe.

Sarah tried to remember the last time Jacob had mentioned his sister. It hadn't been recently. All the stories she remembered were from her first summer or two at Ivy House. Then one year, when she asked about Oona, he quickly changed the subject. At the time, Sarah hadn't thought anything of it; she and Jacob often flitted from topic to topic like bees moving between flowers, and Jacob even more so than she did.

But now, standing around the corner of the alley, Sarah was quite sure Jacob hadn't mentioned Oona in several years. Now she knew why: Oona had given birth to an illegitimate child. If she'd married and then had a child, Jacob would have most certainly mentioned both events to the entire household. Now that child had apparently been orphaned by her mother's death—something that sounded like a recent event. Jacob had taken on the job of caring for her as best he could, all the while keeping her existence a secret due to the nature of her birth. Now, he faced the prospect of losing his niece—the one connection he had to Oona and his mother.

Sarah sighed with resignation, knowing all too well society's opinion on such matters. He'd been wise to hide the connection. *Even from me*, she thought sadly. *Even though I could have comforted him and tried to help.* If she'd known, she might have spoken of the situation at a time when someone might overhear or tried to help in a way that revealed the truth. If she'd learned anything by working for a wealthy family with dozens of servants, it was that the chances of a secret remaining one decreased with every additional person who knew it, no matter how trustworthy they were.

But now she knew about Ellie and had no way to erase that knowledge. She glanced about the street casually as she walked along and then slipped around the corner into the alleyway.

As expected, she found Jacob at the far end, sitting on a metal stair, holding his head with both hands. His shoulders were rounded, and he looked more wretched than she'd ever seen him. For a moment, she forgot that she'd gone counter to his wishes by not going ahead to the market and—worse, surely—by eavesdropping.

Only moments before Mr. Huntsman's appearance, Jacob had wanted to tell her about his niece—Sarah felt certain that the very situation she'd learned about was the one Jacob had hinted at. Perhaps Jacob would be cross with her for discovering his secret; if so, she'd take the blame. But she would also do everything she could to help him—and to carry his secret to the grave.

But first, she had to comfort the man who meant more to her than anyone else.

The cobblestones were angled slightly to allow water and

refuse to flow down the middle, so she kept to one side as she made her way down the alleyway. With each step, she expected Jacob to look up, but he mustn't have heard her footfalls because she drew within a few paces of him before he saw the hem of her dress and looked up.

He quickly wiped one eye and then the other with his palm. Even if she hadn't seen the tears, she'd have known by the redness around his eyes and his bereft expression that he was in pain. "You heard?" he asked.

"I'm so sorry, Jacob."

She went to the stairs, dropped to her knees, and embraced him. Jacob held her tight, and for a moment, neither said another word. He mourned, and she mourned with him. After a time, he released her and scooted over on the stair, an invitation to join him.

"I failed Oona," he said miserably. "I promised to care for Ellie, to watch over her. And now . . . I can't."

Sarah sensed what he did not say. She guessed now why he'd been tardy for the arrival. Who could blame an uncle for spending a few extra minutes with the girl he'd promised to watch over? "What are you going to do?"

Jacob leaned both arms against his legs and stared between them at the cobblestones below. "What *can* I do?" He grunted in frustration and raked both hands through his hair. "And now you're in the middle of it. Sarah, I tried to protect you so the Millingtons wouldn't have a reason to connect you to—"

"Shh." Sarah placed a finger over his lips to stop his anxious rambling. "I'm glad I'm 'in the middle' of this, as you call it. Ellie is important to you. The circumstances of her birth don't matter. What does matter is that you are her uncle and she should be with you."

"Should but won't." He sounded dejected, completely

adrift. She yearned to draw him into a haven from his emotional storm, to smooth the worry lining his face. "I don't know what to do," he went on. "We'd need a miracle—rather, several—to fix this."

Sarah leaned close and spoke into his ear. "You know what they say about miracles?"

At the question, Jacob turned his head, and suddenly their faces were nearly touching. She felt her own breath fail her completely. The two of them had been near each other hundreds, if not thousands, of times. They'd touched in some manner almost daily. But this connection, this closeness, was entirely different—intimate and wonderful and anxious all at once. Like the moment a rail track would be switched—or not. Somehow, their future hinged on this moment.

He didn't pull away, and neither did she, unwilling to stop feeling his breath on her cheek, unwilling to withdraw from the masculine scent that was Jacob—something she'd been familiar with for years, but had never experienced this intensely, this closely, or this long.

He gazed into her eyes, and she felt as if she could drown in the hazel depths of his. "You aren't disappointed in me?" he asked in a whisper.

"About what?" Sarah said, equally breathy. "Having the loyalty and courage of a knight, no matter the cost?" The words thrilled her as she spoke them, for she felt their truth to her core. "You are an even better man than I thought, Jacob Croft—and that is no small thing."

"I could say the same about you," Jacob said. "Though I'd amend the statement to your being an even better *woman* than I thought." He smiled at that, but it was tinged with sadness.

"Thank heavens for that." The words slipped out, like a

prayer of thanksgiving for having a man such as Jacob in her life.

He reached up and smoothed a bit of hair that had escaped her bun. "To think I tried to protect you from my secret, when you would have been Ellie's greatest champion all along."

"Of course," Sarah said. "She needs you, and you need her."

He studied her face, drinking her in. "I need *you* too."

Her heart hiccuped, almost stealing her voice, but she managed, "And I you."

How many more seconds would they stay in this position, sitting so close, their bodies, touching, their faces nearly so? Sarah wanted the moment to last forever. She wished they'd been born under different stars—she with a dowry, he a landed gentleman—so they could be together forever and never worry about keeping their positions with a wealthy family because they needed them to survive. But she could not change their stars, so she wished instead that this moment, which had to end, would bring her joy to look back on.

And it did. Jacob moved toward her until his lips pressed against hers. Her eyes instinctively closed as the warmth of his kiss spread throughout her body. She pressed her hands against his shirt, and he reached up to hold her face, cradling it in his strong hands. When the kiss ended—too soon—he pressed his lips to her temple and held her close. She rested her head against his chest and heard the pounding of his heart, which beat almost as fast as her own. She smiled at the thought that she might have such an effect on him, as he did on her.

"I would do anything for you," she murmured. The words were as close as she'd ever come to saying she loved him—was in love with him.

"You would?" Something in his tone told her that his thoughts had shifted. Where had the bumblebee flitted now?

"Of course I would." She sat up, her back straight, bracing herself for she knew not what. He might insist she go away so as to not sully her reputation by associating with him, to obtain a letter of recommendation from the Millingtons before the truth about Ellie was discovered. She didn't know if she could bear that.

"I have an idea—a way to keep Ellie from being adopted."

"That's wonderful," Sarah said with relief for herself, for Jacob, and for the little girl she'd never met.

"But I need your help."

"Anything. What can I do?"

Jacob took a deep breath. He let it out slowly, but instead of the sigh calming him, he seemed more nervous than ever. For the span of a couple of seconds, he looked everywhere but at Sarah. At last, he shifted to face her, took her hands in his, and spoke four simple words.

"Will you marry me?"

Chapter Nine

Sarah didn't think she'd heard right. Her shock and confusion must have been plainly evident because Jacob broke the silence between them.

"You heard what Mr. Huntsman said. If I had a stable life and were married, then Ellie could leave the orphanage and live with me—us." He squeezed her hands, excitement in his eyes, but Sarah pulled away and stood, trying to make sense of the world that had turned upside down. She took a few steps away and lifted one hand to her lips, which still tingled with his kiss. In the course of a few minutes, she'd gone from desperately worried to being swept away, from floating in the air to dropping to the ground and landing in a bruised heap.

Jacob proposed, she thought, as if repeating the idea would make it real.

Then why didn't she feel happy? She'd hoped that this summer he'd kiss her—and he had.

She'd hoped that he'd come to love her in return. He'd kissed her, yes. But in spite of knowing him for years, she had no experience with how he was with girls. Had he kissed other girls? Would he have kissed any girl who'd been there to show compassion? She hoped he wouldn't, but she didn't know.

And then he'd proposed. Not after an expression of his love, if he had any, but as a solution to save Ellie—all very logical and practical. And entirely void of feeling.

I can't say no. If marrying Jacob helped Ellie, she should do it. He'd make a good husband to any woman, and there was every chance that she'd never again receive an offer. She'd been naive to think she could have what so many others lacked: a marriage based not on convenience, money, or need, but on love.

She felt her eyes watering and fought back tears. She could *not* let him see her weep, not when she was foolishly mourning the loss of a girlish dream. With her back to him, she pressed her eyes closed. Two tears escaped one eye, which she quickly wiped away with her fingertips. She hoped he didn't see the motion.

"Sarah?" He sounded unsure, though not nearly as unsure as she felt.

Not trusting herself to turn around, she answered with several wordless nods.

Behind her, the staircase creaked as Jacob stood. "It won't solve the entire problem, of course."

It? Even if she'd tried to come up with the least romantic way to refer to a marriage, she wouldn't have thought of using *it.* The single word hurt. She hugged herself but had to wipe away a third tear from the other cheek.

He paced behind her as words tumbled out with his energy. "We wouldn't have a home for Ellie, of course, and that would be a problem," Jacob said. "But we could probably find jobs in the city—maybe at a factory. Mr. Millington might be willing to loan us some money to help us get started." When Sarah didn't answer in the brief pause, Jacob barreled forward at full steam like a locomotive. "I know that factory work isn't glamorous, and it's far dirtier than what we're used to, but hard work has never scared either of us, right?"

She nodded and murmured something that he must have interpreted as an affirmative reply.

"I'm glad you think so," he said. "There is the matter of the Millingtons losing two servants at once, but I imagine there are plenty of men and women eager to take our positions, and—" At last, he stopped blathering and took a breath. "What you do think?"

That I'm a fool for letting romantic stories get the better of me. His plan makes perfect sense and would be good for everyone involved. I should be grateful for the chance to marry a good man, no matter how much he cares for me. Oh, how much she wanted her first kiss to have meant something, to represent his genuine regard. To think that it might have been nothing but a response to an emotional moment nearly broke her.

"Sarah? Did you hear me?"

She'd surely stopped listening at some point, but she wasn't at all certain how much longer he'd spoken. What had she missed?

"What do you think of my plan?" From behind, Jacob laid a hand on her shoulder. Not flinching at his touch took every ounce of her self-control. The warmth of his hand, which moments ago would have sent her soaring, now made her heart feel like stone. "Come now, Sarah, what do you think?" he repeated.

How to answer the question? His solution to Ellie's predicament was a sound one, if judged entirely on its likelihood of keeping the girl from being adopted by someone else. That wasn't all Sarah thought of the idea, but she couldn't tell him what she really thought about those parts. Besides, she had yet to answer his proposal.

She swallowed hard, hoping it would dissolve the thick disappointment filling her chest. "I think—" Another surreptitious swipe of her cheeks. "I think your plan will work."

"So you'll do it?" He took her by the shoulders and, before she realized it, turned her around to face him. She smiled as quickly as she could, though there was no hiding the fact that she'd been crying—and far from smiling—a moment before.

"What's wrong?" Jacob looked both perplexed and concerned.

At least I'm not the only foolish one.

She let out a shaky sigh. "It's been a difficult day."

It was as broad a statement as she could come up with quickly, but she hoped he'd accept the explanation. With a trembling hand, she reached into her apron pocket and pulled out the slip of paper with the shopping list, followed by the coins Mrs. Roach had given her earlier. "Would you do the shopping for me? I'm afraid I'm rather unwell."

Jacob took the coins and paper with an open hand, but his brows were drawn together, and he studied her face as if he were a physician searching for the cause of her ailment. "If you're ill, I can't let you walk back alone."

"It's just a headache, and the town house isn't so far. I'll return on my own just fine." She left out any word about the mysterious—and likely fictional—highwayman Mrs. Roach had used as the reason for Jacob accompanying her in the first place. She nodded toward the money in his hand. "But Betsy will have a fit if she doesn't get her pantry properly stocked. If you could do that for me, I'd be most grateful."

"Of course." Jacob closed his fist around the coins and

smiled at her in the way that always made her insides turn to pudding. "Anything for you."

"Thank you." Not trusting herself to say another word, she left the alley, heading back toward Ivy House. When she was sure she'd put enough distance between her and Jacob, the tears fell on their own accord. She wiped them away, annoyed for having pinned her hopes on something more than a marriage of convenience.

I should be happy, she told herself. *Many women aren't so lucky as to have the opportunity to marry, let alone to marry someone they know and care for, someone good and kind and agreeable.* But despite her rational mind lecturing her the entire way back, her heart refused to believe a word of it.

She went down the steps leading to the servants' entrance and said a silent prayer that no one would notice her arrival, especially Betsy, who would likely swoop down on Sarah like a falcon on its prey. If that happened, Betsy would be disappointed that Sarah had returned empty-handed, and Sarah would be unable to maintain her composure long enough to give any explanation for why she'd returned without Jacob or the foodstuffs.

She slowly twisted the handle, then inched the door open, praying that the squeaky top hinge wouldn't betray her. Of course, it whined in protest. She slipped through the narrow opening and closed the door tight. Hoping to avoid anyone seeing or calling out to her, she hurried down the corridor on her toes past the kitchen and Mrs. Roach's room, then turned and slipped through the even smaller corridor that led to the other side of the basement. That was where the small winter kitchen and other rooms were, including the small scullery that was her sleeping quarters.

Once inside the vacant room, she dropped onto a chair

in the corner, and her face fell into her hands. She listened carefully for any indication of someone following her. When, after several seconds, she heard nothing, disappointment spilled out of her in full force. A small, dusty corner of her mind recognized that after this bout of crying, she would have to create a spine of steel for herself and encase her heart in a similar cage to prevent such waves of sadness from ever touching her again. But in this moment, she let out the sadness from being rejected and having her dreams destroyed like a soap bubble popping in the air. Her dreams had been that fragile—and that temporary.

I just became engaged, and I'm miserable about it. She wouldn't have believed such a thing was possible, but there had also been a time when the greatest minds believed the earth was flat. Discoveries such as the one she'd had today drastically shifted one's view, like Magellan's trip around the globe had changed the way the West viewed the entire world. Somehow, someday, she'd find her axis again, and her world would continue to spin as it always had. But for now, the tears flowed freely.

She became so caught up in her isolated grief that the touch of a cold hand on her arm made her yelp as if a ghost had appeared. Sarah raised her head with a jerk, her breath catching in her throat, only to find Mrs. Roach. The woman had such angular features, from the sharp planes of her cheeks and nose to her bony shoulders and thin neck, that most people assumed she was harsh and unkind. To maintain her authority as housekeeper, she tended to encourage the reputation, often speaking harshly and demanding compliance without question.

Though Sarah knew Mrs. Roach had a gentle temperament at times, she didn't know which of the housekeeper's moods had come with her now. So Sarah sat up straight, wiped her eyes, and took a deep breath, ready for a lecture about failing to buy basic items for the pantry.

When Mrs. Roach didn't speak, Sarah tried to explain. "Jacob should be back very soon with everything on the list." Every word felt forced, but she had to do something to preserve Mrs. Roach's favorable view of her, if at all possible. Hands clasped in her lap and face lowered to show contrition, Sarah went on, "I apologize for returning early and not staying with him as my chaperone during such a turbulent time in the city. I was unwell."

"As I can see." Mrs. Roach's voice held no censure at all. In fact, she sounded compassionate.

In surprise, Sarah looked up to find the housekeeper fetching a stool from the winter kitchen. She moved it near Sarah and sat down—lower than Sarah, which seemed wrong, considering their respective positions in the household. Mrs. Roach clasped her hands in her lap as Sarah had and shook her head.

"I suppose it was foolish of me to arrange for you and Jacob to have some time together."

"What do you—Oh." Sarah suddenly understood her earlier conversation with Mrs. Roach.

The housekeeper shrugged. "I've long watched the two of you fall in love, and I was so hopeful it would be a match."

"It is. He asked for my hand today."

Mrs. Roach considered Sarah for a moment. "Then I must have botched the whole of it. I was certain you cared for each other. I am so sorry. You must believe that I had your happiness in mind—yours and Jacob's. I never would have interfered otherwise."

"You have no reason to apologize," Sarah said, though she didn't elaborate. Mrs. Roach most certainly had *not* misunderstood Sarah's feelings for Jacob, but it seemed they both had misunderstood Jacob's.

"I've been dropping hints to Mr. and Mrs. Millington for weeks now about how you two could live in the cottage at Rosemount, seeing as Mr. Kelly is retiring and will soon be living with his daughter in the country. It seemed to be the perfect situation, and they agreed."

"That would be lovely," Sarah said, grateful that her future wouldn't necessarily include factory work. "It is perfect for Jacob and for—" She cut herself off before she revealed anything about Ellie.

"For Jacob, but not for you?" Mrs. Roach tapped her fingers on her knee as she pondered. "Does he have his eye on another girl?"

In a manner of speaking.

Could she tell Mrs. Roach about Ellie after Jacob had taken such pains to keep everything about her a secret? Would the association harm him in Mrs. Roach's estimation? She had tremendous influence with the family, so her opinion mattered deeply. In spite of his secrecy, Sarah couldn't imagine the kind woman calling for Jacob's resignation, but she might counsel the Millingtons not to offer him the position of head gardener after all.

Now that Mr. Huntsman is involved, the truth will come out anyway, Sarah realized. *If all goes according to plan, Ellie will be living with us in the cottage. I might as well tell her.*

"His niece is about to be adopted to a couple from Liverpool."

"Jacob has a—"

"Yes," Sarah said, needing to speak it all now, or she'd never dare to finish. "For him to have custody—she's an orphan, you see—he must have an income, a home . . . and a wife."

"Ah, I see," Mrs. Roach said. "Have you given him an answer?"

"I said yes, of course." Anything else would have been foolish—for her own future, for Jacob's, and that of an innocent child too. What right did she have to prevent Ellie from being with her family?

Mrs. Roach stood suddenly. Sarah braced herself for a lecture or instructions for work to do. She received neither.

"You rest for a spell," Mrs. Roach said. "I'll come for you later."

"Th-thank you."

The housekeeper's stoic countenance had returned. She nodded and left the scullery—and a befuddled Sarah.

Chapter Ten

Jacob returned to Ivy House at a run, hoping the delay caused by Mr. Huntsman wouldn't get him in trouble. He clutched several parcels wrapped in brown paper and a linen sack holding wax paper packets of pepper and other spices. At the top of the servants' entrance, he navigated the narrow stairs carefully and balanced the purchases in one arm as he opened the door. Inside, he nudged it closed with his foot, meaning to head straight to the kitchen, but Mrs. Roach blocked the way, arms folded, one eyebrow arched high. His step came up short. Mrs. Roach with folded arms was never a good thing to see. Neither was her arched eyebrow.

Both at the same time? Something must be horribly wrong. He felt like a lad again, awash with shame and guilt over Thomas's departure.

"Here are the items you requested," Jacob said cheerfully. He held them out. "I apologize for the delay, but I came as fast as I could. And I found good prices. I think you'll be pleased with how much money is left over."

Jacob's words had as much effect on Mrs. Roach as they

would have on a locomotive stopped on the tracks. Her face didn't change expression at all. Wondering if she hadn't heard him, he almost repeated the words, but another look at Mrs. Roach made that idea flee. Why was she so upset?

I returned without Sarah. Of course. That's what this is about.

"Is Sarah well?" Jacob asked. He tried to peer around Mrs. Roach, unsuccessfully. "She assured me she'd be fine returning on her own. I wouldn't have left her side if I'd thought otherwise." He hoped she wouldn't mention the mythical highwayman. When she didn't answer, worry snaked up his back. "She's here, isn't she?" What if there really was a group of miscreants in the city, looking for women to kidnap?

"She's here."

"Thank heavens. And she's well?"

"Yes. In body." Mrs. Roach's words were clipped and curt. Something was wrong with Sarah in spirit, then?

"What is it?"

Mrs. Roach nodded toward the kitchen. "Bring the parcels to Betsy, then step outside."

"Of course." He dipped his head in respect.

She moved to the side to make room, and he scurried into the kitchen, deposited the armful on the wood table by Betsy, and ran out again without so much as a hello to her. He went back out the servants' entrance to the small area between the door and the stairs. There, he found Mrs. Roach standing with her back to him, her toe tapping impatiently. She must have heard him close the door, because the moment it clicked, she whirled about.

"Jacob Croft, are you, or are you not, in love with Sarah Jenkins?"

"Am I—what?" The question took him so off guard that

he couldn't think straight. Why was Mrs. Roach, of all people, asking him such a question?

"And did you, or did you not," she went on, pacing around him in a tight circle, "propose marriage to her not an hour ago?"

How did she know *that*? She walked around him like a tiger circling its prey. He did his best to find his voice—and something to say. "I should have discussed the matter with you and Mr. Millington first, of course. I apolo—"

Mrs. Roach spun to face him, cutting off his words. When she spoke next, she wagged a finger. "And did you, or did you not, make this proposal because it was a convenient solution to an external problem?"

"Well, if you put it that way . . ." He didn't complete the sentence.

"Hmm?" Apparently, Mrs. Roach expected him to.

"Yes," he said, half expecting demons to rain down on him for whatever evil he'd perpetrated. "I suppose I did."

"Men are nothing but dolts." The housekeeper's hands rose in disbelief and then fell to her sides with a slap. "*This* is why I have never married and *will* never marry."

Was she jealous that he'd proposed to Sarah? Surely Mrs. Roach didn't want a proposal from someone three decades her junior, did she?

"I don't understand," Jacob said.

"Of course you don't." She hmphed and then folded her arms this time, to his relief, without the eyebrow. "You also didn't answer my first question."

From the moment he'd returned from the market, she'd had Jacob's mind spinning, and it had only spun faster with every passing moment. He couldn't have remembered her first question if pirates had demanded it of him.

At his look of confusion, Mrs. Roach rolled her eyes. "Are

you," she said slowly, emphasizing each syllable, "or are you not, in love with her?"

His gaze flitted toward the door and back again. Would answering truthfully hurt Sarah in some way? He eyed Mrs. Roach, whose brows threatened to go up again.

She knows. She already knows, so I must tell the truth.

"Yes," he said, and then he had to wipe beads of sweat from his upper lip. "I am very much in love with her."

"I am glad to hear it." Mrs. Roach sighed with something like relief, which served only to confuse him further. "Now to fix this ridiculous mess you've created."

"This mess?" What all did she know? Had she seen him hiding behind the shrub? "Do you mean the trouble with Ellie?"

At that, any attempt at long-suffering left Mrs. Roach's person. "I assume that is the name of your niece?"

"Y-yes." How big was this mess if Mrs. Roach knew so much? What did the Millingtons know?

"She is the external problem I referred to. She is *not* the mess you've created." She stepped closer and lowered her voice, this time speaking in a gentle tone. "You are a good man, Jacob. A dolt, yes, but as men go, a good one."

"Thank you." It came out sounding like a question.

"Coming from me, that is high praise indeed," Mrs. Roach said, and he had no doubt she spoke the truth. "But as a man, you do not realize what you have done this afternoon regarding a kind, equally good young woman who is most decidedly in love with you too."

His heart leapt in his chest. "Sarah?"

"Of course Sarah." Another huff. "Dolts. Every one of them," she said to the air.

"I hoped she might care for me. I suspected she did, but I didn't know for sure. Today, there was a moment when . . ."

He cleared his throat, opting to skip the part about kissing Sarah and how wonderful it was. "Then Mr. Huntsman arrived—"

"After which you proposed without saying a word about your preexisting love for her. Did you give her any indication that you would have proposed at a later date regardless of the situation with your niece?"

"I . . ." The spinning in Jacob's head slowed, stopped, and resolved into a clear picture of the situation Mrs. Roach painted. He ran a hand through his hair. "I *am* a dolt."

"As I said," Mrs. Roach replied with an utterly matter-of-fact tone. "But the situation may yet be salvaged."

"How? The matter with my niece is urgent, and now Sarah believes that the only reason I want to marry her is Ellie."

"*If* you follow my every instruction to the letter, you just might repair the damage done to Sarah's heart—and you'll save your niece too."

"Truly?"

"There are no guarantees, but I'd say the odds are quite good." The arch returned. "Are you willing to do as I say?"

"Yes."

"Will you follow my every instruction?"

"Absolutely. I'll do anything you say." Fear of losing Sarah altogether consumed him. He'd thought she knew he loved her, that he'd made the fact perfectly clear. He just hadn't known how *she* felt. Instead of making sure she knew, he'd bumbled the entire situation.

Mrs. Roach headed for the door and called over her shoulder. "Come with me."

He followed as obediently as a puppy, feeling about as manly as one, down the corridor and across the connecting passage to the other half of the basement. A pit formed in his middle as he realized they were headed to the small scullery. To Sarah.

"I'm not ready to speak to her right this moment," he said to Mrs. Roach's retreating figure, though he kept up a few steps behind. "Won't you tell me what to say and do?"

"Of course."

"Privately, I mean."

"Hardly." Mrs. Roach slowed her step to cast a disparaging look over her shoulder before continuing down the hall. "You said you would follow my—"

"Every instruction," Jacob filled in. "And I will. I apologize."

Whatever she has planned, please work, he prayed, looking at the ceiling.

At the scullery doorway, Mrs. Roach strode right in. Jacob held back in the hallway, unsure what her plans were. But she waved him in impatiently, so somehow he stumbled across the threshold. He was aware of Sarah sitting on the other side of the room but felt too ashamed to look directly at her. He studied the cracks in the floor. Mrs. Roach, however, had no such compunctions.

"Look up, Jacob," she ordered. "No woman wants a man who can't hold his head up."

He lifted his chin and looked right at her. "Yes, ma'am."

That's when he looked at Sarah—really looked at her—and realized that her pretty face was stained with tears. His initial instinct was to hurry over and comfort her, but with Mrs. Roach at his side, he didn't dare. Even so, her name slipped from his tight throat. "Sarah?"

She looked at him hopefully, but then lowered her face. Mrs. Roach, he noted, did not criticize Sarah for not holding *her* head up straight.

He leaned toward the housekeeper and whispered

uneasily, "What do I do now?" Moments ago, he thought he would need to place faith in whatever methods Mrs. Roach decided to employ. Now he wanted *any* instruction from her at all. Something. Anything.

Instead of answering him, she turned to Sarah. "Come," she said, waving her over.

Sarah hesitantly stood from her seat and approached, each step more unsure than the last, until she stopped at Mrs. Roach's other side.

Mrs. Roach looked from her to him and back again. She nodded. "I'm glad we're all here together to discuss a most important matter."

Oh, heavens, Jacob thought. *What is she going to say? Don't say I'm a dolt. Not to Sarah.*

"As it so happens," Mrs. Roach said, clasping her hands together, "Mr. Kelly is readying himself to retire. He's the gardener at Rosemount." The last was directed as Jacob, as Sarah already knew every servant at the estate. But what did this sudden turn of topic have to do with anything?

"Ma'am?" Jacob managed.

"In fact, several months ago, Mr. Kelly informed the family of his plans to live with his sister in the country, although he's stayed on until now, of course." The housekeeper continued as if Jacob hadn't spoken. He and Sarah exchanged puzzled glances. "Of course, finding a replacement takes time, and the Millington family doesn't view such things as permanent staff replacements lightly."

Sarah threw another confused look at Jacob. "Of—of course not."

"Indeed not," Mrs. Roach said, as if she were discussing something obvious. "So it makes perfect sense that I've been actively looking for a replacement for some time—someone who could take on the position and work hard, someone who respects the family and is loyal to them. Of course, that person would live in the cottage Mr. Kelly has occupied for the last twenty years." She looked at Jacob and then at Sarah as if she was about to say something of particular import. "While Mr. Kelly never married, I know from discussions with Mrs. Millington that she and her husband would prefer his replacement to have a wife, and they would raise their family in the cottage at Rosemount."

Now both of her eyebrows went up, and she looked between them pointedly. Her meaning started to dawn on Jacob—and by the looks of it, on Sarah too, but she didn't look as pleased as he felt, likely because of the horrid way he proposed to her.

"Further," Mrs. Roach continued, "I understand that a certain child would benefit from such a marriage with guaranteed employment. And I *know* that both Mr. Millington and his wife approve of the match, for they gave me that very assurance in March."

Jacob looked at her in shock. "March?"

Her staunch affect softened into an amused smile. "I've been watching the two of you for half a decade. I may be old, but I am not blind."

Sarah cleared her throat. "What do you mean?"

Instead of replying to her, Mrs. Roach turned to Jacob. "Tell her what you confessed to me in the outside just now."

For a flash, Sarah's eyes widened with worry, but this time, Jacob knew he would be able to quell her fears, and he felt an overflowing gratitude for Mrs. Roach, who had made this moment come to pass. He turned to Sarah and opened his mouth to speak, but Mrs. Roach shook her head abruptly, cutting him off before he began.

"What?" he asked. "I'm following your instructions."

As before, she looked up and shook her head, as if talking to God. "Must I be so specific?" She sighed. "I suppose I must."

"Because I'm a dolt," he muttered.

"But a lovable and good one," Mrs. Roach said. She patted his shoulder and added, "I suggest you kneel this time."

Of course! Why hadn't he thought of that the first time?

He dropped to one knee on the cold stone floor and looked up at Sarah, who was beautiful as ever, even with her tear-stained face. "I love you, Sarah, ever so much. And I have for so long. I cannot begin to tell you how much I love you and want to spend my life with you. I hoped you felt the same—"

"Oh, I do—I do!" she said, her face finally breaking into a smile.

The sight warmed his heart and gave him the courage to go on. "I apologize for the horrid way I said things earlier today. I was caught up in my worries about Ellie and unsure how you felt about me and—"

Mrs. Roach placed a hand on his shoulder. "Get to the point, my boy."

"Right," he said, glancing at her briefly. He cleared his throat and tried again. "Sarah Jenkins, I love you more than I thought possible. Will you be my wife?"

The housekeeper added, "And live with him and Ellie in the cottage at Rosemount?"

"Yes. Everything Mrs. Roach said." Jacob pointed at the housekeeper. He took Sarah's hands in his, face uplifted to hers. "My heart is yours and always will be. Will you marry me?"

Sarah laughed through new tears. "Of course I will. Yes. A thousand times, yes."

He got back to his feet, and they embraced. Somewhere in the back of his awareness, he heard Mrs. Roach murmur,

"I'll step outside to let you two lovebirds have a moment together."

Next thing he knew, they were sharing their second kiss, this time as professed lovers who would soon be married.

After the kiss, he held her tight. "I am a dolt. The situation with Ellie—"

"Shh," Sarah said. "I understand now." She held him tight. "I cannot wait to meet her and love her as much as you do."

About Annette Lyon

Annette Lyon is a *USA Today* bestselling author, a four-time recipient of Utah's Best of State medal for fiction, a Whitney Award winner, and a five-time publication award winner from the League of Utah Writers. She's the author of more than a dozen novels, even more novellas, and several nonfiction books. When she's not writing, knitting, or eating chocolate, she can be found mothering and avoiding housework. Annette is a member of the Women's Fiction Writers Association and is represented by Heather Karpas at ICM Partners.

Find Annette online:
Blog: http://blog.AnnetteLyon.com
Twitter: @AnnetteLyon
Facebook: http://Facebook.com/AnnetteLyon
Instagram: https://www.instagram.com/annette.lyon/
Pinterest: http://Pinterest.com/AnnetteLyon
Newsletter: http://bit.ly/1n3I87y

Other Works by Annette Lyon

WOMEN'S FICTION
Band of Sisters
Coming Home
A Portrait for Toni
At the Water's Edge
Lost Without You
The Newport Ladies Book Club series

TIMELESS ROMANCES
Winter Collection
Spring Vacation Collection
European Collection
Summer Wedding Collection
Love Letter Collection
Old West Collection
Mail Order Bride Collection
A Midwinter Ball
A Night in Grosvenor Square
The Orient Express

NON-FICTION
Done & Done
There, Their, They're:
A No-Tears Guide to Grammar from the Word Nerd

Dear Timeless Victorian Collection Reader,

Thank you for reading *Summer Holiday*. We hoped you loved the sweet romance novellas! Each collection in the Timeless Victorian Collection contains three novellas.

If you enjoyed this collection, please consider leaving a review on Goodreads or Amazon or any other online store you purchase through. Reviews and word-of-mouth is what helps us continue this fun project. For updates and notifications of sales and giveaways, please sign up for our monthly newsletter on our blog:

TimelessRomanceAnthologies.blogspot.com

Also, if you're interested in becoming a regular reviewer of these collections and would like access to advance copies, please email Heather Moore: heather@hbmoore.com

We also post our announcements to our Facebook page: Timeless Romance Anthologies

Thank you!
The Timeless Romance Authors

MORE TIMELESS REGENCY COLLECTIONS:

Don't miss our Timeless Romance Anthologies:
Six short romance novellas in each anthology

www.ingramcontent.com/pod-product-compliance
Lightning Source LLC
LaVergne TN
LVHW021759060526
838201LV00058B/3155